MERCIFUL CONQUEST

Heart of a Viking
Book 1

Violetta Rand

ARE YOU SIGNED UP FOR DRAGONBLADE'S BLOG?

You'll get the latest news and information on exclusive giveaways, exclusive excerpts, coming releases, sales, free books, cover reveals and more.

Check out our complete list of authors, too!

No spam, no junk. That's a promise!

Sign Up Here

www.dragonbladepublishing.com

Dearest Reader;

Thank you for your support of a small press. At Dragonblade Publishing, we strive to bring you the highest quality Historical Romance from some of the best authors in the business. Without your support, there is no 'us', so we sincerely hope you adore these stories and find some new favorite authors along the way.

Happy Reading!

CEO, Dragonblade Publishing

Additional Dragonblade books by Author Violetta Rand

Heart of a Viking Series
Merciful Conquest (Book 1)

The Husband Dilemma Series
How to Fool a Duke (Book 1)
How to Get an Earl for Christmas (Novella)

Highlands Forever Series
Unbreakable (Book 1)
Undeniable (Book 2)
Unyielding (Book 3)

Lords of Hedonism
Duke of Decadence

Viking's Fury Series
Love's Fury (Book 1)
Desire's Fury (Book 2)
Passion's Fury (Book 3)

De Wolfe Pack: The Series
Never Cry de Wolfe

Also from Violetta Rand
Viking Hearts
Raven (Novella)
Belware Bridge (Novella)

*To my mother, Betty,
for gifting me with the love of words and reading
and Kelly Graham,
for believing in me …*

Dedication

It all started with this quirky message: "Hey pretty lady, would you like to join my street team?"

My first thought was that Violetta sure sounds like fun. I quickly agreed and with that simple reply in 2014, my life inexorably changed. I am forever a member of the Violetta Valkyries.

I had nine wonderful years with Violetta as her writer's assistant. But more importantly, I had nine amazing years as part of her life. She often told me, "Star, you are my family." It is true—we were family to one another. Violetta was diagnosed with Lynch Syndrome, which is a treacherous hereditary disease. She was truly a Valkyrie in every sense of the word as she battled multiple cancers in her organs. Her grace and determination helped her conquer each surgery. She would call me to tell me, "I'm still here—thank you for your prayers." In July 2023, she called to tell me that, yet again, she had to have another surgery. But, as usual, she was unwavering in her attitude and assured me, "I've got this." I replied, "You and God together."

And with God she left this world July 15, 2023. She was only 53 years old. I loved Violetta's grace, determination, and creative nature. It was truly as if her soul was the captain of her life for all to see. She was so loved and is missed every day. To her devoted readers and every member of her street team: you undeniably meant the world to her. She felt incredibly blessed you chose to be a part of her writing journey.

A special thank you to Violetta's incredible husband Jeff. Even in the midst of his grief, he has been a dear friend to me. I will always be grateful for his friendship.

On behalf of myself, Barbi Davis, and Violetta's exceptional street team, "Violetta Valkyries", we hope you enjoy this series.

Star Montgomery

Foreword

What happens when you find a master storyteller and allow her to lead you hundreds of years into the past to the country of Norway, a frozen land sparsely populated by barbarians? You experience the thrill of adventure from the safety of your favorite reading spot at a time in history that was far from safe.

The Vikings were known as fierce protectors of their own as well as conquers of new lands. When they wanted something, they didn't ask permission. They pillaged villages, conquered enemies, even kidnapped women when it suited them.

How would I know? I know, because I was born in Norway. Every one of my ancestors on my father's side is, or was, a Norwegian. The history of the Vikings is well documented, but Violetta Rand finds a way to understand the essence of the people and bring that to life in her books. As if by magic, she transports us to a time and place that was cold and primitive, but filled with myths and adventure.

Rand's novels are page turners with characters who embody honor and courage. They are breath-taking tales of redemption, love, and passion. With a backdrop of clashing cultures and religion, you find her brilliantly written books impossible to put down until the satisfying ending.

I'm honored to write this foreword and invite you, dear reader, to be swept into the world of the Vikings. Violetta was not only a wonderful friend, she was also the editor of my first historical romance book. Those of us who knew her personally, miss her dearly. But she lives on in our hearts, minds, and these Viking stories.

Marisa Dillon

PROLOGUE

Orkney Islands

October 6, 1011 AD

RANDVIOR SIGURDSSON PLANTED his feet in the sand and gazed eastward across the North Sea. He raised his war axe high above his head and saluted his forefathers. A yellow-tinged quarter-moon, haloed by rings of light and mist, loomed overhead like an apparition. It inspired the Viking to speak ancient verses to attract Odin's favor. Only six days separated him from Norway and he desperately wanted to go home.

Motionless, he closed his eyes and swore he heard his ancestors chanting the same praises to honor the old gods. Every night for the last three months, he'd walked this shoreline and surveyed the flat landscape. At times, he regretted establishing new steadings in the Orkneys—tonight seemed to be one of them. Barren hollows of sand and withering bushes stretched as far as the eye could see. The only redemptive qualities in these islands were the familiar scent of salt water and the brooding sounds of gulls.

Sighing deeply, he turned and walked toward the flimsy lean-to he slept inside when he chose to stay onshore. As he neared the camp he shared with his men, he spied a few soldiers sitting near a roaring fire, passing wine around. They greeted him and offered the bottle. Randvior shook his head. No spirits tonight, unless they were the kind the gods sent as messengers in dreams.

He kicked open the plank door and stepped inside the shelter.

It was barely large enough to accommodate his bulk. He stripped off his cloak and lay down, stared overhead, and studied the brightening nighttime sky between gaps in the boarded ceiling. Thousands of stars twinkled above. He counted them one by one, as he'd often done as a child. And very slowly, his eyes grew heavy with sleep.

In the middle of the night, Randvior's dreams caught fire. He growled and cursed, challenged and defended, until he rolled off his cot and knocked himself awake. He tried to remember where he was exactly. The shelter was dark, but the vision of a woman's face glared at him through the pitch. Almond-shaped eyes pinned him to the floor.

He thought he remembered that beautiful face, crowned by a mane of honey-colored hair. She resembled one of Odin's Valkyries, perhaps a match to the ones depicted in the tapestries in his hall.

He sat up and she uttered a single word. *Durham.*

But ... why?

CHAPTER ONE

Invasion

Durham, England
October 10, 1011 AD

DARK CLOUDS ALWAYS gathered in Noelle Sinclair's dreams. Hundreds of nightmares had played out in her mind since childhood. Why should tonight be any different?

The smell of burning wood invaded her sleep. Smoke snatched her breath and she tried to purge her lungs by taking deep breaths. She ran for the great hall and all she could see were scorched rafters and floorboards. Guards scrambled to the battlements, while women and children fled the castle. She searched for her sisters among the people migrating outside.

"Fire!"

Noelle's eyes snapped open at the sound of dire warning. By God, this was no dream! She flung blankets aside and rolled over, shook her older sister awake, and jumped out of bed.

"What's wrong?" Margaret asked sleepily.

"The castle's on fire. Get up, *now!*"

Margaret scurried from bed and ran with Noelle to the windows overlooking the eastern edge of the castle. Through the swirling fog, Noelle could make out a tangle of men with torches and weapons in the courtyard below. She further scanned the shoreline where the North Sea pounded against the rocks and dunes. The castle was under siege and poorly defended. Most of the soldiers and her father were in Ireland, leaving only her brother and a skeleton army behind.

Her gaze still locked on the beach, Noelle caught sight of three, silvery-white longships anchored beyond the walls. Their blood-red sails snapped in the wind. She stared in horror as the pattern on the sails came into focus—the shape of a dragon.

"We need to get outside," she said, and gave Margaret a gentle push toward the door.

Noelle grabbed a cloak from a hook, wrapped it around her shoulders, and thrust her feet into the first pair of available shoes. Exiting the bedchamber, Noelle led the way down the passageway, then descended the stairway that ended in the great hall. She halted midway, and Margaret drew back, frightened by the spectacle of violence below. Swords and pikes, fiery torches and axes—a blur of bodies and faces awaited them. The smell of blood and sweat permeated the room instead of the familiar scent of bread baking in the kitchen.

"What can we do?" Margaret whimpered.

"Keep moving," she answered, and gripped her hand.

They reached the bottom floor. Men were fighting everywhere and the sound of metal scraping metal deafened her ears. She searched for a familiar face, someone to help them escape. Luckily, John, her father's favorite captain, met them near the stairs.

"Run!" He lowered his weapon and pointed.

Noelle stumbled, but managed to sneak between two combatants. She looked over her shoulder at John.

"Go!" he screamed.

Before she could take another step, John collapsed. Noelle couldn't move a muscle to help him. Her entire body quaked under the weight of his assailant's steely stare—the man resembled a flesh and bone devil. Trembling still, she sprinted for the main doors with Margaret in tow. They made it to within a few feet of the entryway.

Heavily armored men blocked their route and a flash of movement attracted Noelle's attention. Another enemy charged from their right flank. His mouth hung open as he spoke words she didn't understand. Heathen curses that made her skin crawl. She squared her shoulders and pulled Margaret closer, her sister's heavy panting warmed the nape of her neck. The warrior's mouth twisted into a cruel smile.

"Easy," Noelle whispered. She didn't know where she found the strength to comfort Margaret as her own knees wobbled. Her grasp of reality threatened to disintegrate at any moment.

Just as Noelle contemplated making another move, a battle axe swung and split the offender's skull. Blood spattered across the front of her cloak and Margaret shrieked. Noelle dropped her sister's hand and motioned forward. She lunged and cleared the doorway, catapulting down the stairwell outside. As Noelle's feet hit the ground, she looked over her shoulder and saw Margaret had followed. They ran away as fast as they could.

The forest was the only adequate hiding place nearby and these men, whoever they were, would be more interested in looting the keep than chasing down a couple of helpless females, Noelle hoped. They came closer and closer to the dark outline of trees on the west side. Her father's lands stretched for many miles in every direction.

Flickering light beyond the tree line concerned her. Were other women in the forest already? She sprinted ahead. They mustn't provide a beacon of light for the invaders to follow. She burst through the trees and stopped in a small clearing to catch her breath. Margaret followed, wheezing.

Ten women. But Noelle's eldest sister, Ophelia, and other maids from the household were missing. More women arrived from the direction of the castle and Noelle turned sharply to inspect each one carefully. She took a torch out of a woman's hands and threw it on the ground.

"Put out all the lights," she directed, and rolled the oiled wood with the tip of her shoe until the flame extinguished. "We must remain hidden as long as possible."

There should be more women here. What excuse would she offer her father after he returned from Ireland for failing to protect them? Raids to the north and south had increased over the last few years. If Ophelia and the others were harmed because Noelle had failed to execute their well-practiced escape plan, she'd never forgive herself.

Fear quickly turned to agitation. She also didn't want to give her brother, Brian, a reason to question her competence. Not only hers—any woman's. In all creation, he claimed women were God's *only* failure. Every unfortunate female bore the brunt of his judgment. Whatever it took, Noelle must rescue her sister. Pacing, she considered her options.

She made up her mind and turned to Margaret. "Stay here. There's no reason for *all* of us to risk our necks."

Margaret locked hands around Noelle's arm. "Don't leave me here," she squeaked. "What would father say?"

"Father's not here." Noelle wrenched her arm free. Nothing could interfere.

Margaret's round eyes bulged unattractively as she waited for an explanation.

"Many women are in danger. And Ophelia is stubborn enough to stay behind to defend her dowry. Mother's gold and silver candlesticks aren't worth losing her life over."

"Is saving her from her own idiocy a legitimate reason to die, too?"

Noelle stared. Listening to her questions was a complete waste of time.

"Would father approve?" Margaret challenged. "And if you fail to rescue her, our sire may only have *one* living child to return to."

She actually thinks Brian and Ophelia are going to die. Noelle gave her a stern look. "Nonsense … I'd be more concerned if father returned and found *all* of his children unharmed and his castle burned with his fortune gone."

Margaret's lips twitched as she crossed her arms over her chest. "No wonder father says you are the most disobedient daughter in northern England."

Despite the temptation to match her sister's insult with one of her own, Noelle sucked in a deep breath. She shrugged and adjusted her collar. Not even the Almighty could talk her out of doing this. Ignoring Margaret's continuing protests, she disappeared into the trees.

Randvior Sirgurdson walked along the perimeter of the fore building overlooking the courtyard. Here the heaviest concentration of English defenders guarded the entrance to the castle, and *here* is where most of them perished. He acknowledged their bravery—never failing to recognize men who fought gallantly, although quite foolishly. Outnumbered five to one, at least forty broken bodies were being stacked along the back wall. He'd let the English bury their dead, only after the details of surrender were agreed upon.

After he'd called for a truce, several skirmishes had broken out. His captains put an end to them nearly as quickly as they'd started. A complete waste of time in his mind; why risk his men's lives if he could negotiate terms and bring the castle under his control without bloodshed. In the old days, he would have fought until the last English dropped. After fifteen years of raiding, he was exhausted—finished with pillaging and murdering. His father spent too much time and money on his education and training to piss it away.

My sights are set on the future, where seafaring will be altered forever. Christian kings were uniting in an effort to defend against foreign invaders. Soon, Norway would face its own challenges— the White Christ had already claimed many converts in the south. Quick and calculated strikes yielded the most rewards now.

Of course, it helped that the lord of *this* castle sired a known coward for a son.

He left Aud Magnusson, his most trusted captain, in charge and headed for the great hall. There were many things to discuss. Gold, silver, and a ravishing beauty that caught his attention the moment she appeared on the landing inside the hall. Praise Odin for favoring him this night. He even considered exercising his excellent manners—taught by the best English tutors during his childhood. He could perfectly emulate the speech and behavior of the most refined English gentleman at will. What he never fully grasped was their effeminate nature.

In spite of his limited patience, he entered the hall with good intentions. Confirm reasonable terms and go home. A huge commotion broke out somewhere near the back. He rushed past guards and women—pushed his way to the stairs. The dark bastard he recognized as the heir had a knife in his left hand and a woman's long hair coiled around his right. She struggled to stand, but he kept her bent over in front.

"What's going on here?" Randvior queried.

"This woman has no respect for authority. She's a disobedient bitch," Brian said.

"Drop the knife," he spoke dangerously low, poised for attack.

"Take another step and I'll cut the hag's throat."

Constructed mostly of stone, the castle would survive a fire. But countless wood outbuildings, alcoves, rafters, and floors might fuel one for hours. The closer Noelle came, the stronger the stench of scorched wood. Men were scrambling in the courtyard still. Through the thin torchlight, she could make out bodies on the ground—some wearing her father's colors and others dressed in chain mail.

Getting inside was going to be a challenge. There were only two entrances—the main doors and the entryway along the north end. She hadn't been to that side in a long time. The castle was a sprawling mass and the newest quarters to the north served as barracks for her father's army, close to the cellar.

Convinced she was out of danger at the present, Noelle emerged from the woods and hurried across the clearing. She stayed close to the wall while taking measured steps. Halfway around the wall it started to snow. Her feet were already freezing cold and wet.

Loathing swelled inside her. Not knowing the extent of damage to her home was the hardest thing to accept, and now a throbbing headache threatened to slow her down. Whatever inspired men to conquer and take what didn't belong to them didn't matter, she knew greed and lust drove them to sin, and very little inspired them to seek forgiveness. These invaders were godless heathens, soulless barbarians.

Noelle stopped and crouched to catch her breath. Part of her wanted to run into the open, waving her arms like a madwoman casting spells, and send them slithering back to their ships in fear. Only in legends …

Noelle put her head in her hands and covered her mouth to stifle a scream. She prayed fervently for guidance and strength. She deeply regretted running away before knowing where her sister was. She had acted in haste and forgotten everything her father had taught her.

Upon finding renewed perseverance, she stood. *Only a hundred more yards to the cellar door.*

A frigid wind cut through her cloak, chilling her to the core, and she ran the rest of the way. She peered around the corner. The north side of the castle was near the water, separated by a narrow strip of beach. The cursed vessels she'd spied from her windows were closer. Noelle touched her fingers to her heart and lips and pledged to forever hate the man who commanded those ships.

These ships had a different kind of grandeur about them. They called them dragonships because of the sleek design. Rumors claimed hideous effigies were carved into the bow and stern to ward off evil spirits. From where she stood, Noelle saw none. But that ruddy warrior in the hall could rebuff Satan himself—who needed carvings when mortal men looked like that?

Fear of those murderers using their superior numbers to overpower and torture members of the household haunted her as she crept forward.

If these were the same men who raided villages to the north, only a few months ago, all hope was lost. Those ghastly fiends pushed farther inland than ever before and burned everything in sight. They murdered dozens of monks and priests and stole holy relics. She tilted her head back to take in the full extent of the sail on the closest vessel. Begged Christ, she had been wrong the first time she saw it. The outline of the dragon glowed overhead like an ominous sign in the heavens. She lowered her gaze.

Sticky wet sand and snow clumped on the soles of her slippers as she paced anxiously. Believing them Vikings was one thing, confirming it another. And it had taken her too long to get there. Over an hour if her internal clock was working. No more useless deliberation. She had a specific goal.

As she made to take the last step in the direction of the cellar door, her legs tensed so tightly she feared she couldn't move. *My home. My family. My life.*

Male voices sounded from somewhere close by. Or maybe they were deceptively carried on the wind. Every nerve ending in her body pulsed warning. The noise eventually faded, and Noelle eyed the door. Hand resting on the knob, she went inside.

It seemed the young master of Durham lacked any moral sense. Randvior felt anger coiling inside as he threw Brian a measured look. *Threatening to slit a woman's throat for disobedience is a coward's way. Apparently his reputation is based on more than just rumors.* Randvior felt nothing but contempt and wished he'd never offered terms. His mercy had been wasted on the likes of this spineless creature.

Although the woman was English, he didn't wish to provoke Brian. Innocent blood benefited no one. He chose a less menacing stance. Not one Englishman challenged the heir as he tightened his grip on the dagger and pressed it against the woman's silky throat.

"Let me go ..." she said.

"Not a chance," Brian answered.

"You may think this is what you want, but you're not thinking straight." Her pleas made no difference.

The blade stabbed, cutting off her words as she sank to the ground at his feet. Blood pooled around her slim body.

Gasps resounded through the crowd, and a low growl escaped Randvior. He nearly pulled his weapon, hungered to chop Brian down like a cluster of weeds. But his hands were tied—bound by a promise to spare the wretch's skin.

And Randvior Sigurdsson had never broken an oath in his life.

CHAPTER TWO

Flesh and Blood

NOELLE HAD VAGUE memories of playing games in the storage rooms as a child. But as the years passed, they served a higher purpose—a sanctuary away from her brother's growing insanity. Brian's black reputation drew battle lines across Durham. Some men respected him, but most feared him. Her father did nothing to intervene.

Sons deserved absolute freedom, not daughters.

She stepped off the landing, surprised to find dozens of torches in floor stands down the main hallway. Someone had already searched there. Maybe for her or her sire's gold. Noelle picked her way along the corridor, relying on the walls to provide the support she needed to keep going. As she reached the end, she could hear men talking above stairs.

Such a long way up. *One step, two, and three,* she counted, then climbed. The closer she came to the top, the more heated the conversation grew. Heavy footsteps pounded on the other side of the door, making her fidgety—even tempted her to consider a full retreat. Apparently, the battle was over, but the fight had just begun.

She prayed her brother managed to hold off the aggressors. Or perhaps he was dead and they were fighting over plunder— indulging in what pleasures her home had left to offer. She didn't care about Brian's fate at the moment. What she *did* think about were the women and how these bastards might rape them. Her body tingled with nervous anticipation and she froze at the door. Cautiously, she cracked it open.

Brian's distinct voice sounded above the others. She scowled, while straining to hear exactly what he was saying. *My God!* Noelle nearly fainted. Did he really just reveal the locations of her father's gold and silver? Caches hidden strategically around the castle in hopes no one would find them. Pushing the door wide, she managed to sneak across the threshold unnoticed. She hid in a curtained alcove. From this vantage point, she had a clear view of the long table situated in the center of the room. Brian sat on a bench by himself facing her direction. Five men were seated opposite, clearly interrogating him. Any lingering doubt she had clung to, that might prove her original theory wrong, disappeared. Judging by their armor and long hair, she knew who these men were.

Noelle studied her brother's appearance more carefully. Unscathed. Not a single mark on his body that she could see. Maybe he never had the chance to fight. But something didn't feel right.

A Norse sentry, with a broadsword in his left hand, stood at an angle six feet away. A second man of equally intimidating proportion paced nearby, keeping his eyes fixed on the table. Her father's men were corralled in a corner, and the women were standing together along the east wall. Much to her delight, John was still alive. Faithful John, who had protected her and Margaret so gallantly, looked a bit frayed around the edges.

The room grew insufferably hot and she mopped her forehead with her sleeve. Did her brother just agree to give these pigs three women as bargaining chips for leniency? Her eyes zigzagged across the table. She considered the loose parchment, ink bottles, and quills. Bottles of wine, too, at least eight were open. Her father's favorite vintage. She recognized the bluish-white labels attached to the necks. What would he offer next, a place for these animals to bed the women?

Brian shifted in his seat as his eyes casually perused the room.

She shut the curtain, afraid he might discover her. Noelle blew out a frustrated breath. Slow torture seemed a better fate than witnessing his cowardice. Bargaining continued and her brother was on his way to securing his freedom. She peeked out again. One of the negotiators now demanded thirty able-bodied men as compensation for the fighters he had lost during the siege.

"No more than ten of your own perished," Brian countered. He spoke without conviction.

"Aye," the Viking confirmed. "One of my men's lives is worth at least three of yours."

Noelle's agitation piqued. She pulled the material wider and stared beyond her brother, at John. Dry blood crusted his face and his left arm was in a sling. Other men were seriously injured, a few resting on pallets on the floor. Even some of the women were nursing wounds.

"This is indecent …" She spoke aloud.

Before she realized what was happening, a pair of hands reached inside and extracted her from the enclosure. She jerked violently and broke free. The struggle attracted the attention of the men sitting at the table. She had a few choice words for them; and as for her brother, he deserved the worst of it. Her first duty was to protect her family's interests and, if she were given a choice in the matter, she would dispute any stipulations.

Brian walked toward her as the guard manhandled her into custody. "Where were you?" he demanded. "Several men searched the woods and beach—we found Margaret and her companions over an hour ago and brought them back."

"I've been close enough to overhear *everything* you said."

Noelle squealed when the guard lifted her off the ground from behind. She kicked, but it made no difference. The man hugged her closer and laughed. She wanted to rip his flesh from bone. Instead, she reached between his legs and grabbed a handful of his ballocks. Twisted so hard every muscle in his body stiffened. He hollered like a stuck pig and let go.

She landed on her knees, hands barely breaking the fall. As

she looked up, guards closed in around her with their backs facing in.

"Murderers—thieves!" she screamed. Laughter rolled around her, and much to her annoyance, this all seemed nothing more than a form of entertainment for them.

She stood and paced like a caged animal, couldn't see beyond the ring of bodies. But she knew where Brian waited and prayed for him to intervene on her behalf.

He didn't.

"Where are my sisters?" She let her anger take hold.

"Margaret is upstairs," he replied. "I told you *all* the women were accounted for, save you. Now quit this foolishness and act like a proper lady."

What absurdity. We are prisoners in our own home and at the mercy of wicked interlopers, and he dares to command me to act like a lady?

"I despise you," she hissed.

He chuckled.

She moved around the ring and shoved at the men with all her might. *Immoveable bastards …* "Get out of my way!" she demanded through clenched teeth, pounding a soldier's back with her fists.

"Cease the dramatics or I'll be forced to restrain you," her brother threatened.

He would do it. But she didn't feel like acting like a lady just now. For once, she actually wanted to be more like him and crack skulls. But if she dared strike one of these brutes in the head, the only thing that would break would be her own tiny bones.

"Let me through."

Surprisingly, two guards stepped aside.

"Is this your idea of defending our home?" she asked, breathless.

"Look around you," Brian said much too flippantly for comfort, spinning with his arms outstretched. "Are the walls standing? Are father's men and servants alive? I made a conscious decision to protect our home and assets. Live with it."

He clasped his hands behind his back.

Ah, the infamous stance he takes after he decides he's made a brilliant point in an argument and considers the discussion closed. She resented the fact that she was going to be forced to spend more than a minute in his presence. Brian reminded her of a squawking gosling running unrestrained. Amused by this illustration, she laughed out loud. He frowned disapprovingly and raised his hand to silence her.

"You'd sacrifice thirty of our men to these heathens?" Noelle asked.

"Before you so rudely interrupted our negotiations, I decided to reject that particular demand."

"Oh." She nodded approval. It troubled her to see her people forced to sit in the same room with these savages, witnessing these demoralizing proceedings. "Where is Ophelia?"

Brian coughed, then motioned her away.

"Did I ask something so personal you refuse to answer me in public?" She stared suspiciously. *And to think he's actually admired in the northlands by some men.*

"This is a delicate matter." He gripped her right arm and dragged her further away from earshot. The Norse seemed unconcerned, but still kept watch.

He stopped near an east-facing window. Distressed over what he might say, Noelle blocked him out of her mind for a moment and prepared for the worst. She stared into the darkness outside. Thinly threaded moonlight reflected off the water.

She faced him. "All I want to know is where Ophelia is. Whatever else you decide is your own business. Is she in her room or in the kitchen with the servants?"

Peace could never be achieved between them. No matter what he did or how he accomplished it, Brian *always* looked out for himself. Some men were honored in their lifetimes for observing laws of chivalry. Others were revered for displaying talent as diplomats or distinguishing themselves on the battlefield.

In any of these ways, a man gains the respect of his peerage. Not Brian. He displayed no such talent, but his cunning was of an evil sort. Like the serpent's in Eden.

His gaze traveled up her body and rested on her face. "Ophelia ..." His body language suggested the worst. He didn't need to finish his calculated lies, she shrieked.

She slammed her hands against her sides as long-suppressed emotions came rushing back. He had played her false from the moment she had arrived. Avoiding truth to keep her pacified.

"An accident," he finished, disregarding her outburst. "She suffered injuries in the fight this morning."

Empty words—not an ounce of compassion laced his voice. Under any other circumstances, she would have flung herself on the floor and wept. Instead, she felt numb all over. Noelle chewed on her bottom lip and imagined what it would feel like to beat him to a bloody pulp.

"Who *murdered* her?"

He stared through her, oblivious to her presence.

Roiling emotions cramped inside her gut. "*Who* killed Ophelia?" Noelle threaded her fingers through Brian's in an effort to regain his attention.

He turned, fingered a strand of her hair, and sniffed it. "So pretty ..." he mumbled.

"What happened?"

"I'll tell you. We were attacked in the middle of the night and I was caught with my breeches down like a mindless boy. Half the guards were drunk, and the others barely put up a fight. So I accepted the terms these bloody bastards offered—a way out. Instead of dying, we were spared." His poor excuses did nothing to aid his cause.

Although he hadn't exactly answered her question, he seemed to be getting closer to a legitimate response. Perhaps if she manipulated him just enough, tweaked his delicate ego in just the right way, she might get the answer she needed.

"If father fails to acknowledge your success, tell him he's a fool for overlooking everything you've done to preserve us."

He shook his head. "I failed plain and simple, Noelle. Sometimes a man's honor is stripped away forever if he exercises poor judgment in such matters."

"Ophelia is dead." This reality had hardly started to sink in as she feigned a smile. "The rest of us are alive because of *you*."

"Ophelia?" His voice grew markedly agitated, most likely brought on by the mention of their sister's name. "You're so obsessed with one set of circumstances you fail to see the depth of our troubles. The dead are already dead, I can't change that. As tragic as it is, father is only concerned about one of us."

Bleeding a rock was easier than getting answers out of him.

"His *only* heir is alive and well," she said matter-of-factly, biting back tears that pained her eyes.

He rewarded her last observation by gawking at her as if she were the village idiot. "You really are the most stupid girl." He clutched her hand, applied pressure between the base of her thumb and ring finger until it hurt.

"You have no idea why our father is really in Ireland do you? Sweet, naïve, Noelle, always walks around with her head in the clouds. When is the last time you actually admired yourself in the looking glass? I'd wager a bit of gold and say never. Ophelia and Margaret are lovely, but you are the rare gem. A diamond in the rough as father likes to say. You're in desperate need of a firm hand and a punishing ride in the sack to break your spirit, but a splendid girl by any man's standards."

Noelle's jaw dropped.

"I was counting on your bride price father was going to collect from your future husband in Ireland to finance a larger army next year. And now you've ruined my chances by flaunting yourself before the Norse chieftain like a whore." He jerked her toward the wall and flattened her left cheek against the stone. "You disobeyed my orders. Instead of staying in the woods with, Margaret, you pursued your own interests. I believe you *wanted* to attract his attention, to find a way out of here."

"Who? I have no idea what you're talking about. And why on God's green earth would father go to such extraordinary measures to find a husband for me when he has two elder daughters to forge alliances with?"

The freezing stone numbed her face. Instead of answering her question, Brian twisted her arm and bent her wrist back until she let out a yelp.

"Deceptive little bitch."

He let go, and she faced him. The whites of his eyes were bloodshot.

He grabbed a handful of hair and snapped her so close she could smell ale on his breath. "No matter where you go, I'll hunt you down." He bashed the back of her head against the window frame. "I'll hunt you down and kill you!"

Cringing from his brutal words, Noelle finally burst. Through the blur of tears, she saw a warrior of tremendous proportion storm across the hall. He seized Brian's arm and pried his fingers loose from her hair. She heard a loud snap as he curled Brian's arm behind his back. Her brother stumbled and hollered, then dropped to his knees.

"Say it," the colossal warrior demanded, visibly applying more pressure to his hand.

Brain tried to wrestle him down, but the stranger was larger and stronger—controlled him with little effort.

Although she detested her brother, her first instinct was to protect her own flesh and blood. Yet, it seemed a fitting punishment. Let Brian suffer the same mortification she felt whenever he embarrassed her, which happened too often.

Brain quit struggling. "Mercy," he begged.

The Viking released him, and Brian staggered to his feet as gracelessly as a drunk.

"Is this how you treat your own kinswoman?" her rescuer asked.

"She's faithless—no blood of mine. We've made our bargain Norseman, take her." He stood rooted in place like a stubborn mule and faced her. "You're a whore." His words ripped through her.

How quickly he turned on her like a rabid dog. And for no good reason. Now he spoke about a bargain she knew nothing about and called her horrible names ... *Ophelia is dead and her murderer is walking freely amongst us, but my soulless brother speaks of anything else. Where is her body?* Noelle's anguish increased.

"So long as I serve a purpose I am your blessed sister, but the moment an opportunity is lost, you cast me aside like trash. What have I ever done to deserve this treatment?"

Brian threw his head back and laughed, then stared her down. "You killed my mother."

Heart splayed-open, she felt dead inside—like she had slammed into a brick wall at a full run. Noelle covered her ears in an attempt to block out his vicious words. Blaming her because their mother died after giving birth to her was simply the cruelest thing he'd ever done. How can anyone hold her responsible for something she had no control over? *Cuts and bruises always heal, but a wicked tongue destroys.*

"Never again," she vowed.

"Never what?" Brian repeated mockingly.

"What happened to Ophelia?"

The giant wedged himself between them as if he were preventing a fistfight. She didn't like the stranger standing so close and backed away. His gray eyes washed over her like a torrent of hot water.

"He's unworthy of your devotion, failed to tell you the truth—why *he* killed your sister."

She nearly howled as her eyes flitted between them. Who should she believe? *Why would this man lie? But how could Brian be guilty of killing Ophelia?*

"Tell me," she pleaded. "Convince me this is all just a misunderstanding."

Brian ignored her, made no attempt at denial. He stared at the Norsemen with a lurid expression that made her insides churn. She wanted to run far away. Instead, she only wandered a few feet. She stopped in front of the windows again and watched the sunrise.

Noelle wanted answers. She whipped around and stalked across the hall with one man on her mind. She stopped in front of John. "Tell me, does the Norseman speak truthfully?"

The old soldier nodded, sadly. All the guards agreed. Regardless, she went down the line one by one just to confirm it. And after she finished with them, she looked upon the women. She shook her head.

"You shall not commit murder." She recited the sixth commandment over and over again to keep herself from committing violence against her brother. Just barely, she managed to restrain herself.

The world altered as sunlight seeped into the hall through the windows. Evidence of fire and bloodshed was much clearer in the light. The thick beams near the stairs were charred black and damaged more severely than anywhere else in the room. Floorboards and flagstones were stained in pools of dry blood. Stones in the main hearth—the loveliest feature in the room— were chipped and broken. Chairs and tables upturned in corners and tapestries her mother painstakingly collected from all over the world were shredded or singed. *The house of Sinclair is finally reduced to ash and rubble to reflect the emotional ruins we've lived in for years.*

She closed her eyes, willing the image of a perfect life into her head. Her mother alive—four children lovingly gathered at her feet. And her doting father eating nearby at the high table with a twinkle in his eyes. It was a heart wrenching fantasy.

Noelle returned to Brian's side. He wore his customary arrogance like a war medal. Time stopped and everything moved in slow motion. Her eyes were painfully dry from lack of sleep, itched like they were filled with gravelly dirt. Her hair and clothing reeked of smoke and sweat, and her lungs ached. There was nothing worth saving in this cursed house—honor be damned. Not sire or friend could comfort her right now.

"Why?" she finally asked.

"Ophelia risked our lives by retaliating. Even after the truce was made, she stabbed one of their captains. I put her out of her misery once and for all."

She swallowed yet another scream and flew at him, prepared to use the only weapons she possessed. Like a feral cat, she dug and scratched his face, intending to scar him for life. Brian recoiled and blotted his cheek—shocked at the wet stain on his hand. She raced behind him and jammed her fists into his spine—punching him over and over again.

He whirled. His heavy boot connected with her belly and sent her flying backward. She crashed to the floor and stared up at the ceiling in a daze. It had been a moment of foolish rage to think she could retaliate so boldly without him winning the fight. He abused women—sisters and lovers alike. A burst of pain broke her thought and she rolled onto her side, crunching her knees into her chest for relief.

She raised her head in time to see the Viking circling Brian like a predator stalking its prey before the kill. His hand rested on the hilt of his sword. Maybe he wanted to cut Brian's head off. *Do it.* He was the most polarizing force in her life. *Rid us of this disease. Everything he touches withers and dies.*

He chanted something in that malignant tongue she'd heard him speak before and backhanded Brian so hard he stumbled several feet. Brian didn't move again. But they stared hard at each other, rage arched between them. Then the Viking half-walked and half-shoved him across the room. Women along the east wall parted and scampered for safety. He didn't stop until the back of Brian's head hit the wall. Not giving her brother an opportunity to recover, the Viking punched him in the face and Brian's legs buckled. He landed another blow, kicking him to the floor with a fluent sweep of his right leg.

Noelle's blood pounded as she stood and hurried across the room. Rage had clouded her judgment. Although she wanted

Brian to pay, let him face an English executioner with his bloody head firmly planted on a wood block, not die at the hands of these Norse invaders.

The Viking was unstoppable. She considered the look of violence in his eyes and slowly edged away. He unsheathed his weapon and raised it high above his head, but a guard intervened.

"Hva vil du gjøre med henne hvis hun hater deg før du går til ektesengen?" the guard said.

Judging by the severity of his tone, they must have been words of warning. She didn't know if these men were organized by rank, but the larger of the two—the one who attacked her brother—froze with his sword midair. Brian lay at his feet, muttering nonsensically.

She knew little about these people. Only that they sailed superior ships and worshipped a deity named Odin. She believed his god's fury filled his mind as he leaned over Brian. She shrank a bit when he grabbed a handful of her brother's hair and lifted his head.

"I made these generous arrangements to spare the girl's feelings. Not for your bloody convenience. You owe *her* your life. She's the only reason I'll spare you. And if your other sister wishes to escape this hel, I'll claim her, too." Brian's head hit the floor with a thud. "Worthless bastard ..." he muttered, spinning on his heels, and staring down at her.

Stormy eyes threatened her sanity. She tried not to be deceived by his excellent features. Or drawn in by the smoothness of his bronzed complexion. The Viking seemed as harmless as the sharp end of an ice pick. And that voice—God help her.

His baritone possessed the ferocity she'd fantasized God's might have, thundering from the burning bush. It put the fear of The Divine in her. Blond hair hung well below his shoulders, tightly braided at the temples. His broad cheeks, aquiline nose, and shapely lips were perfectly symmetrical. She marveled at his savage beauty. Although she resented everything he represented, secretly, she was grateful for his sudden appearance. What kind of a barbarian invades a castle and offers terms of surrender to its inhabitants?

She stared pensively at him. He wore a knee-length, chain mail shirt over leather. His boots were embossed with strange circular patterns and dyed a rich bluish-purple. Silver medallions were sewn around the toe line, very different from the rest of his men's shoes. He had an air of regality about him. A chieftain, of that she had no doubt.

The longer she stayed in the room with him, the more her sense of reason fragmented. Nothing would ever be the same again. Brian was guilty of more than cold-blooded murder. He abused his power. But even now, she knew he could do no wrong in her father's eyes. Noelle hated him for that. And the fact that she found herself regrettably obligated to this barbarian for rescuing her crushed her spirit.

What bleak future prospects. She folded her hands over her stomach and stared away as long as possible. Found her mind wandering back and forth between Ophelia and this arrangement that her brother spoke of. She didn't care to add more weight to the burden she already carried. Mere speculation would only drive her crazy.

Instead, she drifted around the room in a silent frenzy and watched as the Norsemen came and went. They carried away piles of loot, depositing them on their ships. She attempted to memorize the faces of her father's soldiers, surmising which men had died in battle. Her father found little use for keeping formal ledgers. In a situation such as this, it would have proven much easier than merely guessing who the survivors were.

She remembered the identities of the women easily. Thirty-three maids were grouped together. The children were obviously cloistered somewhere upstairs. And Brian wisely kept his place on the floor, probably too afraid to move. There was nothing more she could do here. It seemed a selfish way to think, but if she didn't leave, she might do something she'd regret later. Like kill her brother ... Noelle slipped away.

CHAPTER THREE

Eyes of a Stranger

R ANDVIOR HALTED AS the beauty made her way to the doors. His men started after her, but he stopped them. No harm in letting her go, for now. Give her time to work through the torture and torment. Wherever she went, he knew he would eventually find her.

The climate in northern England made him appreciate the place even less. He forbade his men from drinking more because he feared it might affect their already diminishing spirits. Nothing would have kept them from overindulging in food and drink, except for his direct command. And *his* men, like any, might resort to violence once their gullets were wetted. This place had a way of picking away at a man's soul.

The only light he had found within the suffocating darkness of Durham seemed to be the girl. Her unwavering allegiance to her kinsmen and servants restored his faith. It made him reconsider his long held opinion that women served only one true purpose. Pleasure … He remembered only a handful of accomplished females he'd met in his travels. They were spinsters and widows who had dedicated their lives to attaining wisdom. Although young and stubborn, Noelle was composed of the same commendable qualities. And she fascinated him.

Randvior entrusted the management of the takings and preparation of his ships to his men, then found a private space to sit and clear his head. He propped his head on his hand. He'd never imagined coming here, but Odin's vision determined his path. The elusive deity was known to favor his family, and if he demanded an unplanned stop, who was he to defy his patron god?

His men were restless after a season that yielded little profit and *no* action. *These are the risks I am willing to take to solidify my holdings and establish new steadings.* The prospect of a quick raid south ended all complaints. Bound by oaths of allegiance, his captains and foot soldiers went wherever he commanded. And if the gods denied good fortune, blood sacrifices compensated for whatever bad omens attracted their disfavor.

Fortunately, Durham yielded enough silver and gold to go around. And a woman he felt an instant attraction for. She broke his concentration too easily already. He grinned, felt an uncomfortable stir between his legs, and cursed his rebellious body. The last thing he wanted was to run around with an erection, when he didn't even know where its inspiration had fled.

Randvior's pleasant reflection changed course. Noelle needed time to exorcise the demons from her mind before he took her on ship. Many a seasoned warrior had chosen a watery death over another year of raiding if they didn't want to go. Always a coward's way out. And he refused to give the girl a chance to dive overboard. With the burden of her sister's death on her mind, she was in no shape to think clearly yet. And the way her murdering brother treated her—his tongue should be carved from its English mouth. How dare he refer to her as a Norseman's whore?

But he couldn't delay their departure. The evasive girl would simply have to accept her fate. The thought of running his hands over her lithe form nearly drove him insane. He wanted to master her body. Something told him she was more than just a pretty face, though. And he truly wanted the opportunity to explore the complexities of her mind, experience the world through her eyes.

Convincing her to accept him was going to be difficult. He refused to resort to rape as most men in his position would. But he wasn't opposed to relentless seduction.

He left the alcove and headed directly for the stairs. Noelle's sister would provide the information he needed to find her. English castles were a maze of endless rooms and hidden chambers. It could take a man a week to discover the places where a young girl would hide in a structure that took three centuries to build. He knocked on the bedchamber door.

Margaret answered.

He studied her delicate features. Blue eyes as round as a serving tray darted nervously between him and the empty hallway behind. "I know you blame me for Ophelia's death," he paused, surmising her state of mind. "There is no time for formalities. I need your help finding Noelle."

A faint smile flickered across her tear-stained face. "You may be different from the Norsemen the village women describe, but what makes you think I'll provide you with any information?" she asked. "Many of those women were left with child after the raids and will never forget the beasts who assaulted them."

He also exercised better judgment than most jarls. His men had not inflicted such indignities on the women in this household for good reason. The gods directed his hand in this endeavor, and temperance was divine.

"I offer my deepest sympathies for the women who suffered so needlessly." His statement was true for the most part. Resorting to violence was necessary sometimes to bring conquered peoples under control. "Tell me what I need to know."

She scrutinized him with a lingering stare. "I'll only tell you to spare my sister further pain."

"Prudence should prevail, lady. You are in no position to deny me anything."

"There's nothing you can do to make my life any worse. You'll leave my home in shambles and I'll be the one tasked with putting it back together. Do you really think I'm afraid to die after what occurred here today, Viking?" Her eyes brimmed with tears.

"I can't challenge or negotiate for Noelle's freedom, I've nothing to give. So you'll take her by whatever means necessary, I know this. But I'll tell you. If you harm a hair on her head, I will damn your soul every day for the rest of my life, and believe me, God will hear my pleadings."

Bewildered by this sudden display of feminine mettle, he could do nothing but admire her and further loathe her brother's cowardice.

"My sister only seeks refuge in two places, the woods or the old cellars." She rubbed her nose and looked over her shoulder, in the direction of the windows. "She's in the cellar."

As Randvior turned to leave, she fastened her hand around his arm.

"A priest could never hear my brother's confession, there's no salvation for such a man. I beg you not to be such a brute where my sister is concerned, she's only eighteen."

Why was she saying this to him? He inhaled and blew out a frustrated breath, fisted his hands. *By Odin, what evils did she speak of?* And just what had he bargained for?

"My brother is obsessed with death."

"Some men are born killers."

She nodded and changed the subject. "How *old* are you?"

"Twenty-eight."

Her gaze drifted to his eyes. "Old enough to take care of my sister, *I hope.*"

"Aye," he said, and left.

The cellar door was open, a clear indication *someone* was inside. After his men finished exploring the storage rooms for gold, Randvior had ordered them to remove the torches and secure the door from the outside. He ducked under the stone archway and lifted his torch high so he could see down the stairs.

It was an ancient passageway with narrow steps; the kind a man could fall down and break his neck. As he descended, he admired the carved stonework. Two torches burned in a floor stand—Noelle was definitely there. He knew this wasn't the kind of place a young woman would customarily seek solace. But any place must seem safer than near her brother.

He searched the cellar, rummaging through piles of debris. There were three subchambers off the main room, and small, round windows hewn in the stone allowed natural light to filter in. No one was there. He sighed and searched the first subchamber. Dozens of empty barrels and crates were stashed in a corner, but no girl.

He didn't wish to frighten, only wanted to show her a bit of kindness.

"Noelle Sinclair," he called, walking slowly. He sincerely hoped to lure her out of hiding without resorting to physical force. No matter if she resisted, the terms of surrender were *not* negotiable. She was his greatest prize—not intended for slavery, but true companionship after years of meaningless trysts with faceless wenches all over the world.

No words could describe the emotions that stirred inside him once he met those somber eyes searching for an escape from the besieged hall. It compelled him to abandon his men and concentrate on her safety alone. Attraction turned to pure enchantment after she came face-to-face with his fiercest fighter and didn't utter a sound. The rare bravery she demonstrated sparked a passion inside him long forgotten. An attribute greatly admired amongst the Norse. He rubbed his chin and suppressed a smile.

He explored the second room. A hint of shadow moved across the wall. *"Min lille dukke, komme til meg, jeg vil ikke skade deg,"* he whispered. "Why are you hiding in the dark?"

No answer.

He waited a moment longer before speaking again. "Come out."

A rustling sound from behind a stack of dilapidated crates alerted him to her exact location. He took four steps and stopped, kept a safe distance so she wouldn't feel cornered.

"Noelle, I'm here as an ally, not an enemy."

"Hah!" Her face appeared. "You have a strange way of showing it."

"You're right," he agreed. "But situations change as quickly as the direction of the wind at sea. You must be brave a little longer."

Momentarily distracted, he took full advantage and inched closer. The graceful curve of her mouth and the pinkish color of her lips did not escape his attention. Unfortunately, his first opportunity to get closer was impeded by a pile of rotting wood. Blast his misfortune!

She didn't seem to mind he was within arm's reach and stepped from behind the crates. He watched the expression on her face change as she studied him. He'd give her plenty of time to admire his features once he got her on ship. Until then, every second that passed represented increased risk—her father's army could return at any moment.

"It's time to go."

"Where?"

With her face streaked in soot and dirt, she looked more like an orphan than a lady. Her long tawny hair was little more than a mass of dirty tangles, and her shift was badly stained. By Odin, she was still beautiful. His gaze moved slowly up and down her tiny frame and stopped on her feet. *For the love of Odin* ... "Where are your boots?"

"I never had a chance to put them on. I was rather preoccupied with getting out of the castle, because you set it on fire." Her voice was thick with sarcasm. "Am I not suitably dressed?"

Randvior actually preferred his women naked. But this point might not foster feelings of cooperation.

"Under the circumstances, I cannot fault your state of dress. Come with me, you need to change into something warm before you catch your death."

She ran her fingers up the side of a crate, avoiding his stare. "I want to stay *here*. I need to oversee the preparations of my sister's body—plan her burial."

"Impossible." Although he deeply sympathized with her loss,

nothing could extend their stay. "My men are expecting us. There is much to do before we depart."

She inclined her head. "I cannot say I'll be sorry to see you go."

He had been awake for two days straight, and if she didn't hurry up and cooperate, there was going to be a price to pay. "Surely you understand what your brother meant by this arrangement—we bartered for more than just gold. *You* are a large part of my takings."

He turned and searched for an empty floor stand, found one, and placed his torch in it.

He lacked what most educated men considered *virtues*, or the moral ingredients that truly made any nobleman noble. These traits were loosely based on the Greek *Pillars of Wisdom. Humanism. Rationalism. Love of Freedom. Moderation.* Patience was the hardest, of which he usually possessed none.

"Enough." He waved a hand and swore silently at the unnecessary gruffness in his voice. "You *will* accompany me back to the hall."

Her eyes fluttered erratically. "But I don't want to go with you! You've no claim on me—no right to make any demands."

He drew a sharp breath. *Be patient, her world is crumbling before her very eyes.* "I know you need time to mourn your sister, time to digest everything your brother—"

"Stop talking," she said shakily. "My brother will pay for his sins one way or another. He is a subject of the English crown, not you. And a subject of Christ's vengeance—an eye for an eye … As for anything else, I've nothing to say about it." She looked like she wanted to be anywhere else but with him.

She flapped her arms and barely managed to finish. "All of this is beyond my capacity to work through. I hate you—you destroyed my home and it might as well have been your hand on the knife that slit my sister's throat, it's your fault!"

She started to shake uncontrollably, gulping for air between hiccupping sobs. Randvior wanted to snatch her up and hug her close. Show her how he could ease her pain.

Between breaths, she found the strength to explain. "I'm sure you overheard my brother blame me for my mother's death …"

Randvior nodded.

"She died from birthing fever. And I've lived with the guilt of it since I was old enough to speak. My brother, even my sisters at times, harbor ill feelings for me. All I have left of my mother is right here in this castle. Her books, collection of tapestries, and trunks of clothes. Her scent still lingers on some of her gowns."

"You can choose anything to take along," he said. This simple gesture seemed to soften her a bit.

"It's not the same. Her spirit roams freely here and if I am gone, who will look after her?"

He believed her. Who was he to deny the existence of a loved one's ghost? Norse believed in many things they couldn't see or explain.

"And to hell with you, or whatever the equivalent is in your religion if you don't like it!"

He looked at her.

"Please," she begged. "Just leave me alone."

Randvior shook his head. *Impossible.* By Odin, there were instances when a man could easily lose control. This might prove such a circumstance if he didn't get her out of the cellar. The flickering light reflected hauntingly in her cloudy eyes. Tempted him … Made him burn insatiably for just a brief taste of those sweet lips.

"We've tarried long enough."

He had fulfilled his obligations, spent enough time in this wasteland. The gods increased his wealth. The only thing left was to go home—back to the Trondelag before ice prevented him from crossing the North Sea.

As if reconciled to her fate, she offered her hands. He reached, but was rewarded with an unforeseen punch to the chest and a kick to the shin. She jumped back and grimaced. Shook her hand out in obvious pain, cursed the chain mail … He eyed the scrapes on her knuckles and drew her in, wrapped his arms around her little frame. Her body fit so nicely against his.

"Let go!" She tried to wiggle free.

No woman had ever resisted his charms before. He held her close, hoping she'd quit struggling. Randvior supported her body with one arm and let his other hand roam freely across her back. She made some funny noises at first, then exhaled, shifted on her feet, and surprisingly laid her head against his chest.

Breathe.

She gazed up at him. Those dark eyes warned him not to push her any further, but she felt so alive in his hands. He tipped her chin and her eyes fluttered closed. He smiled and slowly touched his lips to hers, then dipped his tongue inside her mouth. He teased her at first, allowing her to make the next move. Then her tongue moved with his, swirling and exploring the depths of his mouth. A branding heat suffused his whole body until his ears burned. But as quickly as she started, she stopped, pushed him away, and stared up at him. Whatever thoughts played in that feminine mind he'd have to worry about later. Willing or not, she was accompanying him, and *right now.*

He pulled her hard against him again. His hand followed the curve of her spine and cupped her arse. She sputtered and slapped him. Randvior withdrew his hands. And for a brief moment, his rage surged dangerously close to the surface.

"If you were a man …" he growled.

"If I were a man," she said. "Your hands would have never strayed to my arse, you rutting beast." She clutched at her breast. "You'd use a woman's grief as an opportunity to seduce her?"

He laughed. "*Min lille dukke*, enough nonsense, I've no time to play these childish games with you—after we are on my ship, we can play whatever you like."

Much to his pleasure, she stomped a foot obstinately and made her own growling sound. "My brother told me you intended to make me your *thrall* or *concubine.*"

Randvior choked back another laugh. *A slave—never. His*

concubine, close enough. "Do you even know what a concubine is?"

"No," she answered stiffly. "But I know what a thrall is, and I won't be anyone's slave!"

Her eyes darted wildly around the room, possibly searching for an escape. He'd better say something to calm her down. "In my homeland there are laws that protect nobles from being enslaved. I would never expose you to such humiliation, even if you were a conquest of war. If it eases your conscience, you have my solemn oath. You will never become a slave."

Her eyes shot daggers as he finished pledging his oath, his hand placed dramatically over his heart.

"And your word is to be trusted? I think not." She whirled and sprinted for the door.

Before her foot touched the landing, he grabbed a handful of her cloak and pulled her toward him. He was delighted, always enthralled by the prospect of a good chase. But there was no time for that kind of sport right now. Of course, it deserved some consideration later. All patience lost, he spun her around like a child's top and flung her over his shoulder. She yelled and kicked, cursed as well as any seaman he'd ever met. *Light as a feather*, he smiled, *with lungs as powerful as a screeching banshee's.*

Randvior chose to take the longest route back to the great hall to give Noelle a chance to recover her dignity. As they exited the cellar, the bitter cold overpowered them. She shivered and squeaked hoarsely. If she persisted in screaming, she might lose her voice altogether. Not a bad thing. But if she sucked in too much cold air, she risked catching her death.

He spanked her bottom and gave her a firm shake. "Enough!"

In turn, she slapped at his arms.

"Didn't you learn the first time that armor scars hands?"

"I'll risk it again if it means you'll put me down instead of carrying me around like a sack of turnips!"

He rewarded her with another deep-throated chuckle, which seemed to irritate her even more. Her flailing feet made contact with his chest. Like a fish on a hook, she flopped around until he stopped abruptly.

"I'll give you one chance," he said, and she went stiff. "Your sister or yourself—fate rests in your hands."

"Violence *and* trickery," she said. "Not as stupid as you look."

"Bite your tongue, woman," he warned, thrashing her backside, reminding her of her rightful place. He did have limits. If he were any other man, she would have been spread across a bed hours ago, feeling his manhood deeply rooted inside her, no regard for her feelings at all.

He tossed her into a snowdrift. "Perception is everything." He grinned.

When he saw the rage in her eyes, he regretted not doing it sooner.

She stood and dusted snow off her front and backside. "Yes," she agreed. "And shall I tell you my first impression?"

"I think you made that clear—never call me that again."

She pointed angrily at him. "Never put your oversized paws on me again!"

Randvior wished he had a muzzle—she had a wicked tongue as fiery hot as a branding iron.

Blood stirring, he stepped closer. "Make your choice, *now*."

"Did you ever really give me one? Are you teasing or simply testing my allegiance? I'm not the kind of woman to push my misery onto someone else, especially my sister. Don't underestimate me, Norseman. I may be younger and weaker, but I'll fight you every chance I get. This is my home. No matter how flawed it seems to you, it's all I have."

She held her ground as he came even closer. Nearly on top of her, he pressed his forehead to hers. "We've reached an understanding. If I must tie you up and carry you away for all of England to see, so be it."

She opened and closed her mouth, wet her lips, and stared hard and long before she spoke again. "Try me ..."

Mediocrity never graced Noelle's life, always feast or famine. The Viking, whose name she didn't even know yet, manipulated her into agreeing to go with him. Oh, that she had a blade to run him straight through! Trailing slowly behind, she imagined a hundred different ways to overpower the libertine. But a girl's fantasies and stone cold reality were anything but the same. The form walking in front of her couldn't be taken down by ordinary measures.

There were ways though, big men required plenty of rest, and unless he slept with his eyes open, a moment of opportunity would eventually present itself. She'd already challenged him. And what did he do? Laughed in her face and embarrassed her beyond comprehension.

It struck her that she might never see Durham again, her sister, or her father. She twirled slowly and absorbed the open countryside covered in snow. The forest and ocean, the open meadows and sandy beaches. This land had something to please anyone. *This is my playground, not some frozen tundra where men live lecherously beyond the grace of God.* If Brian's babbling nonsense about her father going to Ireland to finalize a marriage contract for *her* was true, she'd be forever bound to some faceless groom and still forced from her homeland. Why must she be the one to rescue her family from the brink of poverty, when she had an elder sister more than willing to marry?

They reached the courtyard and he introduced her to one of his captains guarding the doors, Harud Ostberg. The man towered a full head taller than him, if that was even possible. She offered no salutation, but didn't resist as the man took her by the arm and led her inside, leaving the Viking lord to his business.

"A moment with your sister," Harud said, pointing to a tiny closet by the stairs. He paused in front of the archway and flashed his weapon. "No games," he said, patting the blade like a dog.

She nodded.

Margaret was waiting, and flung herself into her arms. Touching Noelle's face tenderly, she began to weep. "Everything is falling apart at the seams. Brian is completely unrepentant, claims his actions were justified because Ophelia posed a threat.

Father is overdue and you are leaving me forever."

Noelle wrinkled her forehead and sucked back her own grief, again. Margaret's body quivered in her arms like a terrorized child. After a long time, they broke apart and she brushed strands of falling bangs aside so she could see her sister's eyes.

"Don't let these heathens have the satisfaction of seeing you shed tears."

Margaret's body jerked one last time. "Your clothes ..." She pointed to a chair.

An overdress, chemise, and pair of wool stockings were neatly folded and waiting. She looked around the small space as she kicked off her ruined shoes. Her leather boots were on the floor. Margaret stepped aside, picked up a sheet, and spread it wide for privacy while Noelle stripped out of her damp garments.

Modesty forced Noelle to keep her face to the hall while she changed, just in case roving eyes tried to peek inside. Harud was only a stone's throw away, which did little to settle her nerves. *This is the most shameful thing I've ever experienced.* Resentment grew as she tied the silver ribbon at her neckline. Margaret balled the sheet up, threw it aside, and laced the back of her gown.

"There's little time, Noelle. Have faith and remember I love you."

"Come." Harud's voice sounded.

"Beast." Noelle whispered in her sister's ear, swallowing the lump in her throat. She was also afraid to let go of the only person left to love.

This seemed a defining moment; how she reacted might shape her future amongst these men. Give in too easily and they'd consider her no more than a twit. If she resisted too much, punishment was sure to follow. Noelle chose to disregard him completely and gripped her sister harder. She might have to go with them, but not so willingly.

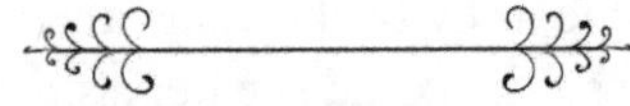

CHAPTER FOUR

Realization

AFTER HARUD HAULED Noelle from the alcove and dragged her across the room kicking, her stomach wallowed. With home incessantly on her mind, she couldn't concentrate on anything else. And it didn't help that a pair of foul-tempered Norsemen were escorting Margaret upstairs. She shook her head. Margaret might be out of sight, but never far from her heart. After inspecting the room, she noticed the servants were gone, too—even Brian had mysteriously disappeared. Noelle wondered if this was the chieftain's way of controlling her. Isolate her from everything familiar so her heart broke *before* they boarded his ship.

Crates were piled near the doors where the Viking Chieftain stood. She imagined this scene resembled her future, all alone with a legion of warmongers, who scared her out of her skin. No chaperone and no one to provide comfort.

The giant strode across the room as if he reveled in the fact that he was temporarily the master of the keep. He grinned boyishly at her, revealing perfectly straight white teeth.

"Come." He tugged at her sleeve and she followed him to the hearth. A platter containing bread, cheese, and fruit was on the table. "Are you hungry?"

"A little," she admitted with cool courtesy, quite intimidated by his hulking physique.

"Woman," he said dispassionately. "You are in no immediate danger from me."

She looked at him in exasperated wonder. *What was that supposed to mean, in no immediate danger?* Dwarfed by his gargantuan body, she thought him daft to think she felt otherwise. Noelle tried to find the right words to express her feelings, but nothing appropriate came to mind.

"Eat," he said, shoving a piece of crusty bread into her hand.

She glimpsed another smile playing around his attractive lips and wanted to rip them off his face. Being so close to him made her aware of just how dangerous he really was. She mashed the bread in her hand and bit a sizable piece off.

He possessed no manners of any kind, and stared at her lips while she chewed and swallowed. He looked a bit tortured for it. Exhaustion and hunger had finally caught up with her and she reached for another piece.

Rudely, he blocked her hand. "Why did your father leave his lands so vulnerable?"

She could see his self-admiration coming through. God have mercy … Her stomach ached from the first sampling of food. The crumbs had only teased her insides. "Leave me to eat in peace, *please.*" She eyed him.

"Only if I give consent."

Frustrated, Noelle slammed her hand on the table. *Fools play.* Would everything be a competition with him? From the moment she'd met him, an aggravating smile had spanned his face, similar to a court jester's.

"Go to hell," she murmured indelicately, praying for patience and the good sense to keep still. She brooded over whether she should ask him what he found so damn entertaining. Women were often the subject of masculine amusements; but surely, a man of his worldly experience knew they didn't like it!

"Answer my question and I promise you shall eat without further interruption."

Her blood went hot. She didn't like being toyed with. There

must be limits to his patience, she had limits of her own and considered herself more than fortunate with how well he'd treated her thus far. His kindness must be closely linked to how well she performed—how well she amused him. If she cooperated, he'd continue to reward her with everyday necessities. Disappoint him, and she feared he would withhold often-underappreciated luxuries like food and water. Fortunately, Noelle had never truly felt hunger before. But after only a few hours of her home being under siege, the uncomfortable hunger pangs that were currently stabbing at her gut convinced her she never wanted to again.

The hall suddenly hummed with life around them. She absolutely could not bring herself to answer his question and shook her head. His beautiful eyes held many secrets. And another grin creased his face as he clutched her hand, wrapping strong fingers around her fragile wrist.

"I already know where your father went and what business took him to Ireland. I was just curious to see if *you* knew."

She snorted and leaned her elbow on the table.

"My father never thought enemy ships would stray so far south this late in the season."

Hopefully this reply satisfied him.

"Under normal circumstances your father would have been correct, but it's still a costly oversight on his part." He relaxed and released her hand, poured a glass of wine from a bottle on the table, and offered it to her.

She refused.

"Drink." He pressed the glass into her hand, nearly spilling the dark liquid down the front of her dress.

She sipped sparingly. His insufferable personality served no purpose. No need to force-feed her. *Cretin. Men are the same everywhere—making meaningless demands simply because they enjoy watching inferiors squirm and jump at their commands. Someday I'll find my voice of true resistance.* For now, the Viking remained in complete control.

After she finished, she scowled at him from behind the empty glass, turning it slowly around in her hand. "Now I have a question for you."

"I will permit it."

"What is your name?" She didn't see any harm in asking. If she was destined to keep company with this stranger, shouldn't she have the privilege of knowing his given name?

"*Randvior Sigurdsson.*" It rolled off his tongue as prettily as a line from one of her favorite sonnets. The last syllable heavily emphasized.

"Rand for short," he offered with a brilliant smile.

Thank God, a moment's reprieve from his doltishness. She sighed as he moved the tray of food toward her and plopped down in a chair.

"We sail this eventide."

Noelle found it impossible to look at him for longer than a few moments at a time. Something made her feel inconsequential in his presence, which forced her to navigate through a wide spectrum of emotions she'd sooner forget than face.

Smirking at her apparent distress, he burst out laughing. Disgusted by his brutish manners, she looked away. She could easily call him dozens of filthy names … Having a brother as dastardly as Brian had served a purpose after all, it increased her vocabulary tenfold.

"Am I that bloody entertaining?" Noelle simply couldn't harness her emotions any longer and balled her hands into fists at her sides. She threw him a venomous look.

"Yes." His grin broadened.

Noelle's throat went dry with irritation and she blushed. He was purposely trying to aggravate her. A humongous hand brushed the side of her face and she jerked away.

"Why do you assume you can touch me whenever you wish? You care nothing about how I feel or the lives of the people you interrupted here. But I congratulate you on a stunning victory, Jarl Randvior. You've conquered my father's lands without a proper army to defend them. And we shall provide the necessary praise to keep you pacified to keep us from further harm. Must you persist in denigrating me, even after I submit to your every demand?"

His loud chuckle vibrated off every stone in the hall and down her spine. How she desperately wished she possessed the strength to kill him. Instead, she retreated to the other side of the chamber. Immersed in thought, she didn't hear him follow. And without warning, his hands rested on her shoulders as heavy as millstones.

"I've seen the way you look at me, *min lille dukke*," he whispered tantalizingly near her ear. His breath swept across her neck like a hot summer breeze.

Rattled, she knew if her face revealed half the things she was thinking, it was no wonder why he made sport of her. Determined to keep her pride intact, she responded. "And I've seen the way *you* look at me."

"Assume nothing where I am concerned."

"My father says a man's actions speak louder than his words." She faced him, then stepped around him to take her leave.

He caught her by the sleeve before she made it too far. Randvior Sigurdsson was undeniably surreal. God carved his physique with such precision he reminded her of a statue.

"I'm sure your father is an educated and competent man. And I readily admit if *my* eyes reveal half the emotions yours do, consider it the reason why you're going with me."

Her breath caught in her throat. This unexpected confession pushed her closer to hysteria. She should hate everything about him—but he had played her protector and spared her family. He was taking her away from the only world she'd ever known. Godless heathen. And if she surrendered, everything she had hoped for in life and considered special, including honor, would surely be lost.

"Your brother parted easily with you, if I swore to leave this castle standing and spare the lives of his men. It was an astute decision on his part, but a clear indication of where his loyalties lie—with himself. We greatly outnumber your men."

Why did he speak of this now? "But ..." She struggled with her thoughts. "... I saw how many bodies littered this hall and the courtyard. Not all were my father's guards."

"Aye," he said. "Many died, even some of my own soldiers."

"And my sister, Ophelia, was she part of your unconscionable bargain?" She shuddered.

He stood in a warrior-like stance, with his barrel chest pushed out and his nostrils flared. His face darkened. "Her death changed everything."

Noelle found some consolation in the fact that she had ruffled his emotions so easily. Not made of stone. Maybe he wasn't dumb as dirt after all.

"I am not the type of man that condones the unnecessary killing of women and children. Despite what you assume, my men are held to higher standards than most. Above all things, I strive to be a fair man. There are limits to my violence, and my *patience*."

She hung on those last words and shut her eyes to avoid his penetrating stare. But his face was forever imprinted in her mind. She felt her most intimate feelings were on display for him alone to judge. "I don't care if I'm a pawn in your twisted game. But my sister's death is only further proof of why *your* kind should be wiped off the face of the earth—annihilated for the crimes you commit. Have you no shame?" Before she could even think, she reached up and slapped him so hard she left a perfect outline of her tiny hand on his cheek. "When did you find the time to barter for me as part of your plunder?"

He looked at her with amazement.

Randvior folded his hands over his stomach and sucked in a breath. She guessed his first reaction should be to beat her senseless for striking him.

"I did not offer those terms late this morning."

"When then?" she demanded.

"Minutes after I saw you in the hall ..."

Why didn't she remember seeing him amongst the fighters? Surely a man of his impressive stature, whether helmeted or not, would have attracted her attention. Letting the sequence of events play out in her mind, she recalled the red-haired mongrel that had attacked her.

Realization.

Her jaw dropped.

Someone had repelled him. A man she had assumed was one of her father's conscripts.

"You?" she asked severely. "You shielded me so I could escape?" She never meant to say it out loud. *"You* defended me?" It slipped out sounding more like an angry accusation than gratitude. Bewildered, she stepped back.

"The day is fast approaching when you will see things with more clarity."

Something scarily infinite sounded in what he said. And he didn't deny her assertion. Or confirm it. All sense abandoned her and she categorically denied the existence of any obligation to him. Sharp pain in her chest made her wince and she felt suddenly lightheaded. If only she had eaten more before drinking a full serving of wine.

The look on his face changed to grave concern. Before Noelle could guess why, he swept her off her feet. She flailed weakly in protest as darkness closed in. *Don't take me aboard your ship,* she wanted to say, but the words never came. The last thing she remembered seeing was his eyes.

CHAPTER FIVE
Mutual Respect

RANDVIOR FIRMLY BELIEVED Noelle's fainting spell to be a ruse to buy time for her father's men to launch a rebellion. But after seeing the color drain from her vibrant cheeks, he moved decisively and commanded two of his men to escort them to his ship. He deposited her inside his cabin and waited for her to recover. Keeping her away from her kinsmen seemed his best defense in case his suspicions were justified. He eyed her appreciatively as she lay curled up like a kitten on his bed. There had been no hesitation on his part choosing her once he'd encountered her inside the hall. That head of honey-colored curls reminded him too much of the woman in his vision and he would not risk his future by ignoring it. He stared down at her, greatly tempted to kiss her again.

She rolled onto her back and had hardly had a chance to breathe before his passion came gushing out. "Look at me."

Noelle combed her fingers through her hair and stared at the ceiling. "Where am I?"

"On my ship," he answered. "You seem determined to prolong our stay in England."

"Believe me," she thrashed a hand. "I have no desire to prolong anything. Be gone from me, devil."

He snickered and considered the cool fury in her eyes. He already knew her incapable of concealing her emotions—her face was as revealing as a gypsy's crystal. A hint of fascination gleamed in those eyes, too, especially when she looked at him. Willing or not, something unexplainable had already sparked between them. Randvior believed the attraction between a man and a woman was one of the unexplainable wonders of the universe. And he was unwilling to overlook the curious timing of her appearance, no matter how grim her circumstances. The gods dropped her in his lap for a reason. Mere coincidence? Not when he knew Odin's hand had played a role. This involved fate. He curled a finger under her chin.

Such a delectable morsel needed to be tasted. What pleasure she would receive while he worked those narrow hips. And that perfectly formed backside had already brushed against his manhood on more than one occasion. He closed his eyes, visualizing how perfect she must look naked. *"Denne jenta har den strammeste rumpa jeg noensinne har følt!"*

"What perverted things are you saying now?"

His lips curved into a roguish grin. "Not insults, *min lille dukke*, merely observations any hot-blooded man would make."

Lifting a slender hand, she deflected his answer. "Horse manure. And those other words I recognize well enough—*min lille dukke*—I hear you speak them often."

"A term of endearment. It's irrelevant."

Might she offer a smile now? He hoped she would. Instead, her eyes narrowed, confirming her annoyance. "Remind me sometime in the future to tease you with words *you* cannot understand."

"Aye," he said. "As long as it's not spoken in French, Spanish, Greek, Latin, Gaelic, English, or Norse—all of which I am quite fluent."

She rolled her eyes. "Most men flex their muscles to attract the attention of the opposite sex, are you suggesting you showcase your linguistic skills to do so?"

"My tongue is skilled at many things, if you care to find out."

"Vagrant—to think you would speak so shamelessly in front

of me. I didn't grow up in a convent. I know what men mean when they say such things." She tossed her head, her words trailing off.

"I shall say something more appropriate for your pretty ears. *Ma petite poupee … meum pupa …* or *mi munequita,* they all mean the same—what I see before me."

She crossed her arms and pursed her lips much too attractively for comfort. He admired her self-control; most women would have thrown something at him. Noelle simply shut her mouth whenever she was particularly irritated.

"Damned to spend an eternity with a mindless churl."

"Careful," he warned, grabbing at her. "Remember, there are consequences for everything you say."

"I meant no—"

"I know what you intended."

Her fingers fumbled nervously with the long gold chain around her neck, twisting the cross pendant. "I'm your captive— this I must accept. Will you keep me from speaking freely as well?"

He'd suspend all hostilities if she'd only offer him a blasted smile. Willful girl. "If you disrespect me or my captains, I will deal with you no differently than anyone else under my care. I cannot allow insults to be overheard by my men."

"Does it undermine your authority or force you to confront the malice so deeply rooted in your soul?" she asked poignantly.

To hell with self-restraint! He wanted to tie her hands to the bedposts and fill that virginal hollow between her legs. *I have plenty of authority,* he thought. And he'd love to give her a firsthand demonstration.

CHAPTER SIX
Sea of Reckonings

A STEADY WIND filled the sail of Randvior's flag ship, *Odin's Eye*, as the last ribbons of sunshine colored the eventide sky. Noelle wrapped her arms around the polished mast as she stared forlornly at her homeland fading away, swallowed by clouds and waves. Her heart was broken. Randvior seemed conveniently occupied at the moment, so she focused her attention on his other two ships following behind. Any distraction would serve her purpose right now—keeping her mind off the people left behind. Especially Margaret.

A strong northerly cut across the deck and quickly reminded her of the season. Shivering, she knew it would only get colder where they were headed. To the wretched northlands, a place where men worshipped carved stones and sacrificed innocents to their gods.

After she'd woken up in Randvior's cabin, he'd given her an opportunity to witness such an act before their departure. She'd accompanied him to shore and watched breathlessly as his men constructed an altar from flat stones on the beach. They'd sacrificed a suckling pig from her father's barn as recompense for Odin's favor. Randvior's personal entreaties were sacrilegious, and she should have turned away. Even though he spoke in a foreign tongue, the power behind his words had captivated her.

She couldn't keep her eyes off the soldier who slit the animal's throat. A second man laid its bloody carcass across the altar. Meanwhile a light rain had started to fall. But it made no difference to her; she had never seen a pagan ritual before, only heard stories told amongst the men in the hall when they were drunk. Deciphering between truth and exaggeration was impossible until she had witnessed it herself.

The sacraments Noelle observed were paramount to her salvation. But she never dismissed the faiths of others. Better to remain silent than risk God's wrath. Besides, these men voiced no concerns over her faith. And their commander hadn't exercised intolerance. After all, it wasn't her soul he craved.

Randvior courteously ushered Noelle around deck and introduced her to many of his soldiers. Aud Magnusson seemed to be his best warrior.

"I have three daughters of my own," Aud announced proudly. "One near your age, perhaps you might become friends someday."

Randvior patted him on the back. "Ask my friend who runs his household."

Noelle believed three daughters would run any man ragged. "I needn't ask," Noelle turned her attention to the imposing figure. "Judging by the look on your face, your daughters are in full control." Even though he was a barbarian, Noelle couldn't help but like him.

Aud laughed appreciatively. "Aye," he agreed. "And we'll see in a few weeks, once you're settled in the Trondelag, who runs my master's house."

The men exchanged mirthful grins. Noelle curtsied, for lack of a better response, and walked on with Randvior.

"Now that we are under way, you may ask me whatever you wish."

Noelle rubbed irritably at her nose. She'd had plenty of questions when they were still in Durham. How dare he show her around his ship as if she were an old acquaintance he was escorting home? Now he was all smiles and acted as if nothing had happened. Ophelia and her father's men were dead and nothing could alter the ugliness of that reality.

"You've given me hardly any time to recover from this atrocity. And now you expect me to parade around this ship with you and exchange niceties with the murdering heathens who attacked my home and stole me away as chattel? And beyond this ..." Her body trembled. "... now you want me to ask questions?" His casualness enraged her. "You make little of what happened in Durham."

Randvior gripped her by both shoulders and nodded.

His unspoken acceptance left her mind a jumbled mass of confusing thoughts and left her heart full of contradictory emotions.

Though one question did come to mind.

"Why me?"

Randvior had promised clarity. And she deserved the truth in measured doses. They walked to his cabin, very much in need of privacy to continue the conversation. He opened the door and they went inside. He sat down on a chair next to the narrow bed, folded his hands behind his neck, and stretched his long legs out.

"I'd never considered targeting your homeland. If I yearned for a lucrative raid, my ships would aim closer to Ireland. A week ago, I was in the Orkneys preparing to return home. Father Odin sent me an incredible vision—showed me his banquet table in Valhalla. A rare thing for a mortal to behold while he still lives."

Noelle sat on the bed and for the moment appeared enthralled by his tale.

"His fierce maiden warriors, the azure-eyed Valkyries, who serve and choose the men who sit at his table, offered me wine from his chalice. No man can refuse this honor. I drank, but much to my dismay, I realized the table wasn't decorated for celebration. It was prepared for a funeral feast. Not to honor warriors slain in battle, but those wretched souls condemned to Hel. I dropped the sacred cup and ran. Once I escaped, I mysteriously appeared on the lands surrounding my home. Funeral pyres burned in every direction, columns of black smoke rose above the earth, very near my own hall." He dropped his hands from behind his neck and leaned forward.

"I hastened for miles through ice and snow to reach my steading. Before I crossed the border, *disir*, women who decide men's fates, were waiting. I greatly mistrust these spirits and attempted to elude them. But they followed me and called out to me.

Why do you run from your destiny? There are two possible ends for you, and we have revealed both. You have drunk from Odin's cup, an honor bestowed on few mortals. Yet you remain only half a man. Sail to Durham on the eventide and discover the troth the gods have chosen for you. If you reject this gift, your wyrd will be altered—given over to forces beyond Odin's control."

"Tell me what wyrd is?" Her skepticism was evident.

"Fate."

The hairs on the back of his neck stood up at the retelling of his tale, yet disbelief still remained on Noelle's face. She resembled the wraith in his dream. Randvior studied her features more closely. Unable to resist the urge to touch her, he moved to the bed and pulled her onto his lap as he sat down again.

She bristled. "So I am to believe that a warmongering prince succumbed to the demands of spirits he doesn't trust, then sailed for distant shores? If my father's army were present they would have overpowered you and sent you back to Norway in burning ships."

He arched a brow, completely unprepared for how to deal with such an undisciplined, feminine tongue. A few unsavory methods crossed his mind, perhaps a gag and a firm throttling to her backside to start.

"I didn't realize Norsemen relied on mystics to determine their futures."

He nodded agreement and loosened his grip. "My people pay homage to countless deities, and seek the council of many when mapping out the course of their lives. Our stargazers are the most famous in the civilized world and have successfully predicted the futures of kings and military leaders—earning them many enemies. I know these ancient practices violate the tenets of *your* religion, but we were mandated by our gods to use our skills to help shape the future. Your church unfairly condemns pagans, levies false charges, and executes them."

The *disir* had revealed his fate. They referred to him as *half a man,* and those prolific words beset him the most. A woman, spirit or otherwise, could say nothing more degrading. Randvior had interpreted them correctly, in his opinion, therefore safeguarding his virility from further scrutiny. The gods wanted him to take a wife. *A woman can fill the empty spaces in a man's soul like mortar between stones.* He went where Odin commanded and found the girl. With his blood heating exquisitely, while she squirmed innocently in his lap, he nudged her off to keep himself from losing control.

He stood. She was too beautiful for her own good.

And his. The only way to win her affection would be to woo her.

"That's it?" she complained. "Your silly story ends there? You fill my head with ridiculous notions of gods and spirits—prophetic visions, fire, and mayhem and end it without resolution?"

Keeping a straight face, he let her rant continue.

"My senses tell me you're full of—"

Randvior laughed warningly. "Sometimes a story ends where it must. This isn't girlish make-believe, but an honest recounting of what carried me here."

Most women would have swooned upon hearing how the gods favored him. Not this one. Noelle Sinclair simply rejected him.

Days passed and Randvior spent his afternoons walking and talking with Noelle on deck.

Today, he formally introduced her to Odin and a myriad of deities he worshipped. He also prepared her for the reaction his people might have once they found out she was English. It seemed hatred thrived on both sides of the sea. *Men most fear what they do not understand.*

"Decades of derision lay between our countries. The first Norse ships landed in Lindisfarne over two hundred years ago. My ancestors swept the region, pillaging, and enslaving with such unprecedented success that no one seemed capable of stopping them. Their bloodthirstiness struck fear in the hearts of men. Norsemen have been demonized ever since."

The *only* thing Noelle surmised his people feared was the expansion of what they considered an illegitimate faith, which had already cost thousands of people their lives across the continent.

"Last year," Randvior continued, "a Christian convert named Olaf Haraldsson, returned to my country to claim the crown. He publicly professed his new faith and proclaimed the indisputable right to unite the country under the Pope's banner. Most jarls rejected his idea."

"Why?"

"My kinsmen are fiercely devoted to Odin. We would never abandon centuries of tradition because belief in a new god was carried across the sea by a zealot long absent from his homeland," he said. "There is always increased risk when a man's ambition is driven by religious fervor."

Noelle didn't know what to say. People should freely choose what god they want to worship, and if Christ's blood united nations, well, she would secretly celebrate it.

"Your religion will sweep the world and your god's holy soldiers will kill anyone who gets in the way. Tension is building across Western Europe as I speak, and I believe your Pope will eventually set his eyes on the Holy Land," he said.

"Do you forbid me to practice my faith?"

"No," he answered curtly. "But any open display of your vulgar traditions might draw unwanted attention, and may even prevent you from being accepted by the women. Women you will need on your side one day."

"What traditions do you speak of?"

"Cannibalism," he said plainly. "Eating the flesh and drinking the blood of your White Christ."

Noelle looked at him incredulously. Had she heard him correctly? "You are greatly mistaken. We do not actually eat his flesh or drink his blood. Holy Communion is a sacrament, a symbolic gesture mandated by our Lord. Surely you don't believe otherwise?"

Randvior smiled ruefully. "What I believe doesn't matter. I've traveled the world and seen many things. My faith is unshakable. My tenants and thralls may not be so open-minded. Their worlds are much smaller than mine."

"I made no such judgments concerning you." Noelle knew she wasn't going to be among her kinsmen or friends any longer, but this seemed ridiculous.

The Viking lord had watched her closely on the beach in Durham during the ritual and had even expressed his appreciation at how she approached things with a child's innocent curiosity. People in his homeland might learn something from her.

"A Christian monk visited my home last year," he offered, "and disappeared on the same day. Not by my order, but my men discovered a fresh burial mound a few miles away."

Noelle flushed and swallowed back her concern.

"You have my protection," he promised. "There are no temples or churches, no Sabbath observed amongst my people."

"Where do you worship?"

"Wherever I choose. Under trees, along the riverbanks, or in a place we think the gods hear our voices. There are holy sites. What were you imagining? Secret chambers where we conjure demons or groups of scantily clad women and hooded priests prancing around a bonfire in the middle of the night like a coven of witches? There *are* priests amongst us, elders who serve as mediators." His eyes danced mischievously now, humored by her naivety.

The ship careened, stopping their conversation short. Objects flew off the table in the corner and Noelle ducked just in time before a candlestick flew over her head. She nearly choked while standing back up and bumped her head on the wall.

A loud knock sounded at the door.

Randvior opened it, one of his warriors waited.

"A powerful storm is brewing, you're needed on deck."

Randvior adjusted his belt. "Stay here," he commanded, looking at her. "It may be hours before it's over."

She understood and nodded. Vikings were the most revered and feared men on the high seas. Not only known for their violence, but as explorers, and successful merchants, too. This much she knew growing up in a territory continuously under attack. Against her better judgment, she allowed her gaze to follow him across the cabin, mentally groping his body. Such capable hands, and she felt herself slipping; sliding down an emotional incline with no way of climbing back up. She smiled bleakly as he rummaged through a cabinet and withdrew several instruments he must use for navigational purposes.

She watched his retreating form. Much to her surprise, Noelle realized that she was starting to like him a bit and felt safe in his custody. She had been so intent on hating him that she couldn't recall when the shift in feelings occurred. Should she forgive him for robbing her of a future she had carefully planned out? Or would that be considered the worst kind of betrayal to her family?

Having always lived outside the circle of intimacy that connected her siblings with their father, she couldn't decide. When her sire spent time with her sisters, he seemed contented in the moment. But in Noelle's presence, his eyes dulled. She had earned his respect, but never his love. Randvior undoubtedly offered a new beginning. With this, she became overwhelmed; the time and energy it would take to find a way home seemed pointless in the moment. Her life was irrevocably changed. Brian had sold her into slavery to save his own life. A known braggart and skilled fabricator of stories, he could easily convince her father of anything if she weren't present to defend herself. Her brother's stinging voice rang inside her head. He would swear on the Holy Father's name that she begged to go along with the Norse to escape marriage to an Irish lord. Her father would surely sever any ties to her for the magnitude of such iniquity.

By the time the only candle in the room had burned down to a waxy nub, Noelle had been tossed and turned about the windowless cabin more than a dozen times. She had sailed on many occasions between southern England and Ireland, always nestled closely to the shoreline, but the open sea was perilous. She eyed a bruised elbow, and now her left knee stung, too. Enough was enough, no more tumbles off the bed. She stripped the covers and made a bed roll on the floor.

Howling winds buffeted the ship. She imagined the black-capped waves ripping holes in the polished wood and nearly vomited when the ship went vertical. She grabbed the bed frame to stay stationary. The vessel surged upward again and came crashing down. Noelle bounced and landed hard. The worst jolt yet.

She had to get out of there, trembling as she imagined a watery grave. *Pray Noelle Marie—pray fervently*. With no rosary beads or prayer book to read from, she had to rely on verses or prayers she had memorized over the years. Heart pounding, she prostrated herself. Comforting visions of an earthly paradise eased her mind as she whispered the verses over and over again. Surely, no harm could befall her wrapped in the protective arms of her beloved Christ.

Hours later, the door burst open. A dripping-wet Randvior stepped inside and almost tripped over her. He muttered something under his breath as she turned and watched him walk to the cupboard. He opened it, withdrew a new taper, and lit it by the wick of the nearly spent candle. He placed it in a holder he picked up off the floor as she sat up.

The worst must be over for he would have never abandoned his men in the middle of a squall. She visualized what he must look like working the riggings and sail with those strong arms. In the muted candlelight, his eyes were purely electric, any amusement long gone. With his wind-blown hair and raw masculinity seeping from every pore of his body, he looked as untamed as the ocean. Dangerous conditions could break any man. And she feared a tempest of this proportion stirred her companion's emotions. Eyes are the windows to the soul and his spoke violence.

He knelt and ran his fingers over the curve of her hip. His eyes never wandered from her face. "Stand up," he commanded.

She obeyed.

Randvior looked capable of striking at any moment. Unsure and afraid, she stiffened when he climbed to his feet and towered over her. A moment of silence passed between them, but she heard the thunder of war drums pounding in her ears. A spell of nausea was followed by a wave of guilt because she knew she was wrong for wondering what it would feel like to be buried in those massive arms.

"What were you doing on the floor?"

"I ... was ... praying ... for the soul of this ship," she stuttered.

He nodded.

Noelle lost courage. Nothing could protect her from this man. Suddenly, Randvior leaned down; his tongue was hot and hard as it broke the plane of her lips. Naturally, she wanted to fight, threaten, and scream—maybe escape. Everything seemed wrong as strange sensations seared through her flesh. Hadn't she anticipated this moment the first time they met? A telling premonition or perhaps she needed something only he could offer. Release after years of holding back her deepest feelings and hostility. She knew she should deny him, but this felt too good and she could not suppress her desire any longer.

Randvior's tongue probed deeper and she opened to him. He groaned inside her mouth and it reverberated up her spine. She matched his scorching kisses with virginal exuberance as a large hand cupped her right breast, and the other anchored her against him. Calloused fingertips prodded and tickled the hardening nipple through her dress.

He licked his way down the column of her neck, moving his tongue in tiny circular patterns. His hands dropped lower, utterly delighting her, exploring every inch of flesh between her stomach and upper thighs. He paused when she moaned and she rewarded his ministration with a dreamy smile. Her eyes met his and she nearly melted in his hands. Curse him for being so irresistible. Did Eve's apple tempt Adam half this much?

His beard pricked her skin as he slid his hands up her body again. And those heated fingers left her in a daze as they indelicately unlaced the back of her gown and tugged. She swayed as Randvior pulled the material over her head and yanked her chemise down until it sagged loosely around her hips.

He stepped back and took a deep breath, openly admired her, while his eyes caressed her lazily. "The enchantress in my dreams has sprung to life. You are more beautiful than I ever imagined, Noelle."

She felt the intensity of his need through the quietness of his voice. Her silence was his answer.

The only stitch of clothing left was her stockings and boots. She convinced herself to feel no shame. She needn't love a man to get what she needed. Men sought comfort in the arms of nameless women all the time. And for once in her life, Noelle intended to gift herself with a single indulgence. He rolled her leggings halfway down and knelt; his soft lips made contact with the goose-flesh on her inner thighs. What was left of her wits scattered to the four winds.

She offered herself to him—her eyes meeting his as she braced herself against his chest, almost expecting something cataclysmic to happen.

It didn't. Only the comforting warmth of flesh meeting flesh. Molten-hot hands scaled the soft mounds of her body. Front and back, and she grabbed hold of whatever part of his she could reach. *Oh God ...* Never had she imagined how wickedly good it might feel to be at the mercy of a man.

He pulled away briefly, and she immediately missed his body heat. If he stopped now, she might lose her resolve to keep going. Everything he did tormented her, and she moved closer, desperate to feed on his passion. Randvior chuckled softly.

"Tell me what you want little one."

No man had ever touched her body before. Even so, Randvior seemed to know how to keep her begging for things she didn't know how to ask for. *And words wouldn't come, not now.*

His body promised both pleasure and pain. Noelle yearned for him to make her a woman, to transform her for just one night. The pain of yesterday would be there after she woke up. Tonight belonged to her—and Randvior. He teased her lips with a flick of his tongue. She opened her mouth to say something—anything—but nothing came out. And after he slid his knee between her legs, she could hardly breathe. She reached up and wrapped her arms around his neck, while he shredded his linen shirt with one hand, revealing powerful flesh underneath.

A jagged scar ran along the top of his right pectoral and she traced it gently with her fingertips. He growled and closed his eyes.

Emboldened by his response, she explored even further. Softly massaged his chest and curled her fingers in the thick hair that covered it. She tasted him and pinched both nipples as her tongue moved nervously over the hard contours of his body. He threaded his fingers through her hair and pressed his body hard against hers.

His nipples went pebble-hard as she nibbled on them, changing from a soft pink to a deeper shade of red. He let her hands go and she pinched again. What made her do that? Randvior laughed so hard he coughed. He winced as she squeezed a third time and caught her hands midair. She enjoyed watching his body tighten like a freshly strung bow.

"What are you doing?" he asked.

Noelle's fixation on his nipples gave her time to calm down.

He hugged her. Noelle looked up and admired the finer details of his face—the arch of his brows, the alluring slant of his eyes, and those naughty, ample lips. She captured the bottom one with her teeth, gently digging her fingernails into the sides of his face.

A pair of mind-boggling kisses stopped her destructive behavior. Randvior lightly touched the curve of her mouth, cradling her breasts in his hands. Her back arched as soul-stealing sensations ravaged her body. Ignoring fear, she began mimicking his movements. If he caressed her face or nibbled her earlobe, she did the same. Her heart fluttered at this new discovery—how she could manipulate his body with the touch of a hand or a playful bite.

Everything about him delighted her. Bits and pieces of her morals mentally interrupted the pleasure. But those thoughts were lost in the slow demand of his kisses. *And their flesh shall become as one.* The blessed saints had failed to stop her.

"Show me ..." She curled her arms around his neck.

He growled as he picked her up and carried her to the bed. Randvior pinned her to the mattress with one hand and kicked off his boots. Next, he stripped off his weapon belt and breeches. She eyed every glorious inch of him—fascinated by his maleness. Noelle's obsession faded as her eyes locked on the monstrosity between his legs. She struggled to break free; terrified *it* would rend her delicate legs apart.

"Shhhh," he whispered as he blanketed her.

With a reassuring nod, he took her mouth. Noelle didn't love him, but by God, she wanted him. The Viking showered her body with feather-light kisses as she squirmed pleasurably underneath. Years of frustration were beginning to disperse. Even if only for one night, she needed to feel this joy. *Make love to me ... now ...*

Randvior surged upward, rubbing his sweat-slicked body all over hers. His shaft grazed her stomach, triggering a new wave of excitement. Noelle clung to his hips.

"Not yet," he whispered and rolled onto his side. Randvior guided her hand between his legs until something velvety-smooth grazed her fingertips. Instinctively, she locked her hand around it. After whispered instructions, she stroked him.

Moisture seeped from the tip, making it easier to slide her hand up and down. It felt so good, thick and smooth and hard. A faint pulse thrummed near the tip. She stared unblinking at him, watching his eyes.

Something made him grimace.

"Let me go," he whispered.

He rolled on top of her and gently spread her legs with his knee, skimming her overly sensitive nipples with his teeth. He licked and sucked until her whole body ached. An arrogant grin split his face as she quaked beneath him.

He parted the folds of delicate flesh between her legs with one hand, gripping her hip with the other. She sighed helplessly and lifted her head to peek down at him. But pressure started to build deep inside her and Noelle was lost in something indescribable and unknown as she tossed her head side to side. There was both a gentleness and darkness to his possession. And she never guessed fingers could do that! Oh, she remembered women bragging about such things. They hadn't lied!

How much longer will he torment my poor body? Nothing could have prepared her for what he did next.

The shock of his tongue between her thighs moving in perfect harmony with his agile fingers reminded her of a dance. She whimpered and flailed, and grabbed fistfuls of hair to try and wrench his head away. The sensations he elicited were mind-bending.

He tethered her wrists together with one hand and pulled them aside. A new sensation heated her insides. Her flesh pulsed around his fingers and tongue similar to a heartbeat.

"*Randvior ...*" she moaned uncontrollably. Beautiful bursts of colored light flickered around her.

He slammed his mouth onto hers, flooding her with the taste of her own arousal. This man was surely bound for the fires of Hades. A string of huskily garbled words in that godforsaken language he spoke followed.

Raising his head, he whispered. *"Min lille dukke*, I must …" He didn't finish and she barely managed to nod consent.

He thrust inside her. Liquid heat spread from her loins to belly, followed by pain. Randvior redistributed his weight and cradled her face so tenderly in his hands that she nearly burst into tears. The virginal pain was a small price to pay compared to the pleasure he had shown her already. She knew he would make her forget all that pain.

"Everything is all right, please don't stop."

He didn't hold anything back. He stripped her maidenly fears away, layer by layer. Noelle instinctively raised her hips to absorb the brunt of his powerful thrusts. *He's magnificent!* Randvior's own satiated cries mingled with hers as he appeared to lose consciousness for a moment. Her body shuddered with fulfill-ment.

And then ached with regret. A single, unseen tear trailed down her cheek …

Her life would never be the same again.

CHAPTER SEVEN

Vikings

NOELLE SLEPT FITFULLY—WAKING, then dosing off again. Finally, she decided to stay awake. Unaware of how long they had lain together with their limbs intertwined, she gritted her teeth, didn't like feeling so vulnerable. Weakened from the physical strain of matching her lover's rigorous stride, her legs and mind felt numb as thoughts tumbled in her troubled mind. She sat up. No secrets remained between her and the Viking now, and she needed to get her priorities straight. Preferably before Randvior woke up and saw her tear-stained cheeks.

She reflected on many things, her new status was her primary concern. The hope of ever emulating the good deeds of the Blessed Virgin disintegrated, but there was always the Magdalene to consider. She huffed and swung the bulk of her hair over her left shoulder. In a careless moment of passion, she had lost her innocence. The unforgettable sensation of Randvior surging inside her a last time lingered between her legs. And wanton thoughts made her skin tingle with embarrassment.

She also remembered Brian's stinging insult—calling her a Norseman's whore.

She stared at the wall, resentment stewing. Brian had deceived her. He had purposely chosen her as the sacrificial lamb and sold her into slavery. And she had willingly given herself to the Viking. What a fool she was.

Serious consequences would follow. No wonder the guards and servants cast sympathetic looks her way after the terms were agreed upon in Durham. Forced to witness the proceedings and everyone but *she* knew what fate awaited her. She snuck a peek at Randvior. His eyes were closed and his lips slightly upturned at the corners. *Even in slumber, he finds me amusing.*

Try as she might to forget, Noelle knew she must accept her bitter portion of responsibility for this sinful act. He had seduced her—but she never refused him. Cautiously, she reached and touched the fingers of his left hand. Those masterful hands awakened fantastic feelings inside her. And oh God, when she touched him, his hands alone were a force to be reckoned with.

What a selfish, stupid, girl. Noelle crossed her arms over her center and hugged tight. What if she was already pregnant? Her father's maids told her on more than one occasion that a man's seed is more potent if it spills inside a virgin. And she'd seen plenty of animals mated at home. If it only took one time with sheep or goats, what would make it any different between humans?

Noelle momentarily thought to wake Randvior and demand he marry her. But that would mean he would win. *No, tis better I act the satisfied wench.* She wouldn't give him the satisfaction of winning so easily, of winning her.

Fluffing the thin pillow on her side of the bed, she lay back and heaved a troubled sigh. No matter how much she tried, she simply couldn't get comfortable. She tossed and turned, shifted from one position to another. Finally, she rolled onto her stomach and ended on her back again. Of course, she moved with exaggerated motions, and shook the bed, hoping to disturb her lover's infuriatingly peaceful sleep. The flesh between her legs ached. She stared resentfully at Randvior. What kind of man falls asleep after he deflowers a maiden?

'Tis no more than a casual affair to him, more evidence of his discourteousness. Noelle tapped her closed hand on her forehead in deep thought. As a child, she had pledged to guard her virginity until married. Most of the women in her father's household surrendered to physical yearnings and bedded different men every night.

Shaking her head, she realized it was no longer advantageous to consider escape. Not now.

Randvior opened his eyes. Rolling onto his side, he playfully smacked her thigh. He slid his hand between her legs and gently massaged. Her traitorous body responded to his touch, it felt like a thousand needles pricked her skin at once. Noelle pushed him away.

"If all you desire is a mindless creature to keep your bed warm, you can take a dog as your companion, not me."

He laughed blissfully and started to tease by tickling her from head to toe. Randvior's inability to accept *no* for an answer grew more evident in bed play. Noelle marveled at his tenacity as he played her body like a master musician.

Pausing, Randvior smoothed tangles of hair from her face, grazing the curve of her lips so lightly with his fingertips that she shivered. Already hot and wet, Noelle disliked not having any control. She refused to let physical feelings get in the way. Infatuation is no measure of true love.

"Leave me be!"

Grinning, he shook his head and ran his fingers down her arm. Goose flesh and raised hairs. Randvior didn't give her a chance to move; he rolled on top of her.

She deflated.

Mesmerized by how perfectly they fit together, she latched onto his shoulders.

"Move with me," he said, tugging on her hips.

He positioned himself so his bent knees rested on either side of her hips. His chest and stomach were rippled with muscle. A sumptuous feast for her eyes. He moved again and she felt his shaft throbbing. *If it happens once more, my body will burst …*

"As tight as a new sheath," he whispered against her mouth.

This time, Randvior didn't fall sleep afterward, he crawled

out of bed. Noelle shut her eyes and envisioned a familiar place to escape the reality of the moment. An ancient forest where she had played as a child. His movements were distracting, she heard him shuffling through clothing and lacing his boots. Once he finished, he planted his knee on the mattress beside her.

"You're mine," he said plainly.

She cleared her throat and cracked open her eyes, completely infuriated by his casual observation.

"That is a matter of opinion," she said.

Randvior gripped the back of her neck and her eyes fully opened in surprise. "Yes," he agreed. "A matter of *my* opinion. And I promise you *do* belong to me." He grunted with satisfaction, walked to the door, and opened it. "I'll return shortly."

His departure was a blessing. She shimmied out of bed—legs as unsteady as a newborn fawn's. His fluids were sticky-wet between her thighs, a grim reminder of her mounting sins. She nearly dropped on her knees and begged God for forgiveness— something she found herself contemplating more often than she cared to. Countless hours of instruction on how to conduct herself as a lady had been wasted on a wanton moment.

Her present situation made her think of Ophelia's tragically short, but fulfilling life. Noelle's sister died very much loved. A handsome knight had won her heart three years ago and they secretly met whenever they could. Once her father learned of the unsanctioned relationship, he firmly rejected the man's offer for marriage and sent him away. But not before they consummated their relationship, gifting each other with a precious memory. She envied Ophelia for this, not unkindly of course. Her sister loved of her own free will. And it sustained her through years of unhappiness afterward.

Randvior stole this cherished treasure from her as under-handedly as a thief. She'd never have a chance to experience unadulterated love. Their zeal was of a darker kind—pure lust.

He returned carrying a ewer filled with water and fresh linens and set them on the table. Granite eyes studied her skeptically.

Standing naked, she shyly covered her breasts and nether regions with her hands.

Randvior pointed at the pitcher. "Wash."

She regarded him without any expression. Defiant by nature, Noelle wheedled herself into compliance. She stepped toward the table, but Randvior had already dipped a cloth in water. Without permission, he reached gently between her legs and wiped away the evidence of their sin. It stunned her how easily he performed this intimate task. Jealousy clawed at her. How many women had he touched like this before? Made love to and bathed them like a pampered house pet.

"Always bathe after we make love, good hygiene thwarts disease."

She snorted at him so hard her breasts hopped. As if she needed him to explain how to complete her ablutions for the day. His advice was too parental, like an old maid's.

He reached, but Noelle jumped away.

"You little hypocrite," he grunted. "You permit me to feel the joys *inside* your body and deny me the pleasures outside."

The walls were closing in around her. "I've transgressed!" she burst. "How can I ever forgive myself?"

This time he didn't laugh at her; he stayed silent. He sat on the edge of the bed and left her to take care of herself. Noelle turned her back to him in the pursuit of any hint of privacy and purposely exercised great care while completing her bath. Once she finished, she searched the room for something to take her attention off the Viking. She needed a distraction from his stifling stare. The trunk containing most of her clothing was stowed in the corner and she walked self-consciously across the small space and bent over to open it. She froze. Cursed under her breath for failing to foresee the temptation her bent-over, naked arse must pose.

She cringed the moment his fingers curled around her shoulders.

Noelle tried to shrug his hands off. "You behave like a wild beast," she admonished and turned to face him.

"*Dritt,*" he hissed, rolling his eyes.

Apparently her body was no longer her own.

"*Jeg tar det som er mitt, og til helvete med din Gud.*" His intrusive fingers stroked until she felt dewy-wet again.

Guilt dissolved as his fingertips plied her shoulders. She leaned into him, resting her head on his chest. That secret spot between her legs began to ache. He must have sensed it—his hands lingered cruelly, but never actually touched her in the middle.

"I am master of your body now," he crooned. "Once you accept this, you will find me a generous man."

He released her and left.

Her mouth hung open. How could he abandon her when she was more than ready to give him everything he desired? *So the Norseman wishes to provoke me?* She walked to the trunk and threw the lid open. She selected a dress and shook it out angrily. Fiend— inexorable barbarian. He played her for a fool yet again.

For once she craved strong drink. Noelle needed to erase any memory of him from her mind—forever. Better yet, she wanted to drink herself into oblivion. She laced her boots, then opened the door and peeked outside. She had walked around the ship many times already, talking with Randvior and his men, and felt very comfortable around the crew. If he intended this experience to teach her anything of value, it hadn't. It only convinced her that this newly discovered pleasure shared between a man and woman could be to her advantage … until she found a way home. Her resolve to escape flickered to life again. It might be possible.

Everyone on board served the same master now, and she might as well enjoy her elevated status amongst these heathens, whatever benefits it brought her. She scanned the deck. Randvior stood with his captains on the far end. He looked as if nothing in the world could bother him, as if nothing had transpired between them.

The fresh air renewed her strength. Randvior's gaze traveled with her. *Ah.* Apparently he wasn't as immune to her as she had feared.

A light breeze ruffled her skirts and she turned her face into the wind; the pungent smell of salt water pleased her. It reminded her of home and a sense of sadness struck her heart.

Weather conditions were favorable. She thanked the heavens for this bit of good fortune. When they'd boarded the ship, some of Randvior's men complained she might bring them bad luck. Her paramour disregarded these allegations and called them superstitious fools. Their ships were guided by Odin's hand.

As Noelle gazed heavenward, she smiled; the evening sky was colored with hues of glowing pinks and reds—a good omen. *Red at night sailor's delight, red in the morning sailor's warning.*

As she explored, she further witnessed Randvior's familiarity with his men. They were friends, sharing everything—something her brother had never done with his servants. This affection fostered loyalty. She saw it on every man's face, how they admired and trusted him. Even Noelle's father lacked this level of intimacy with his men.

Unexpectedly, she spotted two familiar faces on deck. Two of her father's soldiers were busy tying ropes. She greeted them, desirous to hear anything a fellow Saxon had to say.

"Lady Sinclair." Samuel Cronin bobbed his head.

"Samuel," she said. "Where are the other men and maids?"

"The women are below and the other guards are split among the other ships, none too happy for it."

"Send my well wishes if you can," she said looking at the second man. "And you, Henry Buckley, how are you?"

"Happier after seeing you in one piece," he spoke hurriedly as he looked over his shoulder. "We *will* find a way home, Lady Sinclair."

Empty words. Noelle imagined a homecoming feast that rivaled any she'd ever attended. A daughter returns much like the famed prodigal son—only she hadn't squandered her inheritance or left willingly. A strange silence passed between them as they stared out to sea. Hundreds of miles separated her from England now, and there was nothing comforting except the ocean.

She left Samuel and Henry and continued on a path toward Randvior.

As she passed, a dozen men smiled with the same cocky amusement she'd grown accustomed to seeing on Randvior's face. An unfortunate inborn flaw, perhaps.

Her attention moved rapidly across the group of warriors that surrounded Randvior. His radiant face made her legs quiver as he stole another glance at her. She rested her hand on her hip. Her addled mind played tricks again. What if he boasted of his sexual conquests the way her father's men always did? If these unscrupulous brigands knew what happened, would they ever respect her? She'd suffered already as the subject of his jokes.

She covered her face, blocking Randvior's eyes from her own. She was only guessing—which never served anyone very well. She whirled, retreating full speed, heading directly for the cabin. She collided with a soldier. Noelle shoved him away in a huff, and tripped over her own feet as she stumbled through the door. She slammed it shut, barricading herself inside.

Confinement was the only escape at her disposal. But that only lasted a few minutes. Randvior tried to open the door. She braced her legs, hoped to keep the rest of the world locked out until they reached Norway. Randvior twisted the knob and pushed, but she stayed stubbornly locked in position. He banged on the planks and demanded she open the door. If she refused any longer, he'd probably just kick it down. She braced herself for what might happen when he came in and reluctantly stepped aside.

"What happened out there? Did you see a ghost?" he asked, entering the room.

"I would consider myself most fortunate if it was only an apparition taunting me." She sat on the bed and wrung her hands nervously. "My conscience troubles me." She raised her eyes to meet his.

He leaned against the doorframe, arms crossed. She couldn't keep herself from sneaking admiring looks at his body. *Only flesh and bone*, she reminded herself, *he's only flesh and bone*. His fine looks did little to relieve her; she was so helplessly riddled with guilt, she didn't know what to do with herself any more.

He closed the door and moved closer. "Remember the things I told you in England?"

"I remember too much."

What she really wanted were assurances for her future. She wanted him to vow he would care for her life as loyally as he would his own kinswoman's. If he wouldn't make her his wife, he should choose someone else. She needed a husband to protect her interests now. Even an inexperienced adolescent or an old man would do. As long as he had a pulse and a respectable name, she'd accept it. This was the only bargaining chip she had left.

"Choose a man from amongst your warriors to become my husband if you won't take me yourself." If he didn't choose her, if she were able to get out of his grasp, she might have a better chance of escape.

"A *husband*?" he repeated it several times as if he didn't hear her correctly. There was half a bottle of wine left over from last night on the table. He tromped across the room and grabbed it, took a deep swig, wiped the back of his hand across his mouth, then slammed it down. "You change your mind as quickly as the wind shifts direction!"

"What are you talking about?"

"Now you want a husband? Your brother told me you were not particularly fond of the idea of an arranged marriage."

"That was before *you* violated every code of chivalry that restrains men in power from taking advantage of their inferiors. I don't care one bit where you come from, I am sure these rules are recognized on your side of the water, too. You have destroyed *any* hope I have for a comfortable future. Any man, if one will still have me, will demand explanation as to why I am no longer a virgin. What shall I tell him, sir?"

"Who?"

"My future husband." *You blundering idiot.*

His mouth opened as if he wanted to say something in return. He must have thought better of it, because he clenched his jaw and simply glared at her so intensely it looked like his head might implode.

"Did you not offer yourself to me with extraordinary willingness for such an innocent?" He nearly paced a hole in the floorboards. "Think you so poorly of what we shared together? Think you so little of me?"

"What can I base my judgment on? As you can see," she moved off the bed and jammed her fingers into the sheets where flecks of blood stained the linen. "Until recently, I was an unfortunate maiden, completely unlearned in the ways of passion. I *never* encouraged your affection, but who am I to refuse my master? I am your slave, am I not?"

Secretly, she burned for him. However her body reacted to his, at least she still maintained control of her heart. And that would never belong to him!

His gray eyes zigzagged around the cabin. He looked away for a long time. And was denied any warmth the moment his attention wandered back to her.

"You displayed ample skill between those sheets," he said, grabbing a hold of her arms. "I might question your reputation if I weren't a gentleman."

She snorted at his preposterous suggestion.

"A gentleman," she scoffed. "You of all things are not. You're a bloody conqueror who pillages and rapes without conscience! If we're going to discuss anyone's reputation," she shot back, "do we have enough time to discuss your history before we anchor?"

"My actions have never been in question, madam." His body swelled with rage; she could tell he was quickly losing patience.

Wearily, she touched his arm. The strength to argue abandoned her entirely. Half a truce was better than none. "I'm sorry,

Randvior."

He acknowledged her effort with a nod.

"Let us make our peace," she said.

But he was not finished speaking his mind. He gripped her arms. "Did I not discuss the proposition of marriage with you before we sailed?"

She twisted and he let go.

"It was my understanding," she said, "that you have a specific use for me. Perhaps offering my hand in marriage to someone for financial gain or to a political rival."

He looked positively disappointed and drummed his fingers on the hilt of his sword. "If my intention was to auction you off or give you to a political rival, why should I risk devaluing my investment by claiming your maidenhead for myself?"

This question was unanswerable. She refused to be part of this conversation any longer and abruptly changed the subject. "What is a *concubine*?"

He threw his hands up exasperatedly. "Something you shall *never* be!"

"What is it?" she pressed.

"A woman who provides the same duties as a wife without the benefit of marriage."

Noelle scowled.

"Damn it, I know what you're thinking, Noelle," he said, taking her by the arms again and giving her a small shake. Randvior seemed to be mentally scrambling to find a way to convince her she wasn't his mistress.

"I owe you nothing," he said, deep lines creasing his forehead.

"Yes," she replied. "You owe me nothing, but still own me." The damage had already been done.

"I underestimated you," he said. "You criticize too harshly for such a young woman. It's a wonder your brother didn't beat you to within an inch of your life before I came along."

"He did, on many occasions."

Randvior stared at her.

Brian preferred to beat her with the hard heel of his boots over the traditional leather strap. How many times had she run away after a good throttling to examine her posterior in a mirror? "Tell me *Jarl* Randvior, what do you intend to do with me?"

He paused in thought. Suddenly, a blooming smile lit his face. "Take you to bed."

After spending the night and half the next day in bed with Randvior, Noelle barely found the strength to get dressed and join him on deck. It was good timing on her part, his men pointed out a group of islands just off the western edge of Norway. She cupped a hand over her eyes and squinted to see the faint outline of her new home against the blinding light of the late afternoon sun.

Randvior approached from behind. He slipped an arm about her waist and tugged her close. She smiled. This was the first time he showed her any affection outside the cabin. His benign touch quickly blossomed into something more fervid and he pulled her toward the cabin.

Her muscles ached and her tender parts were raw. As soon as they got inside, she darted around like a wild goose.

"Stop it," he laughed. "I won't touch you if that's what you're afraid of. We'll be home by morning as long as this wind holds. I know you're a bit saddle-sore from our lovemaking," he teased. "Forgive me. I'm a love-struck fool, so enamored with you I failed to think of giving you a chance to recover."

Love-struck? Did he just say?

She settled down on the bed. "I hurt in places too shameful to name."

"Sleep, *min lille dukke*, tomorrow is a new day." He bent her head back and planted a kiss on her forehead. Randvior unbuckled his belt and put it on the table, and then lay down next to her with his boots still on.

When she woke hours later, Noelle wanted to thank Randvior for his consideration in the night. The space beside her was empty, though. She rolled out of bed and shivered. It was cold inside the cabin, despite the small brazier still burning near the bedside. Always a dreamer—she admitted it. The hatred she felt for this man had channeled away from her heart—if only temporarily. She had resolved she would always oppose him. Not only for what he represented, but because of the type of man he was. No wonder men ruled the world. There was no hope for the weaker sex. It should take more than a day in bed to reduce her to a boneless mass. She braided her hair, smoothed the wrinkles from her dress, and went outside.

The ship had just turned into a narrow inlet. A fjord, Randvior had called it when he described his homeland. And thousands of inlets dotted the coastline like fingers on a hand. High, rocky outcrops surrounded them, and to the south, snow-covered peaks stretched upward and outward for miles in every direction. Noelle looked over the railing; sheets of ice floated on the water, but the ship cut effortlessly through them.

"How far to your steading?" she asked as Randvior joined her.

"Maybe ten miles." He pointed eastward. "This river borders my lands. We'll follow it home."

The idea of bathing and drinking fresh water again pleased her. Luxuries she regretted ever taking for granted. Anything was an improvement over the stale-tasting water rations served from wooden barrels on the ship.

What she regretted most, though, were her actions last night. She looked over her shoulder at Randvior—his face still glowing. After he bade her to go to sleep, she'd tossed and turned for nearly an hour. Unable to settle down, she'd demanded to see the Terms of Surrender her brother had signed. He'd offered it for inspection.

She'd opened the scroll and eyed her brother's grandiloquent scrawl at the bottom of the page. His *B* and *S* were exaggeratedly rounded for a man's writing style.

Her name was written out as insignificantly as she felt. Listed as one of many items the jarl was entitled to as payment for his leniency. She read her name out loud—*Lady Noelle Marie Sinclair,* youngest daughter of Frederick Michael McKenzie Sinclair, the Sixth Earl of Durham. No disputing this contract, she legally belonged to him.

She'd studied the document contentiously, scanned further down the page, and read the amount of silver and gold he acquired and the names of the men and maids he claimed.

"Everything seems to be in order," she'd said with growing apprehension and dropped the contract on the bed.

"Look." Randvior's pleasant voice interrupted her thoughts. He pointed toward a cluster of cottages built along the edge of the water on the last island. People gathered to watch the ships pass by and waved.

She waved back.

"Are you enjoying the scenery?"

Admittedly, his lands were far more beautiful than Durham. More enchanting than anything she'd ever seen. "It's breath-taking."

He raised his head and studied the sky as if he could read the future. "The snow is very late, but it will come, *min lille dukke*. And when it does, we'll be imprisoned together for months with no escape."

She believed him. These were the legendary lands of the dragon people that her countrymen deeply feared. *And now, I am a prisoner in the very place priests in the Sabbath pulpit liken to the torments of Hades.*

CHAPTER EIGHT

Homecoming

WITH THE WEIGHT of the world on her shoulders, Noelle stayed silent once they anchored and Randvior handed her over the ship railing, straight into the arms of two strangers. The men carried her to land and settled her amongst a crowd of people who waited eagerly to welcome them home. A group of lavishly dressed women stared at her. Of mixed ages, even the youngest scrutinized her from head to toe. She breathed steadily and offered her most courageous smile. Not one returned it.

She knew they were trying to guess *who* and *what* she was to Randvior.

Noelle looked past them and focused on her father's former maids; Deanna, Katherine, and Johanna were being brought ashore, too. As soon as their feet hit ground, they scurried away from the men and flocked around her. Noelle smiled radiantly and wrapped her arms around two of them, while she tried to calm the third with comforting words. She reminded them of the small courtesies the *jarl* had shown them already. Even though they had been kept apart for ten days, they appeared unharmed.

"If he wished to mistreat us, I am sure he would have done so by now. He is at liberty to do with us as he pleases. I've sensed no malice in his heart."

"And who are you to judge the *jarl's* heart?" a stern, but feminine voice sounded from somewhere behind.

Noelle turned and locked eyes with a middle-aged woman with slightly graying-red hair. She was statuesque and Noelle instinctively recognized her. Randvior favored his mother.

"Well, girl?" she demanded.

Noelle took a deep breath, reluctant to say anything. Unfamiliar with the customs of these people, she didn't wish to risk offending anyone—at least not until they had been properly introduced. His mother's liquid-steel eyes reminded her so much of her lover's that it made her shiver.

Aud Magnusson walked toward them. He strolled casually up the pathway and stopped next to Noelle.

"You were away longer than we expected," the older woman said coldly.

Aud shrugged. "The *jarl* received a vision before we departed the Orkneys, instructing him to sail to Durham."

"Durham?"

"The English—"

"Yes, yes," she said dismissively. "I know the blasted place, Aud. What riches could possibly lure my son there?"

Noelle crinkled her nose, displeased with the already less than favorable opinion of her homeland. She bit her tongue, remembering what was at stake. This was no longer about her own welfare, the maids clinging to her skirts required protection. If she set herself at odds with Randvior's mother, nothing would go well for them.

Aud looked around uncomfortably while the older woman kept a sharp eye on him. Finally, he faced Noelle again. "The girl ..."

These men spoke truth as easily as her brother told lies. At this moment, Noelle wondered which caused more harm. Finesse, even if used sparingly, would have aided her cause much more.

Randvior's mother opened her eyes wide with surprise. She exuded authority and conceitedness, grace, and power all at once. A formidable woman and she looked Noelle over like a head of livestock under consideration for purchase.

"She's malnourished," she commented unfavorably. "The color of her hair is simply unnatural, dyed I should think. So unlike the women my son typically favors. But who can keep up with a man's passing obsessions? Once we take the shears to her head she'll know her place in his household."

Noelle turned abruptly and stared directly into her eyes. "You'll have no easy time laying a finger upon my head," she warned. "I'm quite aware of my position. My father is no commoner."

To think she dared suggest cropping her hair. *A woman's hair is her crown of glory—cut it and I shall become as insignificant as a bondswoman.* This was a cruel practice, utilized even in England, to distinguish between the classes.

Aud's eyes darted between them. Noelle knew he was very familiar with feminine quarrels, he had three daughters.

As Lauga's mouth dropped open, Noelle prayed a swarm of locusts would descend from heaven and fly inside, shutting her up for eternity.

"Do you know whom you address, girl?" she asked.

"There was never a question in my mind about your identity—Randvior is your son. I shall extend a courtesy you failed to show me by introducing myself. My name is, Lady Noelle Sinclair, and I am your son's guest, *not* his slave."

Her eyes became narrow slits, as gray and frigid as the North Sea. Color drained from her cheeks and she harrumphed, obviously unaccustomed to having her authority challenged. The similarities between mother and son were astounding.

"Yes," she confirmed. "I am Jarl Randvior's mother, Lauga."

Noelle nodded. If they could just start over, she would admit his mother deserved reverence. But if she threatened her again, Noelle was prepared to defend herself.

"I'm surprised my son bothered bringing home an English harridan. There are at least twenty women in the Trondelag more worthy of his affection."

Aud raised an arm above his head, signaling for reinforcements. No need. Randvior started up the footpath and the crowd turned away from the ensuing disagreement and focused exclusively on him. Much applause sounded as he came closer. Noelle met his eyes and smiled; he nodded and jogged the rest of the way, just in time to see his mother's unpleasant face. He stepped in between them, and gave Noelle a sincere look.

"Odin må ha satt vinden i ryggen. Men hans forbannelse er på deg på samme tid, se tispe han sendte over vannet med deg som plager oss alle." Lauga's tone left little to imagination.

"Nok! Du er min mor, men jeg har tenkt å bli viet til denne jenta, og vil ikke tolerere noen fornærmelser," Randvior countered, stepping closer.

They exchanged more heated words before Lauga finally relented and looked away spitefully.

Randvior grabbed Noelle's hand. "I never intended for this to happen. My mother is overly protective of me, even though I'm a grown man."

She managed to veil her truest feelings with a thin smile. The biting chill in the air made her teeth chatter, her fabric cloak poor protection against the rising wind. She searched the ground, frost crowned the wilted vegetation poking through patches of ice and snow. The wide path before them meandered up a hill, and people were walking to and from what she assumed was the direction of Randvior's house.

More than anything, she wanted a hot bath, food, and sleep. Perhaps a night away from her lover's amorous sexual appetite, too. It meant a chance to recover and figure out how she could deal with his antagonistic mother.

"Come," Randvior said. He led her away, through a crowd of cheering admirers.

As they climbed to the top of the hill, she spotted the wood and stone longhouse that Randvior had so carefully described to her. It was situated in a valley, surrounded by forest and pastures. They walked down the incline and slowly approached the facade.

Ornamental stone and woodcarvings of mythical creatures graced the double-arched doorway at the entrance. A gray stone fence demarcated the main courtyard at the front, and dozens of men were seated at tables around a huge fire pit, eating and drinking. Once they realized their *jarl* had arrived, they dropped whatever they were holding and saluted him. Randvior released Noelle's hand and walked ahead to greet them.

One of them handed him an ale horn. He raised it ceremoniously and swallowed. Amber liquid dripped down his beard as he smiled exuberantly, very much the barbarian she'd pictured him as in these familiar surroundings. She had to admit, she enjoyed seeing him this way. He offered high praise in both Norse and English. He thanked them for guarding his lands so loyally. The guards stood and saluted him again. Randvior reached inside his cloak and pulled out a leather coin bag. He tossed it on top of the nearest table.

"Silver," he said.

Randvior pulled Noelle in front of him. "See what else I have brought home."

Catcalls and whistling erupted.

Noelle frowned. How easily he reverted back to that uncivilized nature once he was surrounded by his kinsmen.

Once the laughter and noise stopped, Randvior spoke again. "I present to you Lady Noelle Sinclair. She will be staying here as my personal guest."

Several men expressed their approval and offered their own titles and names. One name caught her attention, *Rafael Long-foot*. She looked at his feet. Completely normal. And Rafael seemed much too Spanish for a Norseman. Noelle couldn't help but smile at their adolescent behavior. *Buffoons*.

Randvior continued, this time in Norse. She didn't understand a word. Judging by the serious looks on his men's faces, it must have been along the lines of *She's mine. Keep your bloody hands off her*. But he had only referred to her as a guest.

Formalities complete, he escorted Noelle inside. The great

hall was more spacious and well-appointed than she had expected. Rectangular in shape, it boasted the largest hearth and finest mantelpiece she'd ever seen. Along the north wall was a raised stage and throne. A less imposing chair stood next to Randvior's seat and she wondered if one day she would occupy it. Her eyes slipped back to the over-sized throne. *Only kings sit on thrones. Just who is this man?*

The chair was shaped as an ancient oak tree in full bloom. Silver and gold medallions, similar to the ornaments on Randvior' boots, graced the tips of the branches. Golden-threaded tapestries depicting famous scenes from history, including what she believed were the infamous brothers, Romulus and Remus, suckling at the she-wolf's teats in what one day would be the gateway to the city of Rome, decorated the walls. The flagstones were covered with luxuriously thick animal skins and soft carpets.

The high table sat on a wide dais steps lower than the throne. She counted eight rows of tables and benches below, where guests would feast alongside him. A room fit for a king.

The kitchens were located off the south end, from which permeated the irresistible scents of roasting meat and bread. Her stomach groaned miserably. Her diet had consisted mainly of salt fish and stale bread over the last ten days. She craved fresh meat. Randvior must have heard her hunger pangs and threw her a sympathetic look.

"There will be a grand feast this evening, *min lille dukke*, perhaps the kind you've attended at court. My storehouses will be depleted, but my stomach will not be disappointed for it. Do you want to take a bath?"

She cheered instantly, willing to forget hunger in trade for fresh water. She felt disgusting, sticky with salt, sweat, and who knew what else from head to toe. Two men came inside carrying her trunks.

Lauga interfered before her son could direct them. "Shall we settle your mistress in the thrall's quarters where she'll be most comfortable, or will she take one of the small chambers off the kitchen?"

Unaffected by his mother's meddling, he waved his hand. "Enough folly, Lady Sinclair is an honored *guest* in this house. She will occupy the suite on the north end of the second floor."

"Adjacent to *your* personal chambers?" She seemed truly scandalized by his choice, her intolerance growing by the second.

"Yes," he answered. "Need I your permission to bed a girl under my own roof?"

Lauga puckered her lips in complete revilement. It was becoming painfully apparent to Noelle why he had revealed very little about his family. He spoke so fondly of his sire, sadly an invalid, crippled in a war nearly a decade ago. But his mother, he told her, was an accomplished *spaewife*. Not a white witch, but one who dabbled in the dark arts. And for this reason, she was both revered and deeply feared by his people.

The men carried her luggage upstairs.

His gaze drifted to the English maids standing nearby—Deanna, Katherine, and Johanna. They were young, the eldest being no more than twenty.

"You may choose one of these women as your personal attendant. The other two will work in the kitchens."

A generous offer—but she hated the idea of rewarding one and forcing the others to work in the kitchen with strangers. She'd choose all three if she could, but if she did, would Randvior withdraw his original offer? Common sense overruled her hesitation, having an English woman as her companion would help. She carefully considered each, remembering how they performed their duties at home. Even-tempered Katherine would serve quite well. She accepted.

"Now that the *lady* has chosen, we can properly prepare the other women for service. Shave their English heads." Lauga struck again.

Noelle pinched herself. Any hope of building a lasting rapport with this woman was fading—her inconsiderate nature reminded her of Brian's selfishness.

Deanna and Johanna cowered nearby, covering their heads. Noelle refused to allow anyone to lay a finger on them.

She rolled her eyes heavenward. "English women *don't* shave their heads, madam," she said, and shifted into a defensive stance in front of the girls. She would shield them with her own body if necessary.

Randvior intervened. "They serve as freewomen, paid a regular salary."

She prayed his word was final concerning household arrangements and deliberated whether this was Lauga's way of retaliating against her only child for frightening her by not sending word of his whereabouts. Thank God, the woman didn't live at his steading fulltime! Her home was located miles away where she lived with her husband. But she imagined Lauga freely exercised her authority in this house in the absence of a proper mistress.

They said nothing more for a few moments, then Randvior looked at Noelle. "Aud will see you to your room."

She inclined her head and waited for the captain to signal their departure. She followed him upstairs and down a narrow hallway. They stopped at the last door on the right.

"This is your suite." He opened the door.

She stepped inside and the door closed. Sunshine brightened the room. She noticed every detail of the comfortable furnishings and feminine tapestries that decorated the walls. Her trunks were on the floor near the bed. Feeling as frolicsome as any child, she couldn't resist the urge to jump up and down on the new mattress. After nearly smacking her head on the beams above, she allowed herself to fall back into the thick padding.

Liberation at last. No Vikings and no smug-faced mother.

A sweet scent drew her to the far corner. A ceramic bowl filled with dried rose petals and heather made her smile. She further explored. The suite consisted of three rooms: her bedroom, a sitting room, and a second bedchamber probably intended for Katherine's use. The furniture looked expensive, likely imported from exotic lands. These rooms were intended for a woman the *jarl* wished to pamper. Her favorite spot was in front of the two large windows, along the west wall, where a carved table and matching chairs gave her a perfect place to sit and view the river.

Noelle opened drawers and cabinets. She found a jewelry box sitting on top of a bureau, and eyed it suspiciously. Perhaps something the last occupant accidentally left behind? She braced herself for anything as she opened the lid, imagined it contained a trinket that Randvior had presented to his last mistress. There was a card inside that simply read *min lille dukke*.

Underneath the paper was a beautifully crafted gold bangle. It felt solid and heavy in her hand. The goldsmith had engraved it with the tiniest shapes. She walked to the windows and held it up, closely examined the intricate designs. Her Christian name was inscribed on the underside. She stared at it in amazement. When did he find the time to have this made for her? And exactly what did it mean?

She wanted him, and reveled in the memory of being close to him—his manly scent filled her head, nearly intoxicated her. Even the first day on ship together, before he touched her so intimately, strange warmth settled into her bones whenever he came close.

No. This was part of his plan. Make her vulnerable and weak, so she'd submit to his demands without a fight. One minute her heart ached for home, and the next she agonized over the man who took her away from everything she loved. The old belief that distance makes the heart grow fonder was an outright lie. What stood in front of her nearly consumed her soul. She must keep the memory of Ophelia alive and draw strength from it. Neither her father nor Margaret could still the whirl of emotions in her head and heart now.

Somewhere underneath the *jarl's* rigid exterior was a man of limitless curiosity and passion. She noticed it on their voyage first—how he immersed himself in everything she told him. He asked questions, sometimes too many. He forced confessions out of her more efficiently than a priest, ones only God should hear. And now she regretted acting too hastily, asking him to find her a suitable husband. She slipped the bracelet on—a perfect fit—like their bodies.

She left England a prisoner and arrived in the north as Randvior's mistress. He could deny it all he wanted to spare her feelings. But truth is truth. Flaunting her so openly in front of his mother reinforced her point. And now this extravagant gift.

Similarities existed between Ophelia's lover and Randvior. Her mind twisted. His gentle hands had worked miracles with her body. And he saved her life on more than one occasion, too. Her sister's lover was no saint; he had threatened to kill her father after he refused to allow them to wed. Both men killed for a living, whether for a king or themselves really made no difference to her.

And the Viking had killed his own conscript so she could escape. He never denied it. That man's blood stained her hands, too. Noelle knew men killed for only a handful of reasons. To protect their lands, for sovereignty, or for the people they loved. The first two were irrelevant.

Randvior is a man, and they always do as they wish. One thing did separate him from most men, though. He revealed secrets so easily—spoke of his gods as if he walked and talked with them every day. A soulless man would say nothing, feel nothing.

What would Margaret say if she knew Noelle was considering a union with the man that nearly destroyed their home? Did it matter? Hundreds of miles separated them now. If she resisted, what benefit would come of it? And if she opened her heart to him …

Her thoughts bounced wildly back and forth. Should she choose loyalty for her family or allegiance to a man she hardly knew?

And for this reason, a man shall leave his father and mother's house and cleave unto his wife … To become one flesh.

She was full of reluctance. If the Viking ever offered her his love, she'd wait to choose.

"You are wrong about the girl," Randvior spat, holding a glass of wine in one hand, banging the other on the table.

Lauga sat next to him, questioning him at every turn. She'd spoken no kind words or said anything useful from the moment he'd arrived home. If he mentioned Noelle, she refused to acknowledge her as anything more than a slave, and continuously referred to her as an English whore.

"If you will not send her away," Lauga said, "relieve her of that English pride before she grows too proud to serve you."

"Silence!" He threw the goblet across the room. It hit the back wall and shattered. "You're twisting words. That tongue is as destructive as a battering ram. I've been home for only five hours and you've managed to set this household onto a path of chaos. *The girl stays. It is not open for discussion.*"

From his seat at the high table, he could oversee all the activities going on in the hall. Occasionally, people gazed in their direction. Public arguments with his mother weren't so unusual—only the current topic. Lauga despised the English. Randvior hoped she only needed some time to adjust to the idea of having Noelle around.

"Sleep with her then," she said, rising quickly. "Bed her until your prick rots off."

He slammed two fists on the table. "Sit down, now!"

Lauga shook her head. "I am not the one that turned this wonderful homecoming into a funeral feast. What would your father say if he knew you brought a Saxon home and deposited her in the most comfortable rooms in your house as if she were your own wife?"

"I said sit down."

She flung herself into the chair.

"I'm sure my sire would congratulate me, considering our family's own history. There seems to be an undeniable attraction between Norse and English that spans generations." He instantly regretted dredging up old memories. But his mother's wicked tongue sent him into a rage.

Her face burned.

"Go ahead," she said venomously. "Make this an occasion to shame me in front of our people." She stood again, sliding her chair back. "I will not be the target of your spite, Randvior. Furthermore, my dearest flesh and blood, I won't allow you to make the same mistake your father did. Your loins are not the center of the universe—think with your head, not your cock. The choices you make today may have serious consequences for all of *us* tomorrow."

He tried to wrap his head around the situation. She spoke some truth. The immeasurable damage inflicted upon his family after his father returned from a raid with a young English woman at his side nearly destroyed his family. His sire publicly declared the girl his mistress. A perfectly legal arrangement, but an immensely stupid risk for a man married to a woman of such renown. Within three weeks living under the same roof, Lauga had stabbed her to death.

According to the opinion of the Thing, the legal assembly that reviewed such cases, her action was completely justifiable. A wife has the right to defend her honorable position in her husband's household.

"I have no wife," he reminded her. "I am entitled to marry *whomever* I damn well please. I am lord over these lands, not some adolescent who needs his mother's permission to go here or there."

Lauga nodded. "And I'm your mother, entitled to choose an appropriate bride for my only son. Is it not a tradition in these lands?"

Yes, he thought, *but merely a tradition. The gods have willed this girl on me ...* "Such traditions are broken all the time," he said, lowering his head. "I'm of a mind to offer her a marriage contract." For the first time in his life he cared deeply enough about a woman to worry about her future.

Lauga's face lighted. "You've claimed her virginity and feel responsible? Is that what this is about?"

"Aye."

"You don't have to *marry* her. Find another man for her. She'll be welcomed by anyone you choose. Preserve our bloodline, Randvior. Don't let it be polluted by Saxon blood. I will gladly help you. She's a spirited young woman and will easily attract a bevy of eager warriors. Imagine how much gold—"

His eyes opened at the suggestion of finding her a husband. He'd kill anyone who laid a bloody finger on her. *She belonged to him.* "Either respect my decision or leave my house until you've had sufficient time to change your mind."

He had enough to contend with at the moment—repairing ships, overseeing the winter slaughter and stocking of his storehouses, settling civil cases, and now Noelle. Had his mother lost control of her senses? No woman had any right to make unreasonable demands of any man. Even if it was tradition for a mother to help select her son's bride, it wasn't written in stone. Odin commanded his hands and the girl his body. Perhaps even his heart.

He left Lauga standing alone and exited the hall. The majority of his men were still unloading merchandise from the ships. He had a list of tasks he intended to oversee before deep winter set in. He was already at a disadvantage because he arrived home so late in the season and needed to catch up.

Repairs to the vessels were the most pressing issue. His ships were housed in four buildings near the river over winter. He needed to get them into dry storage as soon as possible. One vessel would stay anchored for defensive purposes. Although longships were designed to withstand cold, the wood could warp or the hull could crack if temperatures dropped too low for long periods of time. They needed to treat the wood.

He followed the pathway to the riverfront. Only enough time left in the day to coordinate with his men, inspect the storage buildings, and return to the hall for the homecoming feast. Regardless of his state of mind, the feast must go on. Odin deserved his gratitude. The gods delivered him safely home again—wealthier, mightier, and perhaps much happier.

Chapter Nine

Feasting

THE DOOR OPENED without warning. Noelle twisted to her side and eyed Katherine standing at the doorway with a platter of food. How foolish to think Randvior would give her time to catch up on sleep.

"I suppose you've been instructed to stay with me at all times," she commented sarcastically as she gestured for the maid to enter.

She climbed out of bed and inspected Katherine closely. "Turn around."

The maid rotated slowly while her mistress ran her fingers through her auburn hair, which was swept back off her face. Everything seemed right. Noelle breathed a sigh of relief.

"I pray I never live to regret my decision to cooperate with these people."

Katherine nodded and served the food.

"Your bedchamber is over there." Noelle pointed at the door near the hearth.

"Thank you." Katherine curtsied. "I promise to serve you well."

"Of that I have no doubt. We shall act as each other's eyes and ears. We are English above all things and will never accept being condemned to live anonymously in this strange country."

"Might we find a way home?" Katherine's hands trembled as

she poured a glass of wine.

"Home …" Noelle repeated. Durham seemed as foreign a place as Norway. "Home is inconsequential at this point."

Katherine's face grew barren.

"I'd be a cold-hearted liar if I offered you false hopes. Believe me, if we had a choice, I'd choose England. The *jarl* holds legal documents that grant him custody of all of us. I reviewed the contract on the ship."

She knew Katherine was clever enough to understand. "Then we must make the best of our new arrangements." The maid offered her the glass of wine.

Noelle culled over the food—bread, cheese, and fruit. An hour ago, her stomach begged for sustenance and now she could barely handle looking at it. The only thing that appealed to her was blueberries, surprisingly plump and firm. She stuffed a handful ravenously into her mouth. Sweet juices seeped from the edges of her lips and ran down her chin. Katherine giggled and offered a napkin.

"I'm so tired of tasteless bread, and now even cheese." She wrinkled her nose in rejection and turned from the table.

"I've been told to escort you to the bathhouse. The *jarl* promised he would leave soap and oil for us to bathe with."

Noelle didn't care if he offered her a puddle of mud—she wanted to go, and now. "Well, why are we still standing here?"

The maid tapped her fingers on the table as if she were mulling it over in her head. She smiled and followed her mistress out the door.

Below, the hall bustled with life. Men came and went, disappeared below stairs carrying cargo into what Noelle guessed were storage cellars. She wondered how many of those chests came from her father's home. She searched for Randvior amongst the crowd, but couldn't find him anywhere. Katherine led her across the room, passing by groups of men and women who stared curiously. Two doors were opened in the back and Noelle stopped and stared outside. Dozens of buildings stood in the yard.

She identified the stable, horses were lined up outside and grooms were brushing their fine coats.

She spotted Randvior standing in a corner. His lingering gaze followed as she stepped closer to the kitchen. She stopped and fixed her eyes on his face. Could she possibly hide the feelings he stirred inside her whenever he stared at her? He lowered his head in greeting and turned before she could decide.

Curiously, Katherine passed the doors that opened to the courtyard and brought her to the kitchen. Noelle considered the lively room, careful not to disturb any of the women who worked so diligently at the counters and ovens. Racks of fresh bread were cooling near a back door and the familiar aroma of meat pie nearly made her salivate like a hungry dog.

No one bothered to greet her. Not a bloody word from any-one. She might as well be a spirit. Try as she might to distract herself from giving it any more thought, it made her feelings simmer. Every woman laboring away in a kitchen across the civilized world gossiped while preparing the day's meals. She expected a certain level of animosity from the servants, consider-ing where she came from. But something bothered her even more. Why did Katherine bring her here when they could have avoided this room altogether and gone straight outside through the doors in the hall.

"Who told you to bring me here?"

"Lauga."

"Did she offer an explanation?"

"Only that thralls are not permitted to use the main entrances for personal business."

Noelle wiped her hands on her dress and shook her head. The audacity … She lifted her chin and started for Lauga, who was managing the women baking pastries. Then stopped short, realizing it a bad time to confront her.

From the moment she had arrived, she knew things would not go smoothly with the matriarch of Randvior's family. Noelle's feelings were important, though, and she deserved all the small courtesies extended to even the humblest of guests.

I am not here of my own choosing! Blame your son, not me. Her eyes bored holes in Lauga's back.

Perhaps she was overanalyzing everything, but she didn't like the way the woman made her feel. She headed in the opposite direction, toward a doorway where Katherine waited. They walked outside.

Breathing in the fresh air, she enjoyed the warmth that streaked across her face. Sunlight was a valuable commodity in northern England in the wintertime. Noelle knew the farther north, the rarer it became. Randvior had warned it might take some time to acclimate.

Two-dozen outbuildings were arranged in a semi-circle just outside the main house. Katherine identified them all. A barn, shearing sheds, smoke houses, storage rooms, armory, and other infrastructure necessary for every day survival. Beyond the service buildings were dozens of wooden cabins of all shapes and sizes, similar to an English village. This must be where his tenants lived.

The bathhouse stood out amongst the other buildings, constructed of rough-cut logs and sealed with dark mud. Katherine opened the door and Noelle stepped inside first. She immediately noticed the dramatic change in humidity; a foggy heat swirled around them. No one was inside—an arrangement Randvior must have taken care of. Tiny beads of sweat formed on her forehead and in the valley between her breasts. She gathered up the hem of her gown and tried to cool her legs by fanning them.

She walked the perimeter of the narrow room. A natural hot spring bubbled invitingly near the center like a witch's cauldron. Without a second thought, Noelle stripped, kicked off her boots, and peeled off her stockings. She allowed the healing warmth to overtake her.

She continued to tour the room with her eyes. There were two tiled tubs on one side where she imagined families gathered for their weekly baths. The hot spring was banked by warm, flat rocks. She stepped up and the heat penetrated the soles of her feet. She tested the water with her toes. The effervescent heat reminded her of Randvior's searing fingertips. Noelle stepped into the water and waded away from the edge until she was submerged to her shoulders. She had to stand on her toes to keep her head above water by the time she reached the middle of the pool.

After a while, she swam back to the edge and stared toward the back of the room. Tables and chairs were neatly arranged alongside a large fire pit. Several smaller pits and wooden shelves stocked with linens were near the tables. She sat on the stones with her legs still soaking in the water. She watched amusedly as her maid removed her clothing and waded into the water. Her gratifying moans were rewarded with a hearty laugh.

Submerged in the healing waters, Noelle felt as if the world were a perfect place. God's hands alone formed this paradise and she pretended it was an enchanted spring and she a fairy changeling. She raised her arms above her head and breathed in and out, relaxing for the first time in days. Noelle closed her eyes and fantasized about exotic places—beautiful men and women in public bathhouses in Rome. So real were these images, she nearly jumped out of her skin when Katherine tapped her on the shoulder.

"Tender skin—look how red you are."

Noelle inspected her own body. Bright pink splotches covered her arms and stomach like a fever rash. They were being boiled alive! She groaned with disappointment and grudgingly stood and walked away from the pool. Katherine scooted ahead and returned with a pile of linens.

The soft material felt good against Noelle's skin.

Draped in towels, they walked to the tiled tubs. As promised, a basket of scented soaps and bottles of oil waited. Noelle smiled as she disrobed and stepped inside. She lowered herself into the cooler water. Katherine opened a bottle of oil and poured a generous amount onto her hands. She lathered and began massaging Noelle's shoulders. The emotional storm raging inside her eased the deeper her maid's hands penetrated her sore muscles. In time, she'd know what to do.

Randvior slumped forward in his seat. His good fortune had paid off this year. His holdings in Scotland and the Orkney Islands were successfully fortified and manned with dozens of conscripts that would protect his interests in his absence. He considered his mother, seated on his left, and his captains, Harud and Aud, seated on his right. Several kinsmen from nearby steadings had traveled to welcome him home, including his distant cousins, Invar and Hagan, who were seated at opposite ends of the high table.

He watched, rather humored by the spectacle of his cousins consuming as much ale and wine as they could. They always took advantage of his hospitality and depleted his stock of spirits instead of their own. The lower tables were overflowing with platters of roasted mutton and venison, meat pies, boiled cabbage, and vegetables thick with butter, spiced apples, sweet breads, flagons of ale and mead, and his best bottles of German wine. The homecoming feast was an important tradition. But Randvior's thoughts were elsewhere—preoccupied by the empty seat at the nearest table, which was reserved for Lady Noelle Sinclair.

He straightened his back, remembering the glint of rebellion in her eyes the moment he encountered her in Durham. He grinned, immensely pleased she possessed a strong spirit. His only mistake was thinking she'd bend to his will so easily. In bed though, praise Odin, she laid malleable underneath him—as soft as a piece of sculptor's clay. He wanted to shape that tiny body after one of Odin's Valkyries. But there was no time to give her his full attention yet. He closed his eyes and savored the memory of her willowy form and the scent of cinnamon oil on her skin.

Damn it, where was she?

An invitation to the *jarl's* feast was not to be taken lightly. And for Noelle, not a simple request, but a direct command. His eyes roamed the lofty corners and lingered on the landing where he expected her to appear at any moment. All night he had anticipated nothing else and attempted to conceal his disappointment from his mother. Nothing escaped her notice, especially if it pertained to him.

He sized up his mother. Lauga was the furthest thing from what he envisioned a woman should be. Handsome, none could deny it. Dozens of suitors competed for her hand before his father won her heart. Yet even now, as beautiful and respected as she was, scorn reflected in those stony eyes and her lips were always wet for the attack.

He longed for peace, and one woman to warm his bed for the rest of his life. Noelle offered everything he desired.

That's exactly why he was suffering presently. He couldn't get the wench out of his head. He'd slipped into the bathhouse, through a secret passageway, and had hidden behind a curtain. He shifted in his chair. He'd leered at her like a horny boy, watched as she emerged from the hot spring. Her wet hair cascaded down her back, leaving her breasts fully exposed—shiny and beautiful, pale globes bouncing attractively as she climbed over the rocks. And right now, he paid full measure for his intrusion; his erection throbbed miserably. That memory sent sizzling heat pumping through his veins. He moaned, tempted to go upstairs and relieve himself.

"And where is your fine Saxon woman this evening?" His mother's voice shattered his dream.

"Late."

Before Lauga replied, a flash of light green silk appeared on the landing. Noelle stood with Katherine—her gown clung attractively to the hollows and curves of her youthful figure, like a glove on a delicate hand. Her appearance disrupted his guests, too. Aud tactfully crossed the room to usher her to her seat. Dozens of eyes probed the most intimate parts of her body that Randvior had claimed for himself. He moved uncomfortably and watched possessively as she made her way to the table. Nothing had ever aroused him more than watching her glide across the room. Something darkly animalistic in him wanted to spread her across the table like a feast and take her in plain sight. He didn't care if his men watched, or even his bloody mother—*she belongs to me.* He'd leave his mark on her—a more permanent mark than the tattoos his warriors received after battle.

He had purposely seated her next to Sir Brandon McNally, a Scottish noble whose family had been intimately linked to his own since childhood. And across the table, he placed Starri and Unnr Raske, a married couple who had served him loyally for more than a dozen years. Recently deeded a small track of land as a reward for faithful service, they were of kind spirit and would treat her as one of their own. He expected the women would bond instantly, Unnr also being of English decent.

He nodded approval as they welcomed her and served her wine and meat from their own plates. Noelle was an absolute pleasure to behold. Every movement she made perfectly exquisite. She possessed a smile as potent as absinthe. He adjusted himself underneath the table and determined Odin may have gifted him this tiny sprite as punishment instead of reward.

Eyes never straying from his lady, Randvior ignored his captains as they staggered to their feet half-drunk and mumbled indiscernible oaths in his honor. In his periphery, he observed his mother as she hung on everything the girl did. Every word she spoke or move she made embittered her. Lauga even flinched when Noelle's tinkering laughter filled the room as sweetly as an instrument.

His mother had lived vicariously through him for too many years. Anything that threatened to take his attention away from her became the target of her contempt. To preserve his relationship and to keep peace in his household, Randvior had always avoided developing attachments to women.

Noelle changed everything.

He stared deliberately, his eyes moving slowly down her neck and shoulders. Her hands were folded on top of the table, and he glimpsed a flash of gold. She wore his gift, a priceless heirloom from his maternal grandmother that he always carried with him as a good luck charm. He'd had her name engraved on it on the ship, after they made love the first time. He rubbed his chin. That bracelet was a token of his sincerest feelings, but also intended as a pretty shackle to bind her to him forever.

Once the tables were cleared, thralls prepared the room for entertainment. Randvior stepped down from the dais and started to mingle with his guests. He eyed Brandon as he escorted Noelle across the hall. A dozen young bucks followed and swarmed like bees around a pot of honey, vying for her attention. Randvior drifted around the room, intent on meeting up with them inconspicuously. Raging heat infused every inch of his jealous body.

Musicians started to tune their instruments as the tables and benches were arranged against the walls to make plenty of room for dancing.

Music always tamed the beast inside him and he stopped to listen. The lyres and flutes eased his tension, but a snarl still lingered on his lips as the crowd parted to make way for Brandon and his lovely partner. The Scot raised a hand and the musicians began playing a popular ballad. Brandon pulled Noelle to his chest.

Randvior frowned so hard it hurt his face. The couple moved in graceful synchronicity. Spun and clapped hands, exchanged admiring smiles, and pleased the crowd so well a round of applause and demands for a second dance followed. The next was even more infuriating to watch than the first. Brandon dared to lift her by her waist and twirled her in the air, grazing her backside with his hands as he set her on her feet. Their skill inspired other couples to join in. Slowly, the room came alive with swaying bodies.

Randvior's face tightened as his mother joined him. "Sir McNally seems to have warmed considerably to your lady. This would be a strategic match. Surely such a marriage would encourage more trade with his family."

He scowled. "I am quite aware of his quick affection for No-elle. It's only natural to be drawn to your own kind. A wasp is *always* attracted to another wasp." He eyed his mother to see if his illustration had hit home the way he intended.

She placed her hand over her bosom, appearing mortally wounded by his insult.

"A Scot would be naturally tempted by an English lassie," he said sarcastically in his best highland brogue.

This affirmation aside, he would put an immediate end to it. He headed straight for Brandon, maneuvering around dancing couples. He bowed sternly at Brandon's side and offered his hand to Noelle.

"If you would consider giving me the pleasure of this dance." Not a request.

Brandon smiled charmingly and swept a hand toward the lady. "She's all yours, my friend."

Randvior curled her into his arms and kept moving until her cheeks glowed as red as berries. He knew Noelle worked doubly hard to keep step with him on a couple of dances she had never performed before. Breathless after four songs, he led her away from the dance floor.

"You are a vision in that gown," he commented gruffly, meaning to compliment, but wanting her to realize how irritated he was. He took her by the arm and pulled her further away from the crowd.

"And you, lord," she said cheerfully. "I never imagined how well you could dance."

"If I find the need, I am a most willing partner."

"And you found a need tonight?" Her eyebrows arched inquisitively.

In one move, he could pin her against the wall and have her at his complete mercy. "Aye." He nodded. *Not because I'm overly fond of dancing, but near lopping heads off for the way these men stare at you.*

He searched her face while stroking the base of her neck.

Randvior ran a finger between her breasts that were so temptingly pressed together and spilling over the lace bodice like two ripe melons begging to be plucked from the earth. She gasped, positively radiant. Noelle was completely unaware of the bitterness choking him at seeing another man with his hands all over her, even if that man was his best friend. He breathed deeply and tried to focus on something more pleasant.

"Did you enjoy the bathhouse?"

"That water possesses restorative powers."

So does my cock ... He wanted to rip her clothes off. What man could contain his feelings after tasting that virgin flesh?

Noelle drew back and showed him her hand. "I must thank you for this bracelet, it was so unexpected."

He grazed her knuckles with a kiss, while eyeing the shiny metal. Her hands were more the size of a child's than a woman's. *Mine.* He stepped closer—obsessed with her lips. His dark mood flared and he pushed her inside one of the many curtained alcoves along the west wall used for *private* conversations. Out of sight now, he latched onto her hips and hugged her close. She trembled as he covered her mouth possessively with his and stole air from her lungs.

He broke away, leaving her dazed and open-mouthed. "If you find yourself craving male companionship beyond the feast table," he growled into her ear, "ask my permission first." Randvior turned to leave.

"Sir McNally convinced me to dance with him. He told me you were like brothers."

He threw his head back and laughed violently. "That would be as careless as a shepherd placing his prized lamb before the mouth of a wolf's den. Brandon *is* my brother, but still a man. No, *min lille dukke*, don't fret. I'm not angry with you. Brandon will always try to outdo me, it's in his nature."

"I'm not a helpless creature. I can fend for myself." She crossed her arms over her chest and sulked.

"Forgive me." He thumbed her chin. "I failed to identify you as *my* lamb. Does this distinction suit you better? Come, let us find refreshments."

He parted the curtains and she followed him.

Lauga bit her lower lip as she spied her son and Noelle emerging from the alcove. She agonized over his lack of propriety—how he flaunted the girl so shamelessly.

No matter how disciplined a man, in her mind, if he abandoned honor to pursue a woman of questionable reputation, the woman was always to blame. This particular tart thrived on his attention. If Randvior needed to whet his sexual appetite by sleeping with exotic women, let him choose from amongst the Danes or Rus, even a Spaniard. Not a filthy Saxon! Her heart nearly burst at the thought of her son bedding such a wench.

The family bloodline was in jeopardy, one of the purest in Norway. And if her son possessed a sliver of conscience, he would forget this girl and marry one worthy of his name. He needed to produce an heir. Lauga sighed at her misfortune in life—the gods closed her womb after Randvior was born. In her heart, she knew she could have birthed at least a dozen sons.

She hovered predatorily and seized the first opportunity to get Noelle alone. She slithered to the girl's side after her son left her standing while he headed for the tables on the other side of the room.

Lauga gave Noelle a glass of wine she'd poured with her own hands. She accepted the drink.

"I know you are unhappy with me," Noelle said, sipping delicately. "I know you think I'm an outlander unworthy of your son's affection. If you'd only give me a chance, I promise—"

Lauga didn't want to hear her lies and cut her off immediately. Noelle had seduced her son, plain and simple. She raised her glass in salutation, refusing to participate in the conversation. "This wine is not from my son's stock, but from my personal collection. Rennish wine, the most delectable in the world."

Noelle drank more sparingly. "Sweeter than any I've ever tasted."

"Aye," Lauga smiled, so much for intelligent dialogue. She inched away the moment she realized Randvior was headed back.

The musicians were done playing, and slaves reassembled the tables. A troupe of skalds wearing festive robes entered the hall with all the pomp and ceremony expected of their kind. They waved their hands, encouraging men and women to sing. Norsemen have a soft spot for gifted storytellers—a fondness for poets who they believed were divinely inspired. Randvior returned to his seat at the high table and signaled for the performance to begin.

"Lordly *Jarl*, gentlemen, and ladies ..." The master of ceremonies established the credentials of his troupe by introducing each artist individually and listing their accomplishments. Randvior grinned a bit drunkenly, tilted his goblet, and drained it. He banged a fist on the table and held his glass up. A thrall rushed to refill it.

In bits and pieces, the skalds magically wove their enchanted tales, gripping the souls of everyone who listened. Even Randvior sat on the edge of his seat, entangled in the story of Valkyries and warriors. The latest story ended when the bravest and most celebrated warrior in the land shed tears for the woman he would never get to marry, as he laid dying on the battlefield. His only reward was the aubergine-eyed Valkyrie that comforted him by ensuring his passage into Valhalla. *Fear not noble man, Odin has heard your war cry. You are chosen for his table.*

Randvior eyed his lady as she clapped enthusiastically, dazzled by the talents of these men. Most stories were told in Norse, some in English or Gaelic. Brandon leaned close and translated. Randvior tolerated it. He knew of the limited entertainment offered in English courts. Master musicians, acrobats, clowns, dancers, and actors graced King Sweyn's hall, but never a skald. The English were not blessed with an ear for epics. The last performer took his respective place in the middle of the room, a wiry youth with eyes as translucent as a spring.

Randvior felt encouraged, always interested in hearing new

talent. But the young man seemed distracted by Noelle; his voice wavered and cracked like an untrained adolescent. The boy started and stopped, but was promptly rewarded with catcalls from the impatient crowd. With great effort, he bowed toward Randvior and picked up a miniature lyre. Skalds rarely accompanied their words with music, but he began a new verse.

> *A lord shall always honor those who serve loyally*
> *With innumerable gifts of silver and gold.*
> *But this time he rewarded us with a rare flower from across the sea*
> *   of ice,*
> *From a land for centuries laid low.*
> *He brought forth a maiden with a countenance as fair as any I've*
> *   beheld—beneath Odin's goodly skies.*
> *A woman with warmth breathed into her silky curls, a hint of*
> *   winter maiden.*
> *And after the lord jarl is taken up to Asgard, his just rewards to*
> *   collect,*
> *May her womb blossom and be opened in Freya's abounding light—*

"What insult is this?" Randvior bolted from his chair, stormed across the hall with his battle-axe raised above his head.

Never in all his years did he see a performer so eager to part with his head by paying homage to a virtuous woman in public— especially *his* woman. Simply not done! Not in his court. A great commotion sounded from behind as Randvior towered threateningly over the singer who had dropped his instrument the moment he had attacked. The boy cowered and trembled, fell to his knees in complete supplication.

"Wait!"

Randvior turned abruptly at the sound of the familiar voice. Noelle bent down and shielded the skald with her body.

"Go back to your seat!"

"What unforgivable sin did this boy commit?" she asked, her brown eyes opened wide, demanding explanation.

He ran his hand through his hair as if to clear his mind; her obstinacy was an even greater insult than the singer's words. It reflected badly on him. "It's forbidden to single out a woman in verse. It draws unwanted attention, compromises ..." He spoke through tightly clenched teeth.

"Her maidenhood?" she finished.

He knew exactly what the sharp-tongued little shrew was insinuating. *Wait until I get my hands on you ...* Noelle ignited a flame inside him that might never go out.

All of his thoughts fragmented as she suddenly crumpled on the floor at his feet.

CHAPTER TEN

A Matter of Trust

VOICES BOMBARDED RANDVIOR'S ears as he leaned over Noelle. Brandon, Starri, Unnr, and Katherine rushed to his side; but he didn't really see them as he dropped his axe and forced everyone back. He wished now he hadn't acted so rashly with her. He cradled her in his arms. She was burning with fever, her skin scarily ashen.

"Upstairs!" he roared. "Summon the spaewife, find the physicians."

He started up the steps, taking two at a time with Aud at the lead. Randvior crashed through the door and laid her out on the bed. The spaewife must have been nearby; she arrived within minutes. She quickly assessed Noelle's condition and flashed a concerned look at Randvior.

"Clear the room," she ordered. "I can't work with all these people breathing down my neck. If you want a proper diagnosis, *Jarl*, I require complete privacy."

Why should he trust this woman, or anyone for that matter? The spaewife had served his father faithfully while he was growing up. Loyalty for his sire did not guarantee her devotion to him. Perhaps she sympathized with Lauga, or at least feared his mother enough to withhold her skills. He gripped her by the arm. Perhaps a bit too hard, he felt her bones creak.

"I ask you as a subject of my household—overlook her birth-

"

right. Remember what is required by me alone."

She nodded. "I'm a healer, not a murderess. It makes no difference to me where she was born." She walked around the bed and began examining Noelle more closely.

Randvior was the last to leave and paced restlessly just outside the closed door. When the physicians arrived, the spaewife refused to let them in. Hours passed before she emerged, looking haggard, but confident.

Randvior studied her face, savage heat rising in his cheeks.

"'Tis better we speak in private," she said. "Your kinsmen might not agree with my findings."

He cocked an eyebrow at her, didn't like the idea of leaving Noelle's chamber unprotected. He left Aud to stand guard and invited the healer into his own bedchamber.

"Speak."

"Your woman was poisoned."

"Poisoned?" he repeated. Something he would have never suspected.

"Only a few plants native to these lands are toxic enough to cause these symptoms. After purging her body and examining her fluids, I can assure you the main ingredient in the draught mixed to bring about your lady's demise is *Amanita muscaria*. It's a very poisonous mushroom. The culprit underestimated the amount necessary to bring about death. In weaker concentrations it acts as a powerful hallucinogenic. Praise Odin, she lives." She squeezed his hand reassuringly. "Let me stay the night with her."

He agreed. "Take me to her."

Noelle slept fitfully. Randvior noticed the chamber pot on the mattress near her head. The healer immediately walked to the bedside and restrained her hands. Suddenly, Noelle flailed and kicked, called out for her brother, Brian.

The name sliced through him like a knife. Why would she call that sluggard's name instead of his? Dark thoughts plagued him. He remembered Margaret's allegations against her brother—what heinous acts had he committed? Beatings or rape? He possessed the bloodstained sheet from his first night with her to disprove rape.

"Be comforted," the spaewife urged. "She shouldn't remember any of this."

He swallowed his rage. "Stay with her." He needed to get away for a bit. "Tell me, would a man resort to such tactics?"

"No."

Her weathered face reminded Randvior of his favorite wine bag, proof of her years and reason to trust her opinion.

"Undoubtedly the deed of a woman, a very dangerous one," she observed.

"How can you be certain?"

"Men kill without hesitation." She cleared her throat. "Poison is the weapon of choice for women."

Noelle woke with a pounding headache. Every time she opened her eyes, bursts of light swirled dizzyingly around her. Her throat was as parched as a desert. The room was dark, but she crawled out of bed and went to the table near the windows to get a drink of water. It went down like liquid heat.

Oh, God ... The last thing she remembered hearing were Randvior's threats directed at that defenseless boy. Why? If he had performed in an English court, singling out a beautiful woman, no one would harm him—they'd celebrate having been chosen for such an honor. Noelle realized she wasn't in England any longer, and her heart plummeted. She tried to reason, but her mind fogged if she thought too hard.

For weeks, she'd attempted to overlook Randvior's violence. But he seemed intent on never letting her forget who he really was. She refused to accept it any longer. Regrettably, he shared the same tainted blood as her brother, blood that bred tyranny. She swooned—*what's wrong with me?* Memories rallied inside her head. As a child, she'd sworn an oath before God. Had promised to escape the cruelty of her home and seek refuge in a place where she could serve the poor and live peacefully. How could she find any peace in enemy lands? Noelle reached for the pitcher of water and threw up in it.

God has placed my future in my own hands. I must leave and find someone willing to take me home. If England is too far, I'll seek refuge in the first Christian lands I come to—where the Church grants sanctuary to displaced daughters of Christ. Maybe in Scotland or Ireland.

Head still swimming, she limped away from the table and went to the wardrobe. She dressed in the heaviest overdress she owned and wrapped her fur cloak tightly around her shoulders, securing it with two silver brooches. Her legs wobbled. Next, she flung herself in a chair, put on a pair of stockings, and laced on her warmest boots. She had no money to pay passage on a ship, but Randvior let her keep many of her jewels. She pocketed the most expensive pieces.

She opened the door and peered into the hallway. Empty—it must be very late. Noelle stepped outside of her room and listened. Not a sound.

Confident that she had chosen a perfect time to escape, she cautiously made her way downstairs. She stiffened as she came closer to the landing, but didn't see anyone below.

Stopping to catch her breath, Noelle rested her head against the wall, dizzied by blurred vision. Bile left a bitter taste in her mouth. She tried to shake it off, then proceeded to the landing, and managed to slip through the hall unnoticed. The back doors loomed as imposing as Saint Peter's gates. Her passage to freedom lay ahead, and this time Lauga couldn't keep her from using them.

Once outside, she staggered to the bathhouse, feeling weaker by the second. Had she gotten drunk last night? She sought refuge behind the back wall, and once she was absolutely sure she was alone, she hobbled across the clearing. Light streamed outside from the occasional window of a tenant's cabin, but she kept moving.

As she neared the last row of houses, Noelle gazed ahead. The full moon illuminated the river. She remembered to travel westward, toward the ocean. If she were fortunate enough to find someone willing to help, she'd offer *all* the jewels as compensation. They were worth a fortune. Another wave of nausea—Noelle had to stop again.

The ritual ended with Randvior's whispered words. His tenants and servants had gathered at Odin's altar to offer sacrifices and pray to speed Noelle's recovery. Even Katherine attended.

They returned to the great hall and Randvior gathered everyone around the hearth to share a drink. He warmed his weary bones and remembered how terrified he'd felt after Noelle collapsed. It had been the single most horrifying moment of his life. The nerve-racking silence in the room made him uncomfortable, so he scoured the hall with his eyes while Katherine climbed the stairs. He didn't want Noelle left alone for too long. The spaewife went home after two long days of keeping vigil at her bedside. He was satisfied she was out of danger.

"She's gone!" Katherine screamed from above.

Randvior was across the room in seconds.

He ran upstairs and nearly tore the door from its hinges as he entered Noelle's chamber. They searched every corner together. The maid rummaged through her mistress' trunks, while Randvior checked his room and the hallway. He returned. Everything was in its proper place. On a hunch, he opened Noelle's jewel box. Many of the pieces he let her keep were missing, including the pair of silver brooches shaped like turtledoves. He set the box down and checked the wardrobe. Her best cloak and fur boots were gone. She'd left voluntarily.

He flew downstairs and organized two search parties from amongst the men. Randvior sent them north and east, and decided to ride west alone. If he knew anything about Noelle, she was headed where she felt the most comfortable. The girl came from generations of seafarers, as he did, and a mixture of salt water and blood coursed through her veins.

Without a word, he saddled his horse and galloped away, despite the deep snow. She couldn't get very far in her condition and it didn't take long to pick up her trail. Tiny boot prints revealed where she intended to go. He thanked the gods and rode harder and faster. Poison had surely muddled her mind. And only an idiot would have left a woman in her condition alone. His heart skipped a beat. The more people, the greater the chance his gods would grant his request.

What will she say? *I'm a bastard for taking her from Durham, but a savior for rescuing her from her brother. Damned either way.* He recalled the cryptic message from the spirit women in his dream. *There are two possible ends for you ...* He tossed back his head, his heart felt so brittle it might crack.

He came across two sets of footprints in the snow nearly two miles from the house. One headed north and the other westward, along the river. Identical sets. He chuckled. She must have gotten turned around. Something dark flashed in the near distance. A cloaked figure broke into a full run. Randvior dug his heels into the stallion's ribs. As he closed in, he could tell Noelle was struggling to stay on her feet.

"Stop!"

"Why?" she shouted over her shoulder. "So you can ridicule me?"

She tripped and fell face down in the snow. He swung down from the saddle, walked beside her, and offered his hand.

She refused it.

"Everyone is looking for you. We returned from prayers and you were gone. There are patrols to the north and east ..."

Noelle sat and wrapped her hands around her head. Losing his patience or temper wouldn't accomplish a thing. Randvior didn't know what to say. "Are you unwell?"

Noelle gestured angrily. "Did I ask you to chase me down like a nursemaid?" She brushed snow off her cloak and bent her knees into her chest. "Make arrangements for me to go back to England. There's nothing left between us, Randvior Sigurdsson. And I have no interest in being your concubine or any desire to spend another night under the same roof with your *delightful* mother."

Her complaints were justified. And much to his relief, her mental condition hadn't deteriorated; her tongue remained as razor-sharp as always. He couldn't fault her last grievance. Randvior didn't want to spend another night under the same roof with his mother, either. "Be reasonable."

"*I am,*" she snapped. "I hate you, do you hear me? I despise you for bringing me here. And you raped me! Dashed my dreams and destroyed everything I hold sacred!"

Could she choose more negative words? But rape … This was an outrageous accusation. His temper flared. He reached, gripped the front of her cloak, and lifted. "And what lucky bastard would have claimed you if I hadn't?" He was frozen in the spot before her.

"Let me go," she protested and tried to wiggle free. He let her go and she landed on her arse.

"Ignorant marauder … pirate … murderer … beast … godless heathen … barbaric, inferior man … rapist!"

This was about adding insult to injury. Damned if she was going to get away with calling him those cursed names. He lunged and held her shoulders between his hands. He wanted to squeeze every filthy thought from her mind.

Then he caught himself. *What was he doing?* Randvior heaved a sigh as he let her go.

She landed a solid kick on his shin and sprinted away. But Randvior recovered and tackled her. They tumbled, rolling twice before they came to a complete stop, Noelle pinned underneath. She slapped at his face, but he caught her hands midair and pinned her arms to her sides.

"I'm not a rapist!" he denied vehemently.

"Of all the revolting things I called you, why does the thought of being a rapist trouble you the most?"

"I've never forced a woman to bed."

"No, only allowed your men to do it. Is there really a difference?"

"I did *not* rape you."

She quit struggling and he let go of her arms, but still strad-dled her.

"If not rape, what do you call it when a man barges into a room where a girl is praying for her life and you claim her maidenhead without the courtesy of a kind word or promise of love?"

"Seduction," he said, panting. "Not rape. A man conquers and takes what he wants—it's an inherent right."

"Inherent?" she cried. "Decency and honesty, kindness and moderation are inherent. Stealing what belongs to another is simply criminal!"

"Ah." He tipped his head up and gazed at the stars.

Noelle swallowed hard and swatted his arms. "Get off me."

"Not until you understand the difference between men and women."

"It's cold and I'm soaked to the bone," she complained.

"You should have thought about that before you abandoned me."

She made a low noise of contempt. "How can I abandon you if I never claimed any allegiance to you in the first place? As you confessed, it's only natural for a man to take. Well, for a woman in my position, it's only natural to escape."

He was quiet for a long time, suspended between two philos-ophies: of right and of wrong. She had spoken wisely. Not all men pillaged. In fact, most didn't. Generations of Sigurdsson's had, and he'd be damned if a Saxon wench was going to stop him.

"What are *my* rights?" she asked.

If she were a man, he'd beat some sense into her thick skull. "As far as the law is concerned, you have none." Her undisci-plined tongue always caused trouble. He looked at her as she flailed. "Do you want help getting up?"

She hesitated, refusing to look at him, then reluctantly, nod-ded. Randvior staggered to his feet and extended his hand. She batted it away and stood on her own. A twinge of guilt pinched him. They were both frozen and miserable; he wanted to touch her, offer what little warmth his body had left to give. But would she receive it?

"Leave me alone," she said, as if knowing his question.

"Never," he said with a defensive note in his voice.

"I wish ..."

"What?"

"... that I had killed you the first night you fell asleep in the same bed with me."

He reached inside his boot and pulled out a knife. "Take it and strike quickly, every wicked thing that comes out of that mouth feels as deadly as a blade piercing my heart."

She was silent again and cast her eyes downward. Tears streamed down her face. "I want to go home," she said.

He framed her face between his hands, his passion unfurled like a flag. "You *are* home."

She did not respond. He felt his chest tighten at the sight of the pain in her face. "Anything that hurts you, hurts me. I killed for you," he confessed. "I murdered my own man to protect you. And the gods may punish me for it, but I'd kill a thousand more if I knew it proved to you how much I want you. Please," he croaked.

Randvior picked her up.

"I want nothing more than to keep you here with me forever," he said.

CHAPTER ELEVEN
Promises

ONCE RANDVIOR PLACED her on the saddle in front of him, the heavens opened and a bitter wind blew across the field. Noelle snuggled into her fur collar, still suffering from the effects of poison. Something still didn't feel right inside; her ears were ringing and she felt heavy-legged, almost clumsy. But the Viking offered no explanation and she really didn't want to talk, unless it was absolutely necessary. He commented on how impressed he was that she had covered so much distance and how he had underestimated her tenacity and strength. She was tougher than most women; she was glad of the acknowledgement, but frowned. She didn't want his compliments.

"Why did you run away?" he asked.

"You threatened that defenseless boy." She huddled deeper into his warmth. "My brother displayed the same rage through-out my lifetime, and all I could see were the faces of the countless victims of his violence. I cannot live that way, ever again. I never wish to be the reason a man loses his life."

He swore and slapped his thigh. "If that's the way you feel, why risk running straight back into Brian's reach?"

"I have a sister who needs me."

"And a worthless father who did nothing to protect you."

"Aye," Noelle conceded. "But Margaret deserves a chance to be happy."

The elements of this relationship were impossible to understand. One minute she couldn't stand being near him, the next, she wanted to curl up in his arms.

"There are rules we must respect, and if broken, consequences must follow, punishment I must deliver. I cannot change just because you find it unpalatable. If I bend the rules for one man, another will expect the same leniency when his turn comes. Our women are cherished above all things. No man need point out her beauty in public—the scald deserved to die."

The air around them had thickened with disagreement. Randvior tried to diffuse the situation.

"No matter how devoted my men are, or how many oaths of allegiance they keep, they are only flesh and blood. Do you know how many men gazed at you covetously the night of the feast? Even Brandon acted differently when you were around. By Odin, woman, you could force a priest to question his abstinence." His mouth tightened. "I admit I'm not an easy man to live with. And I own a black heart where you're concerned, my sweet." He sighed, slid forward, and tightened his hold on her. "I'll kill to keep what's mine."

"I didn't ask you to bring me here. And you do not *own* me."

It never failed. Noelle insisted on reminding him how miserable she was at every opportunity.

"I know." He bit back the anger that itched to come out.

Time passed quickly in the saddle and they reached the stables without attaining reconciliation. Goddamn it, he needed more time to convince her to stay. To make her *want* to stay of her own free will. Anything less and he'd consider it a failure.

A groom took the reins and Randvior jumped down. He lifted Noelle from the saddle and steered her toward the bathhouse. This conversation was far from over.

Ignoring her protests, Randvior opened the door and shoved her inside. Enough was enough—how could he administer justice and manage his lands if he was constantly preoccupied with the fear of her running away? All the unnecessary arguments were starting to chip away at his willpower, making him consider things he'd sooner forget. He felt foolish sometimes. Maybe even a bit undeserving and awkward.

No woman had ever infuriated him this much.

Randvior knew what she wanted: words, promises he intended to keep, and lovemaking she'd never forget.

The warmth seemed to have a positive effect on her. She relaxed and color quickly returned to her cheeks. He walked across the room, gathered an armful of wood, and built a roaring fire in the largest pit. He peeked over his shoulder and caught her staring at his backside. He chuckled, more than pleased he still possessed the physical charms to catch her eye. And only an hour ago she had declared how much she hated him.

If she loathed him as much as she claimed, why did those liquid eyes penetrate his skin? Noelle could no more live without him than he could survive breathing fire and brimstone.

"Are you warm enough?" he asked.

"Yes."

He touched her cheek and she stiffened. He ignored her reaction and rested his hands on her shoulders. *Pride comes before the fall* ... Words taken directly from her holy book—worthy ones, he thought. He slowly unclasped the silver turtledove brooches and removed her cloak. He didn't understand why she fought the urge. Randvior slipped behind her and massaged her shoulders. He drew his hands together near the base of her spine and blew softly into her ear. His fingers floated over the curves of her bottom, gently plying and kneading. What she needed was a distraction.

He gathered the hem of her gown and pulled it over her head. Next, he untied the shoulder ribbons on her chemise and watched as the thin veil of material pooled at her feet. "Kick off your boots."

She did.

His hands left her body only long enough to remove his own clothing and then he was on her again. Her hair hung down her back like a honey-streaked robe and he buried his face in those fragrant tresses, breathing in the intoxicating scent of spring. Her body drove him crazy. Her breasts shimmered with sweat. *Odin, give me strength to offer comfort and nothing more ...* He wrapped his arms around her. Crushed against him, she still tried to squirm free. His laugh vibrated through their bodies.

The thrill of the chase exhilarated him more than anything. His cock stood at attention, but they would not make love this night. "Look at me."

Slowly, she turned her eyes toward him.

"What will it take to convince you my intentions are honorable?"

She withered in his hands. What had he done now? *"Elsk meg pokker heller."* He kissed her and carried her to the spring. Her head drooped against his chest as he waded into the water and he was suddenly reminded. *The poison ...* He banished his temper and hugged her closer.

"Stay with me, little one. Baptize me with your sweet love."

A week later, after Noelle had fully recovered, Katherine prepared her for a very important feast.

"Many distinguished guests will be in attendance tonight, including lords from nearby steadings, who have gathered to hear and offer oaths of allegiance to the *jarl*," the maid reported, while combing out her hair.

Noelle noticed a slight tremor in her own body at the mention of Randvior. She missed his company in a carnal sort of way. *How did men perfect their lovemaking skills?* She frowned as the only logical answer dawned.

Hundreds of women, maybe thousands—her toes curled with envy. She eyed the gold bracelet around her wrist apathetically, and swallowed the thought down like a bitter draught. If jealousy consumed her, she might go to him full of reckless accusations. If she wanted to win his heart and protect her family's honor, she must set herself apart from other women. Fornication had its price and her need for a husband gave her purpose.

Randvior hadn't discussed his womanizing past. But she knew in his masculine world, a man would never be considered complete if he didn't bed as many women as possible. Dozens of attractive females lived and worked under the Viking's roof. She smiled warily. But it was only *she* he pursued right now … was it not?

This problem required a precise solution. Noelle formulated a plan and walked to the table. She splashed water on her face and scrubbed her hands. If she wasn't going to escape in the foreseeable future, she certainly couldn't risk losing her position. Randvior had mistakenly told her she possessed the necessary charms to tempt a priest, which meant she could easily gain rule over him.

She dressed with only one goal in mind—capturing Randvior's undivided attention. If he wouldn't publicly claim her, she'd force his hand. She selected a richly embroidered gown with a plunging neckline. It was her most provocative dress, accentuating the delicate curve of her breasts perfectly. Katherine swept the sides of her hair off her face and braided it, letting the bulk of her tresses fall loosely down her back. Noelle removed the bracelet Randvior had given her and put it away. *I'll give him something to think about.* She chose a gold choker as her only adornment. Katherine stepped back and admired her.

"If this is how a woman begs for a man's favor," Katherine crooned, "I'd ask for the moon and the stars, too."

Noelle blushed and opened the door.

Aud awaited and heaved a dismal sigh the moment he saw her. He offered his arm and she accepted it.

The burly captain halted at the top stair. "I know you've suffered these past weeks," he said. "Try to understand the predicament my master was in. The gods tortured him with visions of you—on more than one occasion. What can you possibly accomplish wearing that dress?" He drove home his point by eyeing her from head to toe. "Please, change your gown. Judging by that look on your face, which I've seen on my own daughters, you'll regret it. Your point is sufficiently made. This is not an English court; and this is no way to test our *jarl*. I swear to report your displeasure to him."

Surprised by his insightfulness and elegance, she smiled. Leave it to providence to place a voice of reason in the bulky body of a bloodthirsty warrior before she dared to tempt her lover.

She squeezed his hand appreciatively. "How else am I to secure my place in this house? His mother hates me, and I am neither a slave nor his betrothed. I am caught between two worlds and left to my own devices and shall use what the good Lord has seen fit to give me." The matter was closed.

Randvior nearly choked in mid-conversation when Noelle appeared. Many rumors had circulated over the last days concerning the stranger he'd brought home from England. His intention had been to share her in small doses, this night being the first opportunity to introduce her to his extended family and neighbors. As his eyes struggled to focus on her, they blurred and cleared again. An animalistic growl escaped him as his guests followed the direction of his unblinking stare. Noelle's pearly flesh glowed tantalizingly in the candlelight. The gown left little to a man's imagination.

His jaw locked. Jarl Fald Ovesen, his closest ally, patted him sympathetically on the back.

"You've been bitten by the most dangerous creature in the world," the old man mused.

"Aye," Randvior agreed. "By a heartless viper."

The vixen had the audacity to greet him with a casual smile, then simply continue on her trajectory to the table where Brandon waited. The Scotsman stood and bowed. He kissed Noelle's hand. Damn protocol! It demanded Randvior remain indifferent in certain situations. And since he had never formally announced his betrothal to her, although they were lovers, the law offered him no protection. She possessed all the freedoms of an unmarried woman in his court. Perhaps he should have listened to his mother and put an iron collar around her neck, instead of a gold trinket on her wrist!

He focused on the men standing with him near the high table. Black emotions paralyzed him, keeping his attention dangerously split between politics and Noelle. He couldn't avoid the inevitable, but he could prepare for it. Whatever game the wench played would be revealed as the night progressed.

Lauga drifted into the room behind the servants, directing them where to place platters of food and drink. Randvior's gaze followed hers, swept the room as sharply as a hawk's, and stopped on the girl. The gown had a negative effect on her, too. She gasped in astonishment and headed for the table where Noelle sat. He smirked as indistinguishable words passed between the women. Noelle deserved a bit of harassment for wearing that bedgown. Men rarely intervened in disputes between women, but he knew Brandon couldn't resist an opportunity to ruffle Lauga's peacock feathers. The Scot chased her away in a huff.

Randvior gulped down a glass of wine. Noelle looked like an angel with her hair cascading down her back and her slender neck adorned with a thick circlet of gold. His mother stalked her, openly hated her. His stomach roiled. She had every reason to poison Noelle. By Odin, he needn't look any further to find the culprit—she was under his nose the whole time. If proven guilty, he'd punish her, severely.

Guests settled at the tables. Randvior's cousin handed him an ale horn overflowing with beer. He raised it in salutation. "Let the celebration begin!"

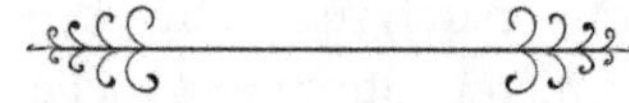

CHAPTER TWELVE
Questions of Allegiance

"J UST WHAT IS an oath of allegiance?" Noelle queried, hanging on Brandon's every word.

"Similar to pledging fealty to a king."

Brandon seemed eager to provide the answers she needed to understand Norse customs. "*Jarls* are considered as distinguished as princes in these lands. Admired and deeply loved because they don't rule from lofty places, but live amongst their people. This country is without an heir, and the men you see sitting at Rand's high table are tasked with enforcing the laws that unify the Trondelag. Your master is an integral part of the future of this territory ..."

She didn't like thinking of Randvior as her master.

Brandon continued, "And if Norway wishes to remain independent, a king will need to be anointed. There are ambitious men living beyond these borders, competing for control of our lands. A kingless territory is an attractive temptation for any man trying to leave his mark on the world." His face darkened. "War is inevitable."

She understood, having grown up in a country crippled by countless rebellions. If Randvior faced half the challenges her father had, she knew what to expect. And ships were the most coveted luxuries of the age. Randvior's vessels carried merchandise from exotic lands back to his country. Taxable goods and high tariffs, if imposed, meant great wealth for any ruler. She fixed her gaze on Randvior. He was the type of man any zealous king would seek as an ally.

But no matter how influential or experienced Randvior appeared, someone needed to instruct him on how to treat a lady. She felt too hot and aware of everything about him, including his stubborn refusal to marry her. An innocent flirtation with a stranger should wake him up.

A perfectly amiable male specimen sitting three tables away gave her hope. Young and potent, he shared similar physical characteristics with Randvior. Brilliant eyes met hers. He smiled and she diverted her eyes. Then she looked back.

He patted the bench next to him. She shook her head. Brandon stared at her, then looked his direction.

"What's this?" he asked.

"Nothing," Noelle fussed with the necklace about her throat. Her eyes fluttered closed, then opened to focus on a glass of wine on the table.

Brandon dismissed the boy with a flick of his wrist. "Give me credit," he winked. "I know a thing or two about wooing the fairer sex."

Noelle managed a pale smile. Uncomfortable with Brandon's intrusion, she searched the room silently. Thralls were shuffling furniture. Much to her amazement, the ten soldiers Randvior commandeered from her father marched into the room and lined up along the west wall. They appeared well nourished and were dressed in clean shirts and breeches. Her cheeks flushed. She had convinced herself that Randvior intended them for hard labor. Or even worse. Again, her chest tightened with guilt.

Forgive me for doubting you ...

Her spirit soared as they greeted her—all smiles. Samuel and Henry were especially enthused.

Randvior stood and signaled for silence. He looked as dominant as a bull. Noelle sat forward and stared. She could see the rigid muscle all over his body through the layers of wool and leather he wore. The broadsword sheathed at his hip and war axe strapped across his back lent an appealing savagery to his appearance. He resembled a bloodthirsty god.

Brandon snorted. "Perhaps your roving eye is cured?" He cast a sidewise glance at Randvior. "He's a man deserving respect from everyone. And I believe he desires an heir."

Heat rose on her cheeks. "I don't know what you're talking about," she said. Despite her misguided attempt to make Randvior jealous, she found herself incapable of following through with it. And now Brandon was on to her.

"Ah …" He wagged his finger. "And what do you think he's doing when he makes love to you lass, playing house?"

She hated the clandestine nature of their relationship. Everyone knew what was going on. Only she refused to admit it. Patience gone, she scowled at Brandon. Noelle didn't appreciate his impertinence—*at all*. Oh, that lousy Scot had a way of getting under her skin. Fortunately, their conversation was cut short.

Randvior stared down at her. Heat jetted from his eyes. "With gratitude we offer thanks to father Odin for bringing us home again. My wealth has increased in Iceland, Scotland, and the Orkneys. We raised shelters, established trading rights, and left behind enough men to protect Sigurdsson holdings until next season. Before returning, we visited Durham …"

"An heir." Brandon whispered tauntingly.

She refused to give birth to bastards!

Moments later, after the toast, the guests mingled freely. Noelle tapped into her courage again and headed for the young man she singled out in the crowd before.

Randvior snatched her arm and swung her back into her chair. He didn't have to say a word; she read everything in his eyes.

"I want you to stay where I can see you," he seethed. A sadistic smile curled at the corner of his mouth. "*Nothing* escapes my eyes, Noelle."

Randvior reclaimed his throne. He couldn't shake his combative feelings or the growing doubt in his mind. Had he treated her so unkindly that she needed to solicit her feminine charms to attract another suitor? Did she think her bad behavior would go unchecked? Or that he wouldn't notice the newly appointed rival tripping over his own tongue to get close to her?

The hall echoed with celebration. The clamor of heavy boots stomping and weapons hitting tabletops made the floorboards quiver. The chanting began.

Randvior, Randvior, Randvior Numerous men recounted his accomplishments. The unprecedented success of his western expeditions, his continued dedication to safeguarding trading routes and honoring treaties with rival kingdoms, and his influence amongst the Varangians benefited nearly every man in western Norway. These men gathered to renew alliances and swear oaths of protection. His home would be well defended next season. *Jarls*, both great and humble, arrived with conscripts from their personal *huskarlar*, warriors they would leave behind as testament to their loyalty.

Dozens of men came forward and kneeled at his feet. Some would accompany Randvior on his next expedition and serve in his *comitatus* as members of his prestigious war band. His gold sword lay across his knees with hundreds of gold and silver oath rings set in the pommel. One by one, each man stood. They latched onto the hilt with one hand and grasped the oath rings with the other and swore on Odin's countenance to protect him.

"By seizing this sword I pledge my life in service to Jarl Randvior Sigurdsson and his captains. Defying all others."

Once sworn, they lined up behind the high table. Sixty-seven warriors swore oaths of protection. Afterward, the English soldiers were offered the same opportunity. They pledged their lives in service. *Anything* promised greater reward than slavery.

Everyone drank. Even the slaves were allowed to celebrate as long as the master's cup was kept full. Thralls provided an endless supply of ale and wine. Randvior wanted to get pissed—filthy stinking drunk. He needed to forget everything before he took his frustrations out on an innocent man. He slammed three servings of ale and called for another as he urged a voluptuous thrall onto his lap. She giggled and held the horn to his lips.

He teased, prodded her arse, and pinched her nipples, his eyes coolly fastened on Noelle's astonished face. *Let her feel the depth of my bitterness before she ever considers flirting with another man again.* He knew drink and wenches were a volatile combination. And Noelle was definitely not the kind of lady to sit timidly and watch him indulge in the pleasures of another woman's body. She bent over Brandon and whispered something in his ear. Brandon shook his head, adamantly. Noelle shrugged and disappeared.

Randvior's lips curled malevolently. He brushed the woman from his lap and staggered to Brandon's table.

"What did she say?"

A haughty grin split Brandon's face. "She asked for my assistance to restore her family's honor. She asked me to marry her."

Randvior wanted to slap the egoistical look off his face.

"Are you of a mind to accept?"

"You'd consider me a damnable liar if I denied any attraction for the girl."

Randvior grabbed a glass of wine off the table and choked it down. He wiped his mouth dry. "If you were any other man, I'd kill you for that admission."

"Aye," the Scotsman agreed. "And if I *weren't* your friend, I'd conveniently forget to tell you to take that enchanting girl as your wife before another man does."

Randvior grunted and shot him an appreciative look. "I intend to."

Desperate to escape the humiliation of Randvior's drunken display, Noelle bolted outside. The only place she felt safe was in the bathhouse, shielded from inquiring minds. She shivered, finding herself once again poorly equipped for the cold. Shelter stood only a few yards away. She hurried and nearly lost her footing as her silk slippers skated across the ice.

She slammed the bathhouse door shut behind her. Randvior's

unpredictability and his mother's conniving and interference were driving her crazy. She had lost too many people she loved to simply accept her precarious position is this household. But it seemed futile to resist Randvior. She sat on a chair near the large fire pit, warmed her hands, then rested her head on the table.

After a while, a noise pulled her from her racing thoughts. The door opened suddenly and she jerked. Half expecting to find Randvior leaning against the doorjamb, she gasped at finding the young man she had flirted with instead. A beatific smile lit his mouth.

"Mistress Noelle." A head of dark hair, tied back in a tail, framed a handsome face. Mischievous blue eyes appraised her leisurely.

"Remember me?"

As if I could forget a face like yours. "Yes," she answered.

"*Dimwitted fool …*" she mumbled self-deprecatingly. The object of her teasing had taken her attention more seriously than she had intended. His unnatural good looks were rivaled only by Randvior. She caught her breath as he came closer. He knelt. Maybe if she ignored him he'd go away.

"My father is Jarl Fald Ovesen, our steading only a day's ride north," he informed, not offering his name. "He sat at Randvior's right side during the feast."

"Yes." She remembered the stocky warrior very well. "It is an honor to sit at the *jarl's* high table. I am sure your family deserves this privilege."

He smiled and plopped down in the chair across from her. "I am greatly encouraged by your favor this evening." He leaned forward and took her hand. "Should I consider myself the most fortunate man on earth to capture the eye of the loveliest woman at the feast?"

Warning sounded in Noelle's head. Extraordinary sensations titillated and punished her body all at once. *I'm absolutely devoted to Randvior,* her heart spoke—but she didn't understand.

"*Stjernene blek i sammenligning.*"

Bloody heathen tongue. She scooted away.

The stranger rubbed his chin and grinned rakishly. He spread his legs, the outline of his engorged shaft visible through his leather breeches. She must concentrate on other thoughts. Were *all* Norsemen concupiscent swine oblivious to rejection? If she screamed, Lauga would blame her, and she refused to give that woman another reason to find fault in her. If she ran away, he'd chase her. She didn't possess the strength to look up and instead rose to her feet, hoping to discourage further advances. It didn't have the desired effect. Rather ... encouraged it. He leapt and gathered Noelle in a tight embrace.

"My dreams are answered," he petted her head. "Could it be that you remain unblemished by any man?" Amusement tinged his voice.

"Let me go."

Too late.

The door burst open. With her back facing the entrance, she was at a disadvantage, but she recognized the bestial sounds of Randvior. She flinched at each heavy footstep she heard.

"Hva faen gjør du?"

"Hva enhver mann ville gjort i nærvær av en slik skjønnhet," Ovesen shot back.

Roughly shoved aside, Noelle turned just in time to see Randvior's fist connect with the younger man's face. *Oh, God.* Reminiscent of a Greek epic, she ran for cover and ducked behind a set of shelves. Noelle peeked around the corner, heart pounding. Ovesen shook his head and hurled his weight at Randvior. They crashed to the floor, a tangled mass of fists and curses.

Randvior rolled onto his side and sprang to his feet. He landed a solid kick to the man's head, reached down, and let out a ferocious growl, lifting him by the front of his shirt. Randvior shook him and hurled him across the room. A pile of firewood broke his fall.

Randvior turned away from the scene and looked at her.

Shaking like a leaf, her life flashed before her eyes. *He's going to kill me.*

Perhaps if she confessed, explained why she chose to wear the dress and flirt with another man, it would put an end to this misunderstanding. Surely, he couldn't blame her. Self-preservation demanded action, nothing more. Rage uncoiled inside her, too. Lauga acted the cold-blooded bitch at every turn and Randvior continuously isolated her. The indomitable Viking never provided her a means to keep her mind or hands occupied. She felt useless. Bravely, she stepped out and went his way. Randvior's eyes swelled from silvery half-moons to spitting flames.

The truth must be revealed, and now.

"Before you punish me," she said, attempting to take control of the situation. "Answer one question. What do you want from me?"

His body shook convulsively as he laughed. Rage and bitterness distorted his face. He glanced over his shoulder at his rival, who remained unconscious on the floor.

"Answer me!" she demanded.

He fanned his fingers and cracked his knuckles. His usually bright eyes were lackluster and red. Her fascination with him deepened because of his fierce possessiveness of her. But she deserved to hear him *express* his feelings; at least hear what he wanted.

"Tell me or I'll be forced to take matters into my own hands. The good Lord doesn't cease his labors above to give a man time to catch his breath to muster the courage to speak plainly with a lady. Much time has been wasted—on both of us."

Randvior resumed his preoccupation with his hands.

"Tell me!" She jabbed a finger in his chest.

He trapped her arms. *"Tell you?"* he repeated incredulously. His voice fell to a whisper. "Perplexing wench." He looked at his hands, then straight back at her. "Making demands of me when it is *I* who should make them. See the damage you've reaped by taking matters into your own hands—attracting the attention of a man who risked his life by following you into the shadows." He dug his fingernails into her tender flesh. "I'll answer, but I warn that you may not like what I have to say."

"Tell me."

He shook his head, burdened by something she didn't understand. "First, you're confined to your rooms after the feast. Your quick departure has sparked a new round of damaging gossip. Do you know how many throats I'd have to cut to stop wagging tongues from weaving wicked lies about you throughout the Trondelag? I haven't the time or resources to do it. But consider *this* while you stew in your icy pot. It has been my intention, since the moment I set eyes on you in Durham, to bring you home as my bride."

Her heart liquefied. *By Jesus, what have I done?*

"You *will* yield to me."

Her heart fluttered as his hands locked around her waist like a tight chain.

"I want you, goddamn it," he lowered his mouth and kissed her violently. "And by Odin, I'll have you."

He raked his lips across her tender mouth.

Forgive me, she thought.

They returned to the hall and Randvior escorted her to her seat. "Stay here."

"No." He still hadn't convinced her of anything. "I find my circumstances too awkward to bear."

The creases around Randvior's mouth deepened. "What is this about, Noelle? Are you purposely challenging my authority to prove something to my guests?"

"This isn't about you." Noelle stood. "It's about honor—my honor." In a huff of tears, Noelle ran upstairs.

CHAPTER THIRTEEN

Odin's Altar

RANDVIOR WATCHED HER climatic retreat, along with his guests. What else did she want? Hadn't he made his feelings remarkably clear? He'd admitted his desire for her from the moment he'd set eyes upon her. Flippant female, she goaded the devil playing around with Sveinn in the great hall. Even worse, she was prone to disobedience and emotional outbursts, had complete disregard for protocol, and no respect for her elders. And now everyone knew how undisciplined his little vixen truly was.

But in truth, Noelle wreaked havoc on his heart. She infuriated, delighted, and branded the deepest regions of his soul in the process.

By Odin, he loved her. Everything inside him went hot and still.

He swallowed a bit of wine before he stalked upstairs. Her door sat ajar and he went inside. The sound of her tears stabbed him. He squinted and had the misfortune of imagining Sveinn's hands all over her body. With this agonizing picture inside his head, it was hard to control himself. He swaggered closer, more intoxicated by bitterness than spirits.

If he must choose—here and now—he knew she was constituted of the most charitable nature and loyalty he'd ever seen in a woman. And those damnable eyes ignited his libido in a second. Her slow smile rivaled the glory of any sunrise. And those delicate colored cheeks and lips begged for an endless supply of kisses. She breathed sensuality, intentionally or not. And that arse, the gods cracked the mold. She rolled onto her side.

He cursed himself for being an infernal beast.

"Did I hurt you?"

She smoothed her hair and sat up, sniffled, and addressed him unchallenging for the first time in days. "I know your duty lies with your tenants and countrymen. Yet, I dared to hope to be a small part of your life, especially after what we have shared." Noelle swung her legs over the bed, feet dangling. "I realize I have no right to make any demands. But if you feel anything for me, or possess an ounce of mercy where I'm concerned, I beg if you find it necessary to seek pleasure in the arms of another woman, give me warning so I don't have to see it ever again."

She loves me …

More than he had anticipated. She looked so helpless gazing up at him. And hot enough to melt the cold fury that still ravaged his body.

"Have I not proven myself worthy of your trust and protection? I'm no longer the gullible maid you abducted from Durham after experiencing the pleasure of your bed. At least I fully understand now why men seek out women. I apologize for my reprehensible behavior. I didn't want another man, Randvior. I only seek what any woman in my position would—a way home—or a husband to shield me from humiliation. Grant me protection and I will work my fingers to the bone to earn my keep in your household. No task too menial, no position too humble." A new round of tears began to fall.

He didn't like her behavior one bit. But if he walked in her shoes … "What safeguards did you employ to protect your reputation when I found you in the bathhouse with Sveinn Ovesen?" He inched closer. "I declared my feelings and you still defied me."

"My brother made it abundantly clear what you intended. And I'd sooner serve Lauga than be attached to a man who doesn't love me."

"Before you act too rashly and choose spinsterhood over my bed, come with me. I want to show you something."

"Where are we going?"

He didn't answer, but unlocked the door connecting their chambers. She'd never been invited to his rooms before; this was *his* sanctuary. Noelle seemed amazed by the lavishness of the décor. He opened a wardrobe and picked a cloak and boots for her to wear. Gracefully, she didn't comment on the fact that he kept an array of women's garments in his bedroom. He wrapped the fur around her shoulders and pinned it with one of his own gold brooches. Next, he knelt, proffering the boots, and she slipped her feet inside; he laced them tight.

"Thank you," she said.

He in turn dressed warmly, and then led her to double doors that opened onto a small balcony. She walked slowly down the stairs. No one would see them slip away.

Inches of fresh, icy snow covered the ground and crunched noisily beneath them as they walked. Randvior stopped to check her, fingered her chin, and looked into her eyes. Truth always lingered on her delicate features—her eyes were red and swollen. He rewarded her stubbornness with a smile and continued into the woods along the northern boundary of his steading.

They halted at a clearing. A massive, whitewashed stone rested at the center. She stared curiously ahead, then turned to him with a questioning look. He patted her arm reassuringly. Randvior knelt and wrapped his arms around the stone.

He called on the gods, "Come Odin, Hlin, Eir, Frigg, Baldr, Magni, and Tyr ..." Inscriptions were carved into the face of the rock.

Noelle reached hesitantly, and he nodded approval as she ran her fingers along the surface. He watched as she examined the ancient altar.

"What is this place?"

"Odin's altar. We're on hallowed ground, the most sacred on

this steading. The place we invoke the favor of the gods, plead our causes, and beg forgiveness. *And pray for you*," he added softly. "The words inscribed on this stone," he ran his fingers over the carving, "are a message the Valkyries delivered on behalf of father Odin, wisdom to sustain my people." The warrior inside him sparked to life again. The spirits of his ancestors inhabited his body now. "Stay with me, *min lille dukke*, and someday I'll reveal the secrets behind these words."

"Why did you bring me here?"

Before he answered, something flashed overhead. "Look!" Randvior pointed skyward.

She followed his gaze. Colored ribbons of dazzling light were suspended high above, pulsing, and oscillating. Terrified, she covered her face.

Randvior pulled her hand away. "It's a blessing. Don't be afraid, my little one, 'tis a good omen."

They watched the celestial dance in awe as color spanned the breadth of the sky. And as the mystery slowly faded, moving farther north and altogether out of sight, they stared at each other in wonderment.

Once Noelle recovered and could speak again, she said, "I've never seen anything so phenomenal before."

"*Nororljos*—the northern lights. The Valkyries favored you this eventide and donned their armor, a guarantee there will be a place for you at Odin's table."

He fell to his knees again. Only this time, he clasped her hand over his heart.

Her shoulders were rigid. "I can't deny the way I feel when you touch me—kiss me—hold me. In your arms the world I knew before never really existed ..." She clenched her left hand into a tight fist. Randvior knew she had revealed more than she ever intended.

"I want you," he said as he got to his feet. "I've brought you here to swear an oath before the gods." He reached inside his cloak and produced a small dagger. "You speak so poorly of love, *min lille dukke,* as if it will never find its way into your heart." He caressed her cheek with the back of his hand. "The time has come for our love to take root."

Randvior held his left hand over the altar, and with his right, scraped the blade across his palm. Blood slowly dripped onto the stone. "Odin is my master and witness. I offer this troth as an everlasting pledge of my love. Noelle Sinclair, you are now and forever blood of my blood. If the world should crumble around us, reduced to ash and dust, my promise shall endure."

She rocked back on her heels in trance. Randvior pulled her closer to the stone. "Will you take this oath with me?"

She stared beyond the trees, focusing on something in the distance. He wondered *what* she saw through the darkness, regrets or maybe her future with him. He had spoken from the heart, as plainly and truthfully as he could. If she did not accept him now, he'd send her away. To a convent or to Brandon's family in Scotland. But never back to Durham where her brother could hurt her.

She offered her hand and dagger quickly met flesh.

His shoulders rose and fell in contentment and triumph. Because he hadn't coerced her into taking this oath, the gods would consider it legitimate. The act of volunteering her hand was enough. Randvior set the dagger aside and removed a piece of linen from his pocket. He doctored her wound tenderly, blotting the blood, and tied the bandage tightly around her wrist.

"I love you."

He could see the surprise on her face and she swallowed. His heart burned and his loins ached for relief. *She's too afraid to give herself away.*

Randvior covered her mouth and cheeks with fervent kisses. She returned them with equal ardor. All this time she begged him to respond, to confess his undying love, and reiterate it over and over again. Still the girl refused to admit her own feelings. *O my sweet little hypocrite.* He swept her off her feet.

"Where are we going now?"

"To announce our betrothal. A man can only endure so much. I'll be damned if I'll wait another minute." For the first time in many days, Randvior laughed.

Guards saluted as they crossed the threshold into the great hall. The crowd responded unremittingly. Noelle's head rested against Randvior's chest.

"I give you the freedom to manage this household," he whispered. "I want you to be comfortable and happy—we are family now."

He knew they were words she needed to hear.

Randvior hugged her closer as he stepped onto the dais and scanned the many faces of the people standing closest. Noelle snuggled deeper into the folds of his cloak trying to hide.

"Don't be afraid." His eyes penetrated hers. "Everyone wants to celebrate."

"No need to exaggerate, my lord."

Randvior chuckled at her pessimism as she slid from his arms.

He'd hold nothing back now. "I returned from Durham a wealthier man. Of all the treasures hidden in that English fortress, I desired the lord's youngest daughter most. I have offered Lady Sinclair the protection of my home and name. The gods revealed the pathway to my destiny in the Orkneys and I returned with my future in my arms. No man," he paused and looked directly at his mother, "or woman, shall interfere with what the gods have mandated."

Pressing his lips closed, the sting of overwhelming silence both disappointed and angered him beyond words. Had he misjudged the hearts of his people so carelessly? He felt consumed by anything that pertained to her. But once Noelle gifted the assembly with a brilliant smile, they erupted into hurrahs. All they needed to see was that she willingly embraced this marriage.

He relaxed then, savoring the sultry glint in her eyes and admiring the soft contours of her face. He kissed her forehead and called for a cup of mead. The honey taste reminded him of the sweetness of her lips. "A toast for father Odin!" He raised his cup high.

Mugs and fists pounded the tabletops thunderous and maddening, proof of his supporters' joy.

Another blessing had graced his life.

Lauga looked him over reservedly. She stood with a group of women near the main hearth. Their eyes locked. His gaze drifted beyond her and stopped on a man with a badly bruised face who stared unfalteringly at his betrothed.

What a difference a betrothal could make. Noelle felt a bit overwhelmed by the number of well-wishers lining up along the front of the stage to shake her hand. God, she wanted to run away. But she stayed because she wanted to enjoy every second her future mother-in-law was forced to stand by her son and greet his supporters with as much enthusiasm as him. Cunning and deceptive.

All her life she had longed for a mother and always hoped marriage would provide one. But not this marriage, and never this woman.

Brandon's company lightened her mood. He grasped her hand and made a ridiculous fuss over the engagement. "I am deeply disturbed the lady chose you over me. To think you could have had my heart and spent your days with a civilized man …" he teased her relentlessly and grinned at Randvior.

Randvior arched his brow. "Did she ever have a choice?"

No. Noelle held her tongue.

They laughed.

Hours later, after most of the celebrants departed or passed out drunk, Noelle yawned—she wanted to go to bed. Randvior had wandered off with a group of men.

As she walked to the stairs, someone flattened her against the wall from behind.

"You chose life with a bloody Norse, and I warn you, I'll use every inch of that beautiful body to my advantage."

Randvior's musky scent filled her nostrils. His body was flush against hers and he hiked the back of her skirt up. Fingers trailed up her inner thigh and she sucked in an excited breath. He thumbed the sensitive nub between her legs. Within a few meager seconds, her pleasure crested and she collapsed against the wall deliriously. She reached around and caressed the rock-hard bulge between his legs.

"Go to bed," he commanded, and let her skirt fall.

She turned. The muscles around his lips twitched while he stared at her. "Why did you pleasure me?" She craved intimacy.

"So you don't forget."

"What?"

"Anything ..." he mumbled, intoxicated. "Good wives are few, and you have the promise to be the best."

She blushed at the compliment. Drunk or not, she wanted more.

Against her wishes, he sent her upstairs without a proper good night. She looked back and met his gaze unflinchingly as he leaned against the wall, eyes hard, face brooding. Her blood thundered. He had deliberately sparked her desire and sent her away thirsting. This was no reminder, but a warning. Randvior Sigurdsson knew exactly what he was doing, removing lingering thoughts of Ovesen from her mind.

Katherine greeted her and she shared the joyful news.

"A pity you are forced into such an arrangement after your sire—"

"He loves me ..." Noelle didn't want her only friend to disapprove of this match.

"Did he tell you so, my lady?"

"Yes, many times." Although primitive, blood oath remained a form of betrothal in England. Mostly in the northern regions where clans still occupied untamed swaths of land.

"A pagan ritual is no substitute for a true Christian betrothal."

Katherine risked much, speaking so boldly. But Noelle had always encouraged her to speak freely. "I'm not a simpleton," Noelle snapped. "I did what I must to protect myself and my family's interests. I admit that I possess feelings for him, how deeply they go I cannot say, not yet. And could my father have done any better?"

"Your noble birthright is squandered on a barbarian. I'm sure your father—"

"Lord Sinclair never considered my personal feelings in anything, especially in selecting a husband. I admire my father's accomplishments, but he needed gold to pay off his debts more than he needed a daughter."

"But the *jarl* is not obligated to the English crown or even our Church."

"I know." Surprisingly, she felt relieved by this fact. "Somehow, I prefer it that way."

Randvior dismissed his slaves after midnight. His unquenchable thirst was driven by an increasing hunger for Noelle. He'd drink until he collapsed or ran out of wine. Whichever came first didn't matter. Better she not see him this way. Better she not know the new depth of his dark obsession for her. Their blood oath changed everything.

Brandon refused to let him stew and slapped his back, making him choke down the ale in his mouth.

"How many lasses are weeping bitterly this very night because the mighty Randvior has finally chosen a wife? Even more hearts would have trembled if the lady had selected *me* as husband."

Randvior snorted. "And how many heads would have been dislodged from their bloody necks if she had chosen you?" He tore off a hunk of bread and dipped it in a bowl of broth.

"Many," Brandon indulged. "Too many to count." He chucked Randvior on the chin.

He smiled before he wrestled Brandon's hand to the table. He held it down in challenge.

"Ye desire an arm wrestling contest?"

Randvior's face split into a heady grin. "Aye," he said. "But I'd prefer to save the weakest man for last to make it fair. Bring me one of those young bucks first so I might demonstrate my superiority for you, my friend."

Brandon espied the group of eager boys who perked up the

minute the informal challenge was made. They gathered along the front of the stage. Traditionally, anyone who defeated the *jarl* in sport would be granted a reasonable request. Fald Ovesen, who still sat nearby, laughed delightedly and pointed out his eldest son.

"Not a skilled talker," Fald observed, "but he speaks well with his fists."

Randvior grunted. What happened in the bathhouse between him and Sveinn would remain private. However, he wanted nothing more than to purge the rage from his heart. He could easily torture the man for hours before he felt any relief. He chose Sveinn as his opponent.

Strict rules applied to arm wrestling matches, no matter how informal. Brandon would act as referee and appoint seats for the challengers. Massive right hands folded together across the high table.

Brandon circled, checking their form from every angle. Upon final inspection, the Scot straightened their wrists until he was sure neither had a starting advantage.

On the count of three, Brandon whistled and the match began. Sveinn displayed raw skill first and locked Randvior's wrist in a vulnerable position. Randvior indulged the younger man by allowing him to dominate and spend his strength early. Each time Sveinn attempted to slam his hand down, Randvior forced him back to the starting position.

He grinned as Sveinn dug his long fingernails into the palm of his left hand and drew blood. He loved competition for the sake of a fight and twisted Sveinn's wrist so hard it cracked loudly as he banged it down in decisive victory. The sickening sound drew the boy's worried father to the tableside. After a quick inspection, it was realized only to be a severe sprain.

Fald seemed relieved. "It's a long ride home and my son requires rest and time to mend his pride."

"Aye." Randvior agreed. "Go with my blessing." He greatly appreciated Fald, but his son deserved the sharp end of his sword.

CHAPTER FOURTEEN
The Weaving Room

COMPELLED BY TRADITION to leave Noelle untouched until their wedding night, Randvior avoided spending any time alone with her. Days blurred into weeks. And although Noelle enjoyed improved eminence in Randvior's house, Lauga continued to encourage the women to treat her as an outsider.

She searched for ways to keep herself entertained. Conversations with servants and reading books helped some. But she had grown dependent on their daily lovemaking on ship and the days before their betrothal to help keep her thoughts off home. Now, only his eyes spoke intimately to her. Thankfully, they spoke a language she understood—they always undressed her.

Most evenings they ate together and enjoyed the entertainment of traveling musicians who visited the hall to earn coin to support their families. She also took the time to learn the routine of the household, assisting the chambermaids with cleaning and laundry duties. However, the kitchen remained unapproachable. Lauga, who never seemed to want to go home, spent most of her time there planning the meals.

The month of December came and the men slaughtered the weakest livestock and dried meat for storage. Slabs of venison, beef, pork, and mutton were hung or buried in deep pits, left for days or weeks to cure in mixtures of salt and herbs. A smaller building was used for processing fish. The men who worked there gave her strings of smoked white fish to snack on as she watched.

Today, the women pickled vegetables and jarred fruits in the kitchen. Everyone worked together—even Randvior labored between the smokehouse and the great hall.

One particular morning, a sharp rapping on Noelle's bed-chamber door wrested her from sleep. Katherine greeted the unannounced visitor. Randvior stood at the doorway holding a tray of food.

"Come in, my Lord."

"You may leave us." Randvior dismissed her and stepped inside.

Noelle sank further below the sheets. He pulled the blankets back and stared down at her, clearly amused.

She pinched her cheeks and combed her fingers through her hair to avoid appearing disheveled, hoping to win some time in bed with him.

"No need." He assured her. "If you wore rags and covered your face with ashes I'd still consider you the most beautiful woman in the northern hemisphere."

She sat up and hugged her knees to her chest, patted the bed invitingly, and flashed her white teeth, pleased with herself. She needed to put an end to this ridiculous separation.

The teasing obviously irritated him. "I'm only here to eat, and then escort you to the weaving room."

She stopped and looked at him dumbly. His rejection stung and she groaned mentally. Whether he wanted her or not, he was still too handsome to ignore. He motioned for her to precede him to the table.

Fine—the window of opportunity to seduce him slammed shut. Well, it had been worth a try.

She allowed her displeasure to show on her face as she bus-tled ahead and chose a seat. And even managed to keep from yelling … although he had mentioned that torture chamber—the weaving room. It was where women gathered to work—apparently English women weren't permitted. On more than one occasion, she overheard the gossip coming from the room, and most of it centered on her. *No. She wanted nothing to do with it.*

"Has anything changed significantly in the past few weeks where an invitation to the women's quarters will be considered a friendly gesture? I think not. They will consider it impertinence, and I look at it as an intrusion." Noelle nibbled on a piece of cheese.

He stared at her for a long moment and dropped his bread on the plate. "You will be mistress of this household soon enough. These women will serve you, and it's time to establish your command."

"This isn't a military exercise, Randvior." She reached for the robe draped over one of the chairs.

"Don't put anything else on."

First, he cruelly rejects my invitation and now he wants to ogle me in my nightdress.

She didn't want to stay seated at the table with him any longer. The floorboards were very cold against her feet as she slinked to the bed to retrieve her slippers. She bent down to get them and couldn't help noticing the look on his face. His eyes betrayed him.

He blocked her pathway back to the table.

"If I touch you," he said while his eyes clung to her breasts, "I won't be able to stop. And if I hear one more of those little gratifying sounds you make every time my hands make contact with your skin, I'll come in my breeches."

She felt the color drain from her face. She didn't appreciate the uncertainty he constantly caused her. First, he denied her any physical contact. Now, he could hardly contain himself. A tear of frustration wet her cheek. He quickly fingered it away.

This time his face tightened in frustration. "I promise you every pleasure ..." he couldn't seem to find the words to finish his thought and shrugged.

They returned to the table and finished breakfast in companionable silence.

The windowless chamber located off the kitchen appeared to

be as comfortable as any woman needed. Six warp-weighted looms were situated along the east wall and ten metal vats for dying were anchored to the floor along the south. Balls of bright yarn, segregated by color and texture, were stored in baskets near the looms. Women were already sorting or sewing. All activities ceased the moment Randvior's hulking frame shadowed the narrow doorway. He pecked Noelle's cheek before he nudged her inside.

Distress gripped her as Randvior retreated, leaving her standing alone near the doorway. She counted sixteen females ranging in age from fifteen to sixty. Spending time with these women should be a positive experience because she'd likely be here the rest of her life. New kinswomen and friends to help her through the long months Randvior would be gone from their home.

Little could be done to guarantee her contentment though. Men, even the *jarl*, were forbidden from this room—the only exception being an emergency. Noelle knew every form of sanctuary had its price and if she wanted to occupy a respectable position alongside these women, she'd have to earn it. But wouldn't it be easier to let Randvior handle it?

What was she thinking? If a man violated the rules, the women would retaliate by casting dark spells to make his prick wither or would spread malicious rumors that called his manhood into question. As ridiculous as it seemed to her, it could forever damage a Norseman's reputation amongst the women. A superstition *no* man was willing to test.

Lauga proceeded with her work while Noelle stood at the entrance. It came as no surprise and an irritating hush fell over the room. *Say something, please. Anything.* She'd settle for open insults if it encouraged discourse. People's futures were shaped in this room—tenants rewarded or destroyed depending on Lauga's mood. And as future mistress, Noelle would assume this responsibility someday. Only she would never destroy someone's life based on factors they didn't have control over. Including their birthplace.

Instead of worrying, she admired the expansive space. Decorative columns were positioned near the looms and she walked over and leaned on one for support. Colorful tapestries similar to the ones in the great hall covered the walls. A granite hearth and bookshelves with two couches where someone could curl up with a book looked inviting.

"Do daughters of English lords weave?" Lauga finally acknowledged her presence. "Or are your hands too unskilled to fashion garments for Odin's children to wear?"

At this point, Noelle would feast on what scraps Lauga was willing to throw at her. "I'm skilled in the arts of weaving and sewing. My work graces the rooms of my father's castle. Direct me, and I will do whatever you ask."

Lauga nodded. An imbecile could stitch a shirt. Simply voicing her accomplishments would do little to impress the ice queen. Noelle tried to keep her hands from fidgeting as she waited for her future mother-in-law to respond. Gratefully, her words had captured the interest of some of the women, because they too waited for Lauga to speak. A small victory, she'd take it.

Unable to refuse her offer, Lauga began. "The looms are occupied for the day," she said, "but if you are capable, you may sit at that table and work." She pointed across the room.

A linen overdress, dyed the boldest shade of purple she'd ever seen, awaited someone's skilled hands. Noelle admired the garment, a sweet design with intricately embroidered rosebuds sewn along the shoulder seams. She sat and continued the pattern of red and yellow buds, adding a personal touch by stitching leaves on the stems of the tiny blossoms. She worked for hours, happy to use her skills.

Margaret had always warned, *idle hands are the devil's tools,* and Noelle couldn't agree more!

By late afternoon, Noelle finished the dress and several women gathered around the table to see. Humbly, she accepted their praise.

Thralls set out trays of food on the tables. The midday meal had come quickly and consisted of bread, cheese, fruit, and wine. Noelle allowed Lauga to be served first to keep peace.

The quality of Noelle's embroidery was the subject of discussion during the meal. Five women sat with her and passed the gown around for closer inspection. Noelle sipped at a glass of water while she listened nervously to their chatter. Lauga's tolerance must have been stretched thin because the woman glared ceaselessly in her direction.

Noelle watched as she poured a glass of wine and nearly fainted when Lauga offered it to her. This was a stunning change of attitude and she accepted it without hesitation.

"Randvior will be very proud of your work," Lauga said.

"This is the first opportunity I've had to contribute." Noelle was wild with excitement. Had something so simple opened a door of possibility?

Lauga returned to her table.

Before Noelle took a drink, the woman sitting at her right tapped her fingers against her teeth. She leaned close and whispered in Noelle's ear. "Never accept refreshment from her hand."

Noelle swirled the dark liquid and set the glass aside. "Why?"

"I will only speak of this once." The woman looked around paranoid someone would overhear the conversation. "Lauga will stop at nothing to destroy you."

Noelle gaped at her. She knew Lauga thought Randvior had betrayed her. Realized she didn't want her here. But this tidbit of warning represented something much more sinister. How could she trust this stranger? Only three people besides her fiancé had made her feel welcome—Brandon, Unnr, and Aud. One woman. Noelle cursed her own naivety.

Across the room, Lauga continued to mentor a young girl on one of the looms, seemingly unaware of the present conversation. Noelle's heart sank in her chest. Something seemed eerily familiar. Another night ... weeks ago. There were serious gaps in her memory. But she clearly recalled a set of gray eyes and a brute of a man ready to commit murder.

More memories came in small spurts. Terrible pain and her insides were mangled. She had vomited a dozen times ... seen the leathery face of a wise woman who attended her. And then, the world went completely dark.

"Have I stirred memories?" the woman asked.

"Perhaps." She clamped a hand over her mouth. Now she could see clearly ... the glass of wine Lauga served her on the night of the feast. It didn't take a scholar to figure out the rest.

This confirmed all her suspicions. Her efforts at peace had all been in vain.

She closed her eyes. "It seems I am an unfortunate victim of something greater than I would have ever imagined."

"Aye."

Noelle drummed her fingers on the tabletop. *Wine from her private stock ...* She faced the woman again. "If I commanded you to drink this, would you?"

"No, though I dare not admit it publicly."

Noelle rose slowly from the table. "I shall not forget this kindness."

She picked up the evidence, careful not to spill a drop. Randvior must be told. If he expected her to stay here, his mother *must* be sent away immediately.

Noelle pounded angrily on Randvior's bedchamber door. It finally opened and she shoved the glass of wine in his face.

"If you doubted your mother, as I have always doubted her, why did you withhold the cause of my sickness for all these weeks?"

His eyes surveyed her. "Baseless accusations are worth nothing, but if I catch her in the act ..."

"Hah!" Noelle's lips twitched. "See this witch's brew?" She shook her hand and some of the wine spilled out. "A special concoction your mother offered me today. The same poisoned draught she fed me weeks ago when I nearly died."

She wanted to provoke him. Randvior resented anything that

cast doubt on his sterling honor. At least he still had a reputation to protect! All she possessed was her life, and that had almost been taken away. Twice.

"Perhaps this is a family conspiracy," she accused.

His indifference infuriated her. But her words must have insulted him because he came to life instantly. He knocked the glass of wine out of her hand and dragged her inside his room, slammed the heavy door, and chased her to the foot of his bed. Without a word, he mashed her body into the mattress and climbed atop her, digging his knees into her hips.

"How can you accuse me of conspiracy? Did I not swear to Allfather to love you?"

She grabbed fistfuls of the cover as his brooding stare pinned her to the bed. She squirmed and glowered, but Randvior wouldn't let her up.

"I will punish you."

"How?"

"I don't know."

"I hate you," she said.

"I know."

This conflict had brought her closer to Randvior than she'd been in weeks. It gave her an odd sense of comfort. Something twisted inside and she grinded her hips in frantic invitation. She'd pay him full measure for his negligence. Weeks of involuntary abstinence caught up with her in a single, torturous moment. She raked her nails across his back.

He snared her hands. "If you don't stop, I'll seek companionship in another woman's bed."

Companionship is an arm's length away, you stupid man!

"I'll do the same!"

Absolutely the most asinine thing she could have suggested. He ripped her gown open from breast to thigh and crushed her with the weight of his chest while groping her between the legs.

"Is this your goal?" he croaked. "Do you want another man between your thighs?"

She opened up for him and he thrust inside her, meaning to elicit a measure of pain. She cried out—speared as helplessly as a seal.

She'd take this unusually rough punishment over loneliness, and surrendered as he crippled her body with unrelenting momentum. Within minutes, relief thrummed through her.

"You've pushed me too far this time." He complained as he climbed out of bed.

"Blame yourself."

"There's no pity for a woman who cannot control herself or demonstrate patience and obedience ... serve as a role model for the women under her roof."

"As you did for your men on your ship for ten days?"

He snorted and muttered. "Not the same."

"Aye, it is. You've met your match for stubbornness, Randvior."

He huffed and sat on the edge of the bed. Noelle rubbed his back soothingly.

"Who told you?" he asked suddenly.

She assumed he was referring to his mother's treachery. "No one," she lied. She needed to protect the identity of the woman who revealed the secret. "I pieced it together after Lauga gave me the wine today."

"Unfortunately, 'tis true." he uttered gloomily. "Lauga has resorted to these tactics before. Norse women are overly protective of their children."

"So are the English, but we're not driven to murder."

Another sigh.

She knew his heart struggled with the truth. Any son loves his mother unconditionally. But she'd say whatever was necessary to protect her own life.

"I'll make no demands. Whatever you choose I will accept without complaint. But for the sake of my own life, I must ask one thing. Either send Lauga away or send me home."

"Vengeance fever is in my blood." His face was a mask now.

"I could choke the life out of her with my own hands the way I feel right now."

She was suddenly sorry for bringing this to his attention in such a confrontational manner.

"Or," she offered gently. "There is *my* solution to consider."

He nodded absently, willing to listen.

"End this unnecessary standoff, send me away. My family is no threat—my father would never send his ships to Norway. My king wouldn't risk his fleet. I'll marry whomever my father wishes and we can put this behind us."

She had come to know the extent of his willingness to keep her. She could beg and plead, but Randvior would never let her go.

"It is out of the question."

She breathed hard—realizing her hope of ever getting home was gone. It had ended weeks ago, but he need never know that.

"I'm a man of my word, Noelle. Once I pledged to become your husband, I shed my former life as easily as an old shirt. There is no room for compromise. An attempt on your life is a direct assault on mine." He gripped her shoulders. "Woman, I'm inspired to love you more than anything on this earth. Trust me when I say no one will harm you."

But someone already had, and she told him so. In answer, he kissed her. That silky tongue might convince her of anything now. What a fantastically foolish suggestion she had made.

"I …" She desperately wanted to confide in him, but one last pathetic attempt to hold on to her pride shut her up. She cursed the gnawing pain in her heart.

He saw through her emotional disguise. "Say it."

"I love you." Those cherished words slipped out of her mouth more hesitantly than a lie.

Her eyes flitted back and forth nervously, heartbeat pounding faster and faster.

"Come here." He pulled her onto his lap.

"I can't stand the way I feel," she sobbed.

"Promise me," he said as he loosened the lacings on his breeches. "Swear you'll never leave me for another man." He eased her back on the bed. "Say it, little one." His knee urged her legs apart.

"I promise ..."

CHAPTER FIFTEEN
Another Man's Property

RANDVIOR WAITED UNTIL Noelle fell asleep to sneak out of his room. She was so different than any woman he had ever known and the cause of too many distractions. She'd even made him break his oath …

He went downstairs and studied the tapestries on the walls. His favorites had always been the ones showing Valkyries tending to the warriors headed into the afterlife. He envisioned Noelle doing this honor for him, dressed in golden armor and holding a pike in her tiny hand.

Only subtle differences existed between Noelle and Odin's maidens, eye color being the main one. But her eyes reminded him of the burnished colors of autumn, when the summer warmth reluctantly yields to the winter maiden whose tears cover the earth in snow. Before she arrived, he had grown tired of the common blue and green eyes that graced the faces of the women in his lands. He hungered for something different and Odin had answered his prayer and sent him a girl worthy of his troth. Randvior dragged himself to the hearth, more aware of the forces of nature around him than ever before.

Noelle remained fragile tinder and he, inextinguishable flame. The fire that would incinerate her fears forever.

He charged upstairs, bathed, and dressed. She loved him, and he glowed with pride as he returned to the hall and found his mother.

"Son." Lauga greeted him, unaware of his newly found happiness and the secret he knew about her.

He fought to conceal his anger. If he accused his mother before he had enough evidence to warrant a formal hearing, she might disappear before he had time to set things right with Noelle. If he waited too long, would she try to kill her again?

"Mother ..."

Her exaggerated self-confidence made his stomach turn. Without thinking, he latched onto her arm and hauled her to the weaving room. At least they'd be alone for a few minutes before word spread that a man had violated the sacred trust of the women's sanctuary.

"Tell me," he demanded, unable to hold anything back. "Tell me what evil besets you that you should attempt to murder the woman I love."

She jeered. "You condemn me prematurely. But if I must take credit for it, know I will go to any length to protect you, even from yourself."

He crossed his arms over his chest and stared down at her. He had not thought of this, that she would confess so easily. "Woman, I've been weaned from your teat since infancy. Have I not always held you in the highest esteem, provided you with a seat of honor at my table? I left my father's home because we could never agree on anything, but my love never faltered. My sire no longer provides for my sustenance. I am free to marry whom I please, with or without your approval."

"I can only pray that one day you will fully understand what it means to be responsible for our family name—to raise sons and daughters of your own, conceived with a woman of Norse blood."

As he had hoped, a small crowd gathered at the doorway. Let them stand witness to her treachery.

"Your fiancé couldn't have made it any easier for me to make up my mind about her," Lauga continued. "Her immodesty and the way she gallivants about this steading convinced me she is no better than a common whore."

Randvior stiffened. "She is no whore."

His mother gave an indecorous laugh. "She's inferior."

There was no hope of reforming his mother. Lauga left him with no choice. His first duty now lay with Noelle.

"Summon Aud," he faced the women gathered in the entry-way.

Two maids scurried off.

Aud arrived within minutes, and hesitated at the door, clearly unwilling to enter the chamber.

Randvior waved him inside. "If any of my women dare question your manhood, I'll put a stop to it, you superstitious fool."

Aud stuck his head inside as if testing the air. He started to take a step, but stopped and shook his head. "It doesn't feel right to me."

Randvior rolled his eyes and walked to him, took a hold of the front of his shirt, and yanked him inside. "Remove my mother from this house. Return her to my father, now."

Randvior should have acted days ago when he truly suspected her of wrongdoing. These were the last words Lauga would hear coming from his lips for a long time. He stalked out, pushing past the onlookers.

Like an immovable boulder, Randvior stood in the middle of the kitchen. His mind raced uncontrollably. Women, children, and old men were not held to the same standards as warriors. But Lauga had made it clear she would stop at nothing to see his betrothed harmed.

Not while he walked Odin's green earth. Sharing her bed again had reminded him of everything he cherished about her.

He must work quickly to solidify her position as mistress in his household, before Lauga called on her minions to do her bidding. He returned to the hall with renewed determination. Enough pain had been inflicted on his fiancée. Randvior deeply regretted ever leaving the women to settle this matter alone.

Brandon met him. "I'm sorry I missed the chance to see ye march your mother across the hall as a wee bairn on her way to getting whipped."

Randvior grumbled. Rumors spread like wildfire in the Trondelag. His friend's wagging tongue irritated him.

"And judging by the way Aud raced away with the lady planted firmly on the saddle in front of him, I suspect the two of you have reached a low point in your relationship."

"My mother will stop at nothing to get her way. Even if it means killing Noelle."

"And this surprises you? I've known your family since boyhood, and your mother has always been a provocateur."

Randvior cursed himself for not being able to see things as clearly as Brandon did.

"I'm sending Noelle away for two weeks, until our wedding preparations are finished. I can't concentrate on anything when she's around. She'll be safe with Aud's family."

"Very sensible, Rand … The kindest gesture you've made in a long time."

"But not without selfish motivation," he assured. The pleasant scent of Noelle's sex still lingered on his body.

Brandon chuckled. "So an English lassie has tamed the Viking's philandering heart."

"Philandering heart? He placed his hand over his chest. "That cuts deeply, my friend."

"*Who* corrupted an entire den of virgins in Constantinople?"

"And *you*? I seem to recall a most scrumptious girl who unlocked the gates to the palace because she had her eyes on you."

"And a blessed virgin she *was*." Brandon licked his lips and crossed himself.

"*Was?*"

"Aye."

Randvior laughed, but the current situation weighed heavy on his conscience. "If only things might be as simple as they were in the old days."

"Nothing worth having is free."

He nodded. Brandon always offered tidbits of wisdom as easily as a scholar. Him being one of the only men Randvior trusted with his life. "Stand as witness at my wedding."

"It will cost you—a kiss from your beautiful bride."

Scottish bastard always tries to twist the knife a little deeper. "On my honor …"

"What honor?" Brandon asked. "You're a bloody Viking."

Randvior couldn't keep from smiling. "I don't like you're Christian traditions."

"'Tis only a harmless way to get my lips wet without committing to marriage."

"One I can live without."

"It's a bloody kiss, Randvior. You'll get over it."

Aud Magnusson's traditional long house was fortified by an eight-foot wall. Two guards were posted at the metal gates and greeted the party of riders as they approached.

Randvior spent a few moments saying goodbye to Noelle. He swore a silent oath that if he found rebels amongst his people, who wished to sabotage his future happiness, he'd forgo trial and mount their severed heads on stakes as a deterrent for future uprisings.

Everything about Noelle crippled his mind and he needed time to recover. Right now, her pouty smile, the translucence of her silky skin in the soft evening sunlight, and those eyes—those damn eyes threatened to change his mind about leaving her behind.

He kissed her goodbye and watched as she disappeared inside the house with Aud. Randvior rode outside the fenced courtyard and spent the next hour patrolling the grounds to make sure no one lurked in the shadows. Satisfied, he rode home.

Noelle walked slowly behind Aud as he escorted her inside his hall. Her gaze took in the features of the comfortable room. There were two hearths and his family waited patiently for them.

"This is my wife, Nessa." Aud took her hand and kissed the

soft flesh on her palm. "And my daughters—Tyra, Ingrid, and Eir."

Noelle collected herself. She felt at ease here, but his daughters were so lovely, they more resembled sea nymphs than mortal women. Tall and elegant, they regarded her. As for Nessa, no wonder Aud chattered endlessly about her, his daughters were the spitting image of their mother. 'Tis no wonder the man is incessantly happy.

The girls' curious fascination with her made her smile to herself. Noelle pictured Ophelia and Margaret standing there. A knot started to form in her stomach. The eldest daughter, Tyra, possessed a stern brow as Margaret. Stubbornness showing all over her pretty face, and Noelle greatly missed her own sister's company.

"I am grateful for your hospitality," Noelle said graciously.

"It is *we* who are honored to have the *jarl's* future wife in our home," Nessa declared as she grabbed her by the hand and led her to a table.

They sat for hours, enjoying a simple meal and fulfilling conversation. One of Noelle's two bodyguards, Randvior had left behind, stayed seated in a corner, drinking, and playing cards with Aud's men while the second made rounds. Nessa showed Noelle her family heirlooms and gave her a tour of the house. Four bedchambers were located off the main room, partitioned by painted screens and embroidered curtains. Noelle's guards would sleep on the floor outside her door.

So much had happened over the last few days that nights of little sleep had finally started to catch up with her. Noelle yawned; she could barely keep her eyes open. "Would you mind if I retired?"

Nessa smiled and showed her to a room. Once she was settled inside, Noelle washed her face and hands and changed into a long-sleeved chemise. She crawled under the pile of furs. For the first time in weeks, she felt completely comfortable and welcome in someone's house. The soothing sounds of Aud's family conversing quietly at the table lulled her to sleep.

Violent nightmares, the kind Noelle had suffered from as a child, dominated her sleep. Blood and screams from faceless women and children ricocheted inside her head. She shivered, hated when her dreams took on a life all their own. She woke up drenched in sweat. The recurrent nightmares she had as a child were so severe she'd began walking in her sleep. Once, she nearly hurled herself from the second floor balcony and soon found herself locked in a chamber at night for the next six months.

She stood and put on her robe and slippers. She languished in the heat and parted the curtains to let cooler air into her room. As she stepped out, she gasped.

Her bodyguard lay motionless in a pool of blood, throat slit ear-to-ear. She raised her eyes, looked down at the body again, and fought to keep her composure. Noelle stepped over him. Nothing could be done, so she prayed for his soul and moved to the main room. No one, only the flicker of flames in the double hearths. She explored the shadows, staying as quiet as possible, and discovered another body near the table. Aud's guard this time.

Noelle covered her mouth to keep from screaming. Fresh blood covered the floor. The valuables—silver goblets, platters, and expensive carpets were undisturbed. If not robbery, what was the motive?

"My lady," a masculine voice sounded.

She threw up her hands and whipped around, searching. She froze after she spotted someone sitting on a chair in the far corner. The darkness might conceal his face, but she knew that buttery-smooth voice.

"Where is Aud's family?" She squinted to see.

Bravely, Noelle walked toward him. Lord have mercy on anyone if they harmed Aud's family. And if this man had, Noelle assumed she would die soon, too.

"Safely quartered," he answered to her relief. "Blindfolded and bound together like slaves."

"And the master?" her voice warbled as she visualized the worst for the old Viking—falling prey to this villain.

"Don't concern yourself with Aud Magnusson. Thor's hammer couldn't kill that bastard." A malevolent chuckle followed.

She considered making a mad dash for the back door. But by the time she looked up again, he was on his feet and headed her way.

"I let you sleep, didn't have the heart to wake you." Sveinn Ovesen emerged from the shadows.

She squealed and retreated three steps. "Why … have … you … done this?"

"I've killed no one of consequence. Aud and his family are alive. Bodyguards are worth but a few pennies. The law provides generously for a dead man's family and my father will pay the necessary *weregild* if one is demanded."

"You place so little value on a man's life?" She felt her innards twist inside out.

"If any man stands between me and what I want, he will die."

"Is *weregild* similar to an indulgence? You pay for absolution?"

"Your acumen is already legendary in the Trondelag. And I think I am the man to put your wit to better use."

Mere feet away from her now, Noelle knew what would come next. She spun and ran across the room. She reached for the door latch. But Sveinn's enormous paw slapped her hand away from the lock. Noelle braced herself against the door and let her forehead rest on the textured panel.

"What a tangled web Randvior weaves with you." He kept his hand on the door.

Noelle raised her gaze. She needed to draw a line in the sand before this man forced her to do something she'd regret for the rest of her life.

She stared him down, wishing her eyes were daggers. "How dare you attack this household and murder two innocent men. Did you think I'd be impressed?"

Sveinn's dark laughter made her sick. He cuffed her cheek. "I will not tolerate backtalk. I'm not a spineless fool. Your former master indulged you too much."

She rubbed her cheek, then lowered her gaze and blinked.

Three men, dressed in armor and carrying weapons, entered the hall. Dressed for battle. She knew she better cooperate to safeguard Aud's family.

"Ready the horses."

The guards bowed and departed.

Sveinn moved closer. "I've come here to make you a legitimate offer, to present my bride price and take you to Ireland where we'll be married in the Church. A ship will meet us within a week."

Noelle's mouth dropped open, flabbergasted by his suggestion.

"I think I'd rather die." She backed away. "I am already promised to Randvior."

"Only after I made *my* intentions known. Jarl Randvior made no public announcement of your engagement until after he caught us in the bathhouse together."

"But, but ..." Tongue-tied, Noelle hunched as if she'd been whipped mercilessly. "I don't want to marry you!"

"The *jarl's* hesitation is my advantage. The law will surely recognize my claim over his. By the time the Thing convenes in spring, we will have shared a bed for months and no man will be able to challenge me. Especially if my child is growing inside you." He touched her stomach.

"My father would never approve."

What had she done to deserve this punishment? Yes, she encouraged the oaf for half a minute with a smile. Nothing more.

"If protecting the purity of your bloodline is your concern, fear not, my pedigree is more impressive than Randvior's. My mother is a Conant, born of Irish and Scot nobility."

She inhaled swiftly, head swimming. "Randvior is still my legal guardian."

"Aye." He reached inside his cloak and produced a coin bag,

tossed it carelessly on a nearby side table. "And I would never consider taking another man's property without compensation. There's enough gold in that purse for the *jarl* to procure two brides. I believe Lauga was in the middle of negotiations for one before you arrived. She will be pleased to find her only son free to marry again."

Now he latched onto her, running his fingernails suggestively up her arm. Her eyes widened and she pushed him away. She couldn't think clearly with him breathing down her neck.

"Time is short," he warned. "If you try to escape again I will be forced to tie you up and it will be an uncomfortable ride splayed across my saddle. Come now," he spoke gently. "Gather your belongings and dress as warmly as possible. We have many miles to ride."

"We can't leave Aud's family."

"Don't worry. If his daughters work the bindings hard enough for a few hours they'll be free."

"What about Randvior?"

"Proper arrangements have been made. I've been planning this for weeks, Noelle, and only needed the right opportunity to act."

"How did you know I was here?"

He grinned and pushed her toward the bedchamber. "Spies are everywhere."

CHAPTER SIXTEEN

Confrontation

MISSING RANDVIOR WAS more painful than being stabbed in the eye. Noelle cursed herself for mistakenly planting the seeds of lust in another man's heart! She prayed desperately to see her bloodthirsty Viking come crashing through the doors to rescue her.

As if he read her mind, Sveinn tugged at her chin. "He will never find us."

She didn't challenge him, only followed his instructions perfectly because she didn't want Aud's family to suffer anymore. She dressed in three layers of clothing and packed her satchel. Before Sveinn collected her, she put on the gold bangle Randvior gave her, fearing it might be the only memento she'd ever have from him.

The curtains parted and Sveinn stared in at her. "You followed my instructions well." He stepped inside. "Before we leave ..." He tipped her chin. "... we will finish what we started weeks ago."

Aud and Nessa and their beautiful daughters filled her head and she parted her lips willingly. Whatever she needed to do to keep them alive ... his tongue slid into her mouth.

Blood pounded violently in Randvior's head. Aud had just delivered the bad news. With his countenance on fire, he opened his mouth and screamed.

Men scrambled in every direction.

Randvior stormed across the great hall and grabbed his sacred axe from the wall above his throne. Reserved only for war, he considered this a fight for his life. He couldn't breathe without her, much less be expected to live. He turned to his men and prepared them as if an invading force waited at his gate. Not only had he grossly underestimated Sveinn, he had failed to protect his beloved, again.

Prudence and admiration for Fald Ovesen had prevented him from killing his son before. *Never again.* The next time Randvior set eyes on him, Sveinn Ovesen would die.

Randvior shut his eyes and took a deep breath. "How long has Noelle been gone?"

"Nearly a day." Aud tightened his weapon belt and checked his knives.

Randvior knew his loyal captain burned with hatred, too. He deserved avengement nearly as much as he did. The security of his home had been breached. Curse Odin for forcing him into this situation. Dangling a beautiful woman in front of him, then snatching her away in the middle of the night. If this was meant to test his faith, it did little to advance the god's cause in his eyes.

Donning full armor, Randvior spoke to his men. "Sveinn Ovesen attacked our brother's home and kidnapped my woman. Who will ride beside me and help deliver Odin's justice?"

Every man in the hall volunteered.

The *jarl* swelled with pride. "We shall take him alive if we can." Adrenaline pumped through his body. Randvior slammed his fist against the metal armor covering his chest. "And then, I'll pulverize his skull with my bare hands."

He divided the guards into five groups. Three teams would search north, east, and south. The fourth would stake out Sveinn's home. And Randvior's team, which included Aud, would ride west, toward the sea.

After three days, weariness showing on his face, Randvior searched a broad area while his men made camp. Regrettably, his nemesis had covered his tracks well. He scrutinized everything between the ground and starry heavens above and still found nothing.

He burned for Noelle as badly as a drunk craves a bottle.

Two more bitter nights passed, and finally, Randvior got lucky. He sighted a fire somewhere in the distance. No one lived this far west. Riding ahead, he climbed steadily up a snow-covered hill. His stallion punched through the snow with as much ragged determination as he rode. A rare, blue full moon provided plenty of light as he crossed a shallow tributary and discovered fresh tracks on the other side. He dismounted. A shoulder overlooking the sea blocked his way west; the only direction left to go was up.

Randvior trudged another two miles before he came across a dilapidated cabin. An abandoned woodcutter's shed, judging by the rusty tools and snow covered woodpiles. He circled the structure three times—relying on his hearing. He couldn't see inside, the narrow windows were blacked out. His men arrived minutes later and Randvior directed his gaze heavenward.

"Grant us good fortune, great Odin."

Upon Randvior's signal, Aud's heavily clad foot punched through the plank door.

Seven men were huddled around a metal brazier, sleeping comfortably with no weapons at the ready. Randvior spit curses at them as they scrambled to their feet, groping the floor for their swords.

"Your master left juveniles to guard his gate." Randvior taunted.

"And your negligence cost you a woman." The swarthiest of Sveinn's guards wore a wolfish grin.

A torrent of rage rained down on Randvior. He lunged with his axe hefted over his head. The man who spoke so freely edged away. His words lost to silence. The *jarl* brought the blunt edge of his weapon down on the man's skull. With his axe bloodied and Odin's fury on his face, he turned his rage on the remaining men. They surrendered immediately.

Aud pounded his sword against his shield. "Kill them."

Randvior lowered his weapon, eyeing Sveinn's guards.

He should demonstrate mercy. "Pledge loyalty and I will spare your miserable lives."

Aud's face twisted. Randvior stifled his complaint with a wave of his hand before his captain had a chance to voice his dissent. "They will serve as slaves."

Sveinn's men fell to their knees and pledged as Randvior had commanded. This decision was final. As his rage leveled for the moment, Randvior studied the interior of the cottage.

Another room straight ahead.

He reached the door in two strides and pounded on it. "Sveinn Ovesen, come out and face me as a man!"

No answer came.

Without pause, Randvior shouldered his way through the door, quite unprepared for what he found. Noelle stripped naked with her hands anchored to a wood beam above her head and tightly gagged. Her eyes flashed warning as she jerked her head left. Randvior understood and lifted his weapon in time to deflect a blow from Sveinn's broadsword. Randvior grunted and turned to see where his opponent stood.

The kidnapper struck again.

Visions of Sveinn's filthy hands probing Noelle fueled Randvior's violence. He moved mechanically. Their weapons met midair and scraped together so hard sparks flew. Randvior twisted around and punched him in the gut. Sveinn hurtled backward, recovered his footing, then charged, whirling his weapon over his head.

Noelle's muted cries echoed loudly in Randvior's ears—she needed help, and he slashed his way through Sveinn, landing a damaging blow to his chest and shoulder.

"Kill me," Sveinn provoked, "and you'll never know the truth. Did I bed her or leave her untouched for our wedding night?"

On the other side of the door, Randvior could hear his men yelling. His chest heaved for air and he responded by pulling a dagger from his boot. With his axe in one hand and his knife in the other, they both ran and collided with the force of two rams. Sveinn punched the dagger loose and grazed Randvior's left hand with his own short knife. A loud *thwack* sounded and Randvior jumped aside, his axe head deeply embedded in Sveinn's ribs. The younger man staggered dazedly, falling over furniture in his path.

With the immediate threat neutralized, Randvior ran across the room to Noelle. He scolded her as he freed her hands and mouth. "How dare you leave my side?" Tears wet the corners of his eyes.

He was so tempted to make love to her right now. Instead, he spread his arms wide. She fell into them weeping and laughing at the same time.

"Tell me …" He pleaded as he enveloped her in his arms. The unfinished question was devoid of any vanity. *Promise me he didn't touch you …* He needed to hear it from her lips.

Noelle didn't hesitate—she shook her head slowly and said, "Only a kiss. He took my clothes and bound me because I tried to escape again."

Randvior pulled her closer. His own brave Valkyrie, a tiny warrior the gods gifted him to love for eternity.

He still wanted to bash Sveinn's brains in. A noise from near the entrance made him turn around and he found his men gathered in the doorway—some watching Sveinn and three transfixed by the naked beauty in his arms. "Get out!" he snarled as he released Noelle and walked to the door and kicked it shut.

"Get dressed, little one." He turned his fury on Sveinn.

Although Randvior was not the type to torment an injured man he felt obligated to enlighten Sveinn before he died. Sveinn was braced against the far wall, his war axe still stuck in his body. Randvior ripped it free. Sveinn screamed in agonizing pain and fell face down on the floor.

"You'll find no mercy here, Sveinn Ovesen. You've shamed

your father's name and assaulted the woman I love. Were you fool enough to think I'd bring such a delicate flower across the North Sea without establishing myself as her betrothed before we landed? I made love to her over and over again. As for you, your fate rests in the hands of my captain."

Fully clothed, Noelle joined him and stared down at her kidnapper. She had no words, perhaps this time she agreed a man should die for his crimes.

Randvior took her bag and directed her to the door.

"Are you hurt?"

"My heart aches." Big, tear-filled eyes stared up at him.

Enough of this place. He opened the door. "Aud! This bastard is yours to do with as you please."

Randvior brushed past his men with Noelle in tow. Once outside, he gave her a brisk kiss and lifted her onto the saddle. He climbed up behind. They rode a short distance and faced the cabin. Aud came outside, leading Sveinn on a rope looped around his neck, his hands bound behind his back. Within seconds, the cabin turned into an inferno.

Randvior mouthed a prayer as he watched the flames rise higher. "To Odin, I am beholden. To Allfather, I am forever grateful. You have delivered mine enemies. Their blood, evidence of your unwavering favor. I am your slave, even after my death, where I beg to sit at your table until the last glorious battle where we must all sacrifice our souls for the sake of Ragnarǫk."

CHAPTER SEVENTEEN

Ashes to Ashes

TIME HAD BECOME a shadow while Randvior was separated from Noelle. Now it drove him, he took no chances riding in the open. Staying vigilant with every inch of ground he covered, he looked over his shoulder continuously. If Sveinn had been shrewd enough to coordinate Noelle's kidnapping, nothing would have stopped him from planting guards along the roadway to ambush them.

He headed northeast, away from the coast.

Randvior was unhappy with himself. Deep down, he still wished he'd been the one to kill Sveinn. But things were changing, especially inside. He'd demonstrated mercy by sparing the lives of those guards. His father had always told him it's easier to kill than not to. And told him once he grew to manhood he'd understand the usefulness of benevolence. All men make war, but few possess the necessary scruples to make peace. Randvior had done that … and now, for Noelle's sake, he allowed those men to live. He remembered her words—why she believed they could never be together. His violence was an abomination in her god's eyes. Though he secretly wondered if her Allfather wore breeches or a dress.

Pallid light streaked the sky, the weather overcast and cold. None of it could penetrate the luxurious heat wrapped in his arms. Noelle's slight form curled close to his heart. He held on tightly, galloping faster and faster. They passed the eastern border of his father's steading and rode through vales and woods before a large lake came into sight. Someone unfamiliar with the landscape might not see it. Beyond the southern shore rose a configuration of starkly white standing stones, almost camouflaged by snow. There they would be offered sanctuary.

He didn't want Noelle to miss seeing the holy place and called to her. People from all over Norway visited this site on pilgrimages during the summer months. She moved, popped open an eye, and quickly closed it again. He laughed delightedly. Anything she did right now would make him happy.

"Wake up, *min lille dukke.*"

She grumbled something unintelligible and peeked up at him. "Do I have a choice?"

Her eyes were puffy from lack of sleep, but she remained as adorable and pretty as ever. He pulled her hood back.

"I want you to *see* where we're going." He pointed across the lake. "This is an enchanted place, where Odin first made his treaty with us. If you look beyond the shoreline and keep your eyes sharply focused northward, where the trees begin to thin out, you can see a group of standing stones. Nine perfectly matched stones."

He knew she adored history.

"And *why* is this place so important at this ungodly hour?" She yawned and tried to lie back down.

"We believe this is one of the places where heaven meets the earth. The gateway into Midgard, the lands Odin gifted the first man and woman, Ask and Embla, to live in."

"Surely you know that's a myth." She was awake now.

"Is it less believable than a garden paradise?"

She considered it. "No," Noelle sighed. "What do the stones represent? Is nine an important number in your world?"

He pinched her hand appreciatively. Her inquisitive mind wouldn't allow her to fall asleep again. "Aye," he said excitedly. "The universe is divided into three levels and nine worlds. Those worlds are Asgard, Vanaheim, Alfheim, Midgard, Jotunheim, Nidavellir, Svartalfheim, Hel, and Niflheim. Each stone represents one of those worlds. And the first Norse king, Harald Fairhair, swore the gods erected these stones as demarcations to show where we should live. They symbolize our sovereignty over the nations of the earth. And each one reminds us of the nine immortal virtues that Northmen strive to live by. If a man abandons them, his soul is doomed—his name forever stricken from the annals of Valhalla. Other legends claim maidens inhabit them, Odin's own daughters as guardians of the realm."

"Name these virtues."

"I cannot, they are forbidden to foreigners. But I shall reveal one, *love.*"

As long as she distinguished between Odin and her god, respected the significance of Allfather's gifts, she would be welcome here. As they neared the clearing, she pointed at a cottage between the sixth and seventh stones.

"A caretaker lives here, a most beloved priest and friend."

Randvior dismounted and she followed. He hobbled his stallion and they walked to the cabin. Before he could knock, the small door opened. A hoary-colored beard covered the stranger's face; he wore a plain wool tunic. Randvior bowed and they exchanged pleasantries before they embraced.

The priest turned to Noelle. "Is this the woman I've heard so much about?"

"Aye."

"Odin has an eye for beauty. Come and warm yourselves by the fire."

The one-room cabin was sparsely decorated, with a crudely made bed, a table, four chairs, and bookcases brimming with ancient scrolls and manuscripts. The priest poured three glasses of wine from an open bottle and served them.

"Does your lady know the purpose of your visit?"

"No." Bloodlust still thundered in Randvior's heart. No, it was time to speak of love now, not hate.

Growing thoughtful, Randvior set his drink aside and approached Noelle, who was standing in front of the hearth. For only the second time in his life, he knelt at the feet of a woman.

"As the priest has suggested, I brought you here for purely selfish reasons."

She touched his face.

Unwilling to postpone their wedding any longer he said, "It is customary to spend weeks planning a wedding—inviting kinsmen and friends and holding elaborate celebrations. We can no longer delay the inevitable. We are still in danger, although I cannot say who wishes to see us both destroyed. I still feel it in my bones. I want to marry you here, on cherished ground. Pledge our hearts to the gods as we did at Odin's altar. To Hel with the rest of the world ... Noelle Sinclair, say once more you'll become my wife."

She swallowed and took Randvior's hands in hers. Rewarded him with an intense smile. He nuzzled his head between her thighs.

"You didn't need to ask me again."

A few minutes later, satisfied she had agreed, he let go and stood. "There are a few preparations before the priest can offer the vows."

In the farthest corner of the room, he unveiled a large chest. After he opened it, he showed her two swords. The first was the one he had laid across his knees during the oath taking ceremony. Randvior lifted the heirloom above his head.

"My sword was forged in the fires of my forefathers and I am meant to guard its tradition. Our eldest son will hold this weapon one day, and it will continue to symbolize everything we hold sacred—our freedom. Odin blessed this blade and our wedding vows will be spoken over it."

He lowered it and lifted the second so she could see it clearly. The thin delicate blade gleamed coppery-silver in the soft light. "This one," he wanted her to join him, "was produced in my armory for you. It's meant to represent your ancestors."

Noelle traced the metal with her fingertips. Her name was

etched along the unblemished edge.

"Why should you honor my family?"

"*Min lille dukke,*" he said. "By custom we equally honor both families during a wedding. *Our* children will share the bloodlines of both our houses. The name Sinclair is honorable. It is only your brother I despise."

"And these rings ..." Noelle inspected the silver and gold rings set in the delicate pommel.

"The first of many oath rings for your blade. These," he fingered two, "symbolize the beginning of our lives together."

He tapped the handle. "Hereafter, every critical moment of our lives—births, weddings, and deaths—will be remembered by additional rings. For a people defined by oral tradition, they will act as a historical record. And long after we've departed this earth, they will serve as a legacy for future generations who will swear allegiances over them, too."

Noelle handled the sword cautiously. It fit her hand so precisely, so perfectly balanced, and she swept it overhead with ease. Her mood improved the longer she admired the weapon. "Thank you."

"Aye," he said, "it embodies the beauty I see in my queen." He took the blade and propped it against the wall.

"Are you ready to face the world as my wife, *min lille dukke?*"

"Only if you promise to quit teasing me so much and if you finally tell me what that bloody *term of endearment* you've called me since the first day I met you means."

You need only ask ... "My little doll."

Noelle raised her eyebrows. "Really?"

He devoured her with his eyes. "I've considered you *that* and so much more since that first day."

She giggled sweetly. "Your honeyed tongue could talk any virgin out of her clothes."

"Aye," he said. "It already did." He hugged her close. "Please believe my words are not practiced. You alone inspire me." He could feel her heart pounding against his chest.

He swung her around like a child.

"Now," he set her down. "More gifts await you."

She clapped her hands as he pulled a powder blue gown and a tawny colored headdress, adorned with sprigs of heather and dried wildflowers, out of the trunk. "My mother wore this bridal crown and her mother before her. Now I wish you to wear it."

"How is it you knew to bring these things here?"

"After Sveinn kidnapped you, I sent Brandon ahead, as my proxy, to receive my father's blessing for this union. He brought the trunk, too. The priest has been waiting for days. I knew in my heart if we were reunited that not another day should go by without us being husband and wife."

"You amaze me."

"No," He cupped her face. "*You* amaze me."

An exaggerated cough disrupted their conversation.

"My Lord Sigurdsson, if you will follow me outside. Please help me set the hay bales, the lady will need time to prepare."

Not wanting to leave her side, Randvior agreed to go, reluctantly. He planted a firm kiss on her forehead before he left.

The priest bowed reverently to Noelle from the doorway. "There is a looking glass inside the cabinet by the hearth if you need it to aid in your preparations."

Noelle's love for her groom increased tenfold once he showed her the gown and headpiece. How many men paid attention to such things? Love had blossomed between them so quickly. Weeks ago, she searched tirelessly for an escape. Now all she wanted waited outside. She touched the headdress and realized its importance. The Norse believed it honored the goddess Freya and brought luck to the bridal bed. The heather and flowers symbolized the harvest and fertility. She pinned it in place.

Dressed, she cracked the door and looked outside. Dozens of celebratory pyres were lit. A ring of fire surrounded her groom and the priest. Most of the snow inside the circle had melted and she could see withered vegetation underfoot as she stepped within the fiery sphere.

As usual, Randvior appeared unearthly, too handsome in his black tunic. The gold sword was sheathed at his hip. His flaxen hair hung loose at his shoulders and his beard had been neatly trimmed for the special occasion. Thank God, she wasn't marrying an Irish lord today!

She had prayed for this moment from childhood. The loss of her mother and the corrupt nature of her brother had affected her life so harshly. After years of strife, she wanted to scream to the world how happy she felt in this perfect moment. How she knew in her heart this was the man God intended her to marry. The snow in the trees surrounding the clearing glistened as brightly as stars, a beautiful backdrop for her wedding. She lifted her skirts and eyed the dainty slippers on her feet—decorated with tiny bell-shaped beads and embroidered with gold thread. Her dress was ornamented in the same fashion.

Clasping a hand over his heart, Randvior greeted her, a slight tremor in the hand he offered. Joyful tears threatened to spill again, but she didn't want Randvior to remember her that way on their wedding day. She must be brave.

The holy man begged their undivided attention, which meant they could no longer stare at each other. But Noelle could barely pry her eyes off her lover. She faced the priest and opened her heart to anything he might say. A pagan wedding vow is better than none at all. The liturgy opened with a prayer spoken in Norse. Noelle cared little if he prayed to the devil himself. She stood at the altar with the man she loved!

Apparently, Randvior arranged for the wedding to be conducted in her language, because the priest started speaking English after the prayer ended. Subtle differences existed in the vows. She stood devotedly and placed her right hand in Randvior's left so he could slip a thin gold wedding band onto her ring finger. Randvior had taken the elegant circlet from amongst the oath rings on his sword. In turn, she presented a ring to Randvior, after the priest blessed and handed it to her.

Once the rings were sanctified, the priest presented swords. They knelt on tiny silk pillows and bowed their heads as he reenacted the moment Odin breathed life into humankind. Noelle's gaze strayed often to Randvior's face, much to the priest's chagrin.

Randvior squeezed her hand. "Behave little one," he whispered, eyes dancing.

They exchanged swords and spoke the vows next.

"The gods have commanded men and women to marry and conceive sons and daughters and to raise them to honor the Old Ways. Noelle Marie Sinclair—do you swear before Odin and his sons and daughters to cleave unto this man, to honor and keep yourself unto him all the days of your life and into the hereafter?"

"Aye."

"Do you renounce your fealty to your English sovereign and pledge allegiance to Jarl Randvior Sigurdsson as your lord and master, husband and protector, spiritual head, and judge?"

"Aye."

"Randvior Sigurdsson—do you swear before Odin and his sons and daughters to cleave unto this woman, to honor and protect and keep yourself unto her all the days of your life and into the hereafter?"

"Aye."

"Do you pledge to guide her correctly and gently through this lifetime and nurture her spirit for Odin's own pleasure?"

"Aye."

"*I Odins navn erklærer jeg dere mann og kone. La ingen utfordring gudene mindre død de søker.*" The priest blessed them and made several revolutions over their heads to ward off evil spirits. "You are bound."

Randvior embraced and kissed her before he turned to the cabin where a black ram was tethered to a post. He carried the beast to the altar. The priest opened a silver horn he'd removed from his belt and prayed. He anointed the animal with fragrant oil from the horn. Noelle's attention turned from the priest to her husband. Another blood sacrifice?

"This will assure our marriage is established on a strong foundation." Randvior raised a dagger overhead and neatly slit the animal's throat.

No words needed—Odin surely accepted this blood gift.

⸙ ═══════════ ⸙

CHAPTER EIGHTEEN
Test of Dedication

DREAMS DID COME true after all. The priest served a modest meal; smoked venison, pickled herring, cabbage, bread, and day-old honey cakes. Ambrosial in Noelle's humble opinion.

Randvior satisfied the priest's demand for a traditional bridal toast. "To Noelle—you have increased my joy and banished sorrow from my soul. I beseech Frigga to bless and give us many sons and daughters who will serve the gods."

"Aye!" The holy man gulped down his portion of wine.

After an hour, Randvior announced their quick departure.

"Folkvar, we humbly thank you for your generosity. Odin's blessings on you, old friend—remember, my door is always open to you and your kinsmen."

"And many blessings on your house," he returned. "But somehow, I think those blessings have already begun." He winked at Noelle.

Once outside, Noelle's body constricted with anticipation, a premonition of feelings of the night to come. Wound as tightly as a chord, if Randvior so much as blew on the nape of her neck, she'd collapse in a chain of orgasms.

After riding east for what seemed a lifetime, they arrived at a lovely cabin nestled between a stream and cluster of trees. Light flooded outside from the only visible window. Randvior dismounted, left her astride, and walked to the door. Aud and

Katherine popped out and hugged him, then smiled in her direction. Noelle stared, shocked and amazed by yet another unexpected surprise. And her husband appeared completely amused. He whispered to Katherine and the maid disappeared inside.

Randvior collected Noelle and they stood by the cabin together. Katherine reappeared with a bowl of breadcrumbs she spread along the front of the cabin.

"Is she feeding the birds?" Noelle thought it a queer thing to do right now.

Randvior's tittering left her feeling a bit dumb. "She's leaving food for the fairies, so they won't curse our bridal bed."

She laughed at his boyish beliefs, never realizing how seriously he took it. "You *actually* believe in the wee folk?"

"I'll not deny their existence after the unexplainable things I've seen over the years. Let's just say I prefer not to tempt anything lurking in the shadows. Ask Brandon, he'll swear on the Blessed Virgin sprites that inhabit these hills and forests."

Before she could entirely digest the notion of her warrior husband believing in such outlandish things, he scooped her off her feet. Aud cheered him on as Randvior carried her over the threshold. A fire roared in the stone hearth near the doorway and the rest of the room was glowing with the soft light from candles and a metal brazier. The dominate feature in the room was a large bed with lush, velvety coverlets.

She blushed at the oversized bed. Only Randvior would demand such a grand mattress to accommodate his athletics between the sheets.

But other things about the room delighted her, too. An ornamented table with two equally impressive chairs, complete with fine linens and platters of food, was placed near the fireplace. The roasted mutton and boiled cabbage made her mouth water. Her eyes feasted on an assortment of delectable pastries and dried fruits.

"How did they know?" she asked, baffled by her husband's

elaborate preparations.

"I stationed scouts along the roadway days before I found you. I planned our wedding very carefully, was not willing to take any more chances. I told you this already, my love."

Regardless, she marveled at his attention for detail. She further explored the room; furs covered the earthen floor and feather pillows were neatly arranged near the hearth. Thick blankets overlaid a bearskin. *Did he expect her to make love on the floor?* A bouquet of fresh roses and violets were arranged in a crystal vase on a bed stand. *Blooms this late in the season—where did they come from?* Noelle eyed Aud curiously.

He shrugged. "It's a secret." He put his finger to his lips.

Why not? Katherine fed the faeries and now Aud managed to produce roses in the middle of winter. Perhaps magic did exist in Norway.

She wagged a finger at Aud. "If I cannot be privy to the secret, I will at least enjoy their beauty." She walked to the table and picked up the bouquet. The soft aroma pleased her.

She turned and watched as Randvior spoke quietly with his servants, clasping his captain's arm with gratitude. "Goodbye," he said.

Aud and Katherine walked outside, and her new husband shut and locked the door behind them. The moment of truth had arrived, husband and wife alone for the first time. Noelle knew the world had altered the moment they exchanged rings. And now Randvior faced her with a flicker of dark desire in his eyes, which was soon replaced by a generous smile.

"Come," he motioned toward the table. "Our *true* bridal feast waits."

Noelle put the bouquet down and joined him. Randvior offered her a chair and she sat. Her lips quivered with anticipation, her insides a tangled mass of bridal nerves.

Acting the gentleman, Randvior bowed and seated himself opposite her. He spooned small portions of food onto her plate and scooped more generous portions for himself. He sampled the meat. Neither of their thoughts was really on the meal, and he looked down at his plate, back at her, and then down again. Then he sprang from his chair and came at her. Noelle dropped her napkin and sighed triumphantly as he claimed her mouth. This is what she wanted—not food—not anything else, but him.

She objected when Randvior broke their kiss and rushed across the room. He rummaged through a trunk and returned with two items in his hands—a gilded box and velvet bag. Noelle took a long sip of wine to avoid the intensity of his lingering stare. Kneeling beside her, he offered the box first.

"In absence of your kinsmen, I offer this as my *mundr*—my bride price."

Overwhelmed by the elegance of the package, she opened it slowly. Filled with gold bullion, English coins! Confused, she raised questioning eyes.

"My share of the takings from your father's house. Wealth intended for your own posterity." He presented the velvet bag next.

Never had she expected such a generous gift, enough gold to make her independently wealthy. With quivering hands, she untied the black ribbon at the mouth of the bag. A strand of perfectly cut rubies and diamonds, fixed between cordiform gold beads—a string long enough to dip between her breasts. The clasp was too intricate for her nervous fingers to work right now. Randvior smiled and did it for her. She gasped, mystified as she fingered the large stones.

"*Morgen-gifu*—my morning gift to my most cherished bride. It is given much too late," he sighed ruefully. "But I ask you to receive it with all the respect a grateful groom might show his bride on the morning after they share the bridal bed."

She nodded. The extravagant gifts he presented were more than her father would have ever offered as dowry.

What am I to do?

"I have naught to give, no wedding gift and no dowry." She lowered her eyes.

He lifted her chin so she had to look at him. "There is nothing conventional about this union. Even if we were blessed with the luxury of time, I would have waived your dowry to prove how much I love you."

"I beg forgiveness," she sniffled. "For the dreadful way I misjudged your intentions."

"Aye, *min lille dukke*, you reacted out of fear and require no forgiveness. I should have handled you more gently." He lifted her from the chair. "Disrobe for me, I want to see you."

She undressed seductively, too slowly, determined to punish and reward him at the same time. The only gift she could offer was her body. And Randvior Sigurdsson deserved it. The moment her clothing dropped, he crashed into her as lethal as a tidal wave.

The heat from her body sent a flurry of wild thoughts whipping through his mind. Impure and animalistic. It nearly strangled every ounce of civility left inside him.

Delicate tinder, hungry flame.

The memory of finding her with Sveinn drove him crazy. He wanted to be inside her *now*, share the joys of her body, and blot that bastard out of her memory forever. Randvior unlaced his breeches and blanketed her from behind. He'd fantasized about this position on many occasions and she wiggled playfully before him—inviting him to do as he pleased.

She squirmed and moaned, welcoming him. His hand glided between her legs and found the sensitive spot that sent her body into uncontrollable tantrums. Her thighs were slick with excitement, and Randvior steadied her, while staring longingly at the heart-shaped cheeks that begged for his shaft to plunge between them. He pierced her like an arrow.

She cried out as he entered and he froze midstride.

"Don't stop," she pleaded.

He grinned lasciviously and continued. It felt too damn good to stop. Randvior locked his hands around her stomach and lifted her off the bed. "Stand up for me."

He gently walked her to the wall. Noelle seemed to know

what he wanted and rested her palms against the boards. She arched to accommodate him. He gulped for air—her tiny ass bobbed every time he moved. He closed his eyes and allowed her to control the rhythm.

Beautiful seductress.

"Randvior …" she purred. "… It feels so good."

"Du kommer til å drepe meg, jente."

Noelle sucked the life force out of him and it took every ounce of mental stamina he possessed not to explode inside her like an unpracticed boy. He withdrew and spun her around. Then draped her across the mattress on her back as she wrapped her legs around him and pulled him down. Within seconds, they finished together.

Loud pounding yanked Randvior from sleep on the fourth night of his honeymoon. He bolted upright and eyed his sleeping bride tenderly. The poor girl was drained—overwhelmed by his bed play. He'd taken her countless times and in many ways, used her wee body to fulfill every youthful fantasy he had.

The knocking grew more intense and desperate. He growled angrily as he got up and grabbed his sword. He stalked to the door and threw it open.

"Speak!" he thundered, standing stark naked over a boy he dwarfed.

"*Jarl,*" he said. "You'll not know me. I'm Matheson, one of your newer stable hands. There's been an attack. Someone set fire to several cabins and many have perished."

At that, Randvior motioned him inside and slammed the door. The servant stared unwittingly at him.

"I've been sent to retrieve you. Master Aud appointed me as his personal messenger and humbly begs you to postpone the rest of your holiday and come home."

Randvior latched on to his shoulder and shook him. "Who died?"

"Three families—burned beyond recognition."

Randvior let go. "Ride boy, tell my captain I'll be on my way.

Gather the women and children and hide them in the cellars. Prepare the steading for battle, arm every man and boy with whatever weapons you can get your hands on—sticks if that's all you can find."

"Aye." The servant bowed and paused at the doorway.

"Go!" Randvior pushed him outside.

Noelle yawned and stretched, and scanned the room. She smiled once she discovered Randvior standing at the open doorway naked. But her smile quickly faded once she noticed the weapon in his hand.

"Get up." He slammed the door. "We must return home at once." Not wanting to alarm her, he offered no further explanation.

He tossed the sword on the bed, grabbed a towel, and washed his face with water from the basin. Disgusted, he threw the linen at the wall and walked to the door. "Lock it after I go out."

A cold bath would clear his head, and a half frozen stream would serve him well.

Sleepily, Noelle stumbled out of bed and latched the door. Had she done something to displease her husband? Deep concern gripped her heart. She could think of nothing under the sun and moon that would lure him from their bed unless it was serious. Judging from the intensity of their lovemaking last night, she was the sole object of his desire, the only person who existed in his universe.

She bathed. Only last night Randvior had threatened to penetrate the layers of her soul—to pierce her heart with his love. Her body jolted at the memory of it.

She dressed hurriedly, putting on a plain wool gown. Despite its lack of adornments, the material was soft and warm. Eager to get outside, she skipped putting on a pair of leggings and laced her boots over bare feet.

She smiled as she hurried to the door. A little love goes a long way—she'd help him recover. As she reached for the latch, Noelle stopped short at the sound of male voices outside. She listened closely and easily recognized Randvior's baritone. But there were at least two others—possibly arguing with him?

She strained to hear more—pressed her ear to the window, the faint glow of dawn sneaking its way around the edges of the old curtains.

"How did you know where to find me?" Randvior asked.

"Look to your mother," a man answered.

She shivered. That woman had her talons buried in every man's hide within a day's journey of Randvior's steading. It was unsettling. Nine days since she had been home, nearly five spent with Sveinn and four with her husband. It was the closest she would ever come to escaping Lauga's destructive reach.

She imagined the dark witch conjuring spirits. Consulting tarot cards or reading rune stones to predict her son's whereabouts or relying on dark forces to threaten Noelle's future prospects of happiness. A flutter of butterfly wings tickled her stomach and she wrapped her arms protectively across her midriff. *Open the door, chase the intruders away.* But a voice inside her head warned she should grab as many weapons as she could carry. Noelle went to the trunk.

Get knives—many of them.

Her silvery blade only waited her hand, and Randvior's sword was too heavy for her to carry. His battle-axe was nearly as long as her body. She chose a long knife and turned back to the doorway. *What are you waiting for?* The same hesitation that often over powered her common sense and got her into trouble growing up nearly took over now. She started for the door after she heard Randvior scream.

She nearly yanked it off its hinges as she went outside.

No one was at the front of the cabin and she started for the stream. She stopped to think before she took another step. Emotional responses *always* ended badly. *Get a hold of yourself.* Valuable advice she remembered from her father. Good thing she stopped. Noelle's stomach felt gravelly and a wave of nausea nearly made her throw up.

Loud noises came from around the corner. "Put him down!" a voice demanded.

Then silence.

Showing herself might distract Randvior and put his life in jeopardy. The unpleasant sensation she felt earlier intensified in the pit of her belly. She decided to listen in a little longer before she made her presence known. Her eyes grew wider, spying Randvior's unclad form partially submerged in the icy water with a man dangling helplessly in his grip. She'd seen him do this to a man before and knew what to expect. Two others with weapons drawn were standing only a few feet away and verbally threatening him with every sort of violence known to mankind.

She marveled at her husband's extraordinary strength. As vulnerable as he appeared—weaponless and naked—he was an incredibly imposing figure in the morning light. From head to toe, he swelled with fury and a rare vengeance shined in his eyes.

Noelle considered their positions.

She estimated twenty-five feet between her and the closest man. If she charged from behind, aided by the element of surprise, she might be able to stab one in the back. This standoff was accomplishing nothing. God help her. Unwilling to watch her Viking sacrifice himself to these nameless brigands, she charged. The man on the left was her intended target.

The sturdy blade cut deep. Randvior screamed as the man she stabbed swung and cuffed her across the side of her face with something as heavy as a mace. She tumbled, and the light faded in and out as she lay on the ground, trying to maintain consciousness. In the confusion of the skirmish that broke out after, Noelle searched for Randvior. She managed to keep one eye focused if she kept the other squeezed shut. Randvior crushed the man's skull he was holding with his bare hands and tossed him aside.

The man she had stabbed lay only feet away, curled in the fetal position—his weakening groans evidence she had aimed well. There was blood everywhere. Lightheaded, her vision blurred again. *Not now, please God, not now ...*

"Stay with me!" Randvior was close; she knew it without seeing him.

"Get back!" a voice warned.

Noelle raised her head, arms flapping uselessly at her sides. The third attacker circled her, blocking Randvior's path. With great effort, she managed to rise up on one elbow and meet her husband's worried eyes. She looked toward the woods and spotted another figure. It moved closer—Brian? She wanted to scream his name out, warn Randvior, but it was impossible. Her brother was in Durham, not Norway!

The world started to spin. She collapsed and vomited, didn't have the strength to sit back up. Noelle heard the unmistakable sound of bodies moving and weapons scraping. The world went black.

Randvior's eyes snapped open. His head felt like it had been impaled on a Rus pike. He wiped fresh blood off his right brow. He could hardly move his left arm, where he found a gaping wound. How much blood had he actually lost? And then, it hit him, *Noelle ...*

He staggered to his feet. Found her withered body some twenty yards away from where he had fallen. He raced to her side. *By Odin, what have I done?*

Noelle had saved his life, defended him with what little strength she possessed. He groveled helplessly at her feet, regretted everything he had ever put her through. The list of violations were endless. He bowed his head. *Forgive me, my love.*

He swept her into his arms. As he made for shelter, more blood seeped from his wound.

He rushed to the warmth of the cabin and slammed the door. Laid her across the bed, undressed her, and examined her from head to toe. A nasty bruise and a small cut along the hairline of her left temple were the only injuries he could see. Dry blood was crusted on her cheek. He suspected a concussion, which sparked fear inside him. He immediately tried to wake her. Called her name a hundred times, but nothing helped. Her pulse was erratic.

"Wake up," he croaked. He'd seen this type of wound before. Watched men in the prime of life succumb to serious head injuries.

There was water in the pitcher on the bed stand and he wet a cloth and sponged her off. "Wake up, *pokker det.*"

His hope deteriorated as he started to massage her feet. Pinched her arms and legs, caressed her cheeks. She needed stimulation and he'd utilize any tactic necessary to rouse her, even pain. Randvior grabbed a knife from the table and quickly made the decision to use it. Gently at first, he pressed the tip into the soles of her feet. No response. He scraped the blade across her toes, nearly drawing blood. Nothing.

"Wake up, god damn it," he begged. *Odin, heal her and this wound in my heart.*

His jaw clenched as he further appraised her condition. They were too far away from home to ride for help. Nothing seemed to work. *The stream!*

He scooped her off the bed and carried her outside. The frosty air made him shiver, reminding him that he had no clothes on. He waded into the frigid water, knelt, and submerged her— letting her head dip under for only a second. As he lifted her, she sputtered and coughed. Those beautiful brown eyes opened in horror and confusion. His heart nearly burst and tears of infinite joy filled his eyes.

Randvior balanced her on his knees and brushed strands of hair from her face. Her lips were dark blue and her teeth chattered, but he was more than just a little bit tempted to steal a kiss. He needed to get her inside by the fire. And to tell the truth, if he didn't warm up soon, he'd freeze to death, too.

⸙ ⸙

CHAPTER NINETEEN
Burning Cross

FEAR AND LOATHING burned Randvior's throat as he deposited Noelle on the bed and wrapped her in blankets. He rushed to the hearth and dropped an armful of kindling, built up the fire until it roared. He returned bedside and looked deeply into her eyes. They were wide open, pupils dilated, and she complained of a throbbing skull—considering the force of the blow she'd ... Oh god, she was lucky to be alive.

Hours later, she slowly became more aware of the things around her. She'd stopped calling him by her father's name and had noticed the nasty gash down the side of his shoulder.

She demanded he let her stitch him up before he bled to death in front of her. Her resiliency astounded him and he pacified her by sitting down on a chair next to the fireplace so she could see. If she needed to use him as a pincushion to stay alert and awake, his body was at her service. She poured half a bottle of wine over the wound and stepped away as Randvior cursed the day. Once the pain subsided, he eyed her speculatively. Maybe it wasn't such a good idea letting her handle a needle and thread right now. Unaware of any formal training she had for surgery, he accepted the fact that he was about to find out.

Medical supplies were always kept in his saddlebags. He watched as she dug around and pulled out sheep gut thread and a needle. She sterilized the needle over the open flame and doused it with alcohol, repeating the process twice. He arched a brow worriedly as she threaded the needle and held it up for inspection.

"Are you ready?" She put her hand on his shoulder.

Practiced fingers sunk the needle under his skin and completed the first stitch. He flexed his fingers on the other hand to keep his mind off the stinging, nagging pain. After careful stitching, she counted forty stitches out loud, cut the thread, and knotted the ends together. Randvior regarded her handiwork and nodded appreciatively.

"It will do," she said.

"Aye," he agreed. Forty tiny stitches—small ones left less of a scar. He smiled. If Aud or one of his other men had gotten their hands on him in the field, they might have sewn him together with twenty. What other skills had she hidden from him? "Your talents are endless."

She mopped her forehead with the back of her hand. "Thank you."

"Do you feel queasy?"

She looked surprised and nodded. "Aye, how did you know?"

"Serious head injuries can do that, although I cannot explain why you're on your feet now."

He had many questions. Like, who taught her how to stab a man in the kidney? Maybe she had witnessed a fair share of violence in her young life. But these kinds of questions would only elicit a feeling of indignity in a woman who risked everything to save him. Instead, he simply gave voice to one. "Why did you intervene? Those men weren't after you, *min lille dukke*, they wanted *me*."

"I overheard one say your mother told them where we were. It made me more furious than anything I've ever heard. She betrayed you, and I'll be damned if she'll make me a widow before I have a chance to live my life with you."

Her words put to rest any lingering doubts. Before, he had wondered if she had only agreed to marry him to protect her family or to gain forgiveness from her god. He looked her over critically, wanted to make sure she was fit to travel. Injuries left them both weak.

Randvior was determined to make it home before nightfall. If she had been hurt worse, to Hel with his tenants, but he knew she was strong and they were determined to face whatever horrors awaited them at home.

Darkness set in as they met a group of riders halfway home. Noelle lowered her thick collar and stared across the field at the horses tethered to trees. She recognized Brandon immediately. He was alive and well. It gave her hope that whatever had happened might not be as bad as originally feared.

Randvior kissed the back of her neck before he slipped from the saddle. Several riders dismounted and met him near the trees. Noelle could see Brandon and Randvior's hands gesturing angrily. Bad news. The men broke apart and Brandon followed Randvior back to his horse.

"My Lady …" Brandon bowed formally.

She nodded. "What news?"

He looked up and pursed his lips. Rarely did Sir McNally frown. "I'll let your husband do the telling. But I'm very happy to see you alive. Randvior told us of your bravery. Once again, you have humbled men of war by showing us purity in spirit."

She received his praise with mixed emotions. Managed to give him a half nod, before Randvior told her to stay put while they made further plans.

Randvior's voice boomed across the clearing as she waited. She couldn't make out what he was saying, but none of it could be good. Bored with waiting, and desperate to relieve herself, she wandered into the woods. No harm with a small army standing nearby. A faint rustling and a whisper drew her deeper into the forest. It sounded so familiar.

Were the Norse gods summoning her?

For some inexplicable reason she wasn't afraid. She jerked around at the sound of leaves and twigs being trampled underfoot. And there he was … whether a figment of her imagination or a ghost, her brother, Brian Sinclair, stood only feet away.

Astounded, she recalled seeing him back at the cabin before she passed out.

"Sister ..."

Noelle searched for an escape route. But it was dark and Brian was faster and stronger. He extended his hand to her.

"I've come to take you home."

"To what?" She realized he was flesh and blood now.

"To Durham."

Noelle sank to her knees. Her mind painted a vivid picture of what misery her life would be back home.

"No. I *am* home." There was nothing he could offer her to lure her back to a life under the same roof with him.

But Brian didn't care about what other people wanted. He came at her—and Noelle couldn't move out of the way in time.

"Life," he whispered as he roughly yanked her to her feet, "is often unfair. Did you enjoy selling your soul to the devil? Didn't I tell you I'd hunt you down?"

She gouged at his eyes, but he clapped his hand over her mouth and spun her around so her back faced him. He held her in a death grip and applied so much pressure to her chest she couldn't breathe. She tried to break free, but he only gripped her harder.

"Help yourself. Come peacefully and I'll let you live until we get home. Keep struggling and I'll slit your throat right now and watch you bleed out like a pig."

At that, she bit the fleshy part of his palm.

"You filthy bitch!" he yelped and shook his hand out while she ran for cover, hiding behind a large bush. Long moments passed, then she heard his footsteps.

"Come out, come out, wherever you are ..."

Noelle bowed her head. Good God—how had he gotten here? Her heart jolted. Lauga ... Of course, they had a shared hatred in common.

"I've been trailing you for days. A touching wedding ceremony, I might add, outdoors for the entire world to enjoy. Did you really think Father would allow you to disappear? Did you think I'd allow you to live happily ever after?"

She could hear him walking around and it frightened her.

"Margaret has been sold off to an English baron and our father is very ill. He met with an unfortunate accident after his return from Ireland, after he tried to banish me."

This news surprised her. Her father would never do such a thing unless the servants and soldiers convinced him Brian had murdered Ophelia in cold blood. Even Lord Sinclair had his limits.

He threw a bit of rope over the bush and it landed by her feet. "Bind your hands and come out."

She focused on the air around her and considered her options, fleeing or dying. She would sleep an enchanted sleep having loved so purely and deeply. Death didn't scare her anymore, but leaving Randvior behind and sailing home with Brian did. She threw the scrap of rope at him.

"I'd rather die."

Her remark hadn't quite registered when she faced him again. Before her brother could respond, Randvior struck as deadly as a rabid wolf.

"You've gone too far." Randvior wrapped his hands around her brother's throat and slammed him to the ground. "I left your home unharmed and allowed you to keep half your wealth. What could have possibly enticed you to risk your life by coming here?"

Brian coughed and struggled to speak. Randvior relaxed his grip.

Noelle knew the answer ... There was no other reasonable explanation.

"To kill her."

With his bare hands, Randvior slammed her brother's head against the jagged stones that littered the ground. Heaving for air, Randvior let go of Brian's body and turned. "I heard your fearless words—say nothing—leave his corpse to rot."

But there was something she needed, someone she wanted. "One thing, my husband."

He nodded.

"Bring my sister home, I beg you." She shouldn't regret begging mercy for her sister's life. *Please my love …*

Randvior came to her and took her hand. "If there is a way, I swear I will reunite you with Margaret."

Tears filled her eyes. Together, they walked back to the horses.

Randvior rode ahead of the guards as they made their way toward home. It took a long while for her husband to speak to her again. When he did, he explained everything.

"Three cabins were burned to the ground last night," he said ominously. "Four families perished."

She turned in the saddle. A great sadness made his shoulders sag like an old man's. Her heart rolled over in her chest. "Why?"

He dropped the reins and fanned his hands across his knees. The stallion kept moving. "It seems my mother, your brother, and other men of opportunity wish to destroy me. They want to force me back to my sire's home so I have no voice in matters of importance. As long as I am a *jarl*, I will protect those who worship Odin."

Her pulse raced as she shook her head in disbelief. Who was foolish enough to try to take power from Randvior? Brandon had warned of war. Although she didn't know all the details of Norwegian politics, Randvior's viewpoint differed from many of the men who ruled here—he refused to convert. He gripped the reins again and they broke into a gallop.

"I haven't a bloody clue whom we killed back at the cabin yet, but rest assured I'll find out."

There was a scary confidence in his voice. She trembled at the thought of him going to war, destroying everything in his path. "I don't want you to leave me …" she mumbled under her breath, never intending him to hear her private thoughts.

"What did you say?" he asked.

Suddenly, she blamed herself for the unfortunate circumstances they had faced over the last weeks. Even the deaths of his tenants were her fault. If she had stayed in the woods with Margaret and escaped, she would never have been brought here and Randvior would have never married her or been caught naked in the creek back at the cabin.

"What did you say?" he asked again.

"*Behold, I come like a thief! Blessed is he who stays awake and keeps his clothes with him, so that he may not go naked and be shamefully exposed.*"

An uncomfortable silence followed, then he broke into violent laughter that shook her body. She gave him her best scowl.

"Leave it to my witty bride to navigate through the canon of Christian scriptures and find the words to chastise me for bathing in a creek. I confess my sins—I am a fool. And yes, caught with my pants down."

"You misinterpreted my intentions."

"No, my sweet." he disagreed. "I fully appreciate the wisdom you show in times of danger. Be careful, the Virgin Mother may be replaced if you keep espousing such words on behalf of your Church. *Intended or not.*"

They reached the cabins located along the northern side of his property and Noelle's heart sank at the sight of the burning cross. Randvior wrapped his arm around her to keep her in the saddle. This was not the way the Church intended for the most sacred symbol of her faith to be used.

She covered her eyes to keep herself from staring. "Wicked mockery—sacrilegious representation of Christ's divine mercy, this is not the work of Christians."

"No?"

"No," she assured him. "It's obviously a trick to mislead you. But what kind of man would do something so outrageous?"

"One who wishes to send a clear message."

He got down and went to the cross. The burning effigy stood near the smoldering ruins of the cabins.

Brandon led them to the bodies draped with canvas. Noelle's eyes filled with tears.

"Turn away," Brandon warned.

She refused. "I will witness this tragedy as anyone else would be expected to." Though she indeed dreaded the moment he would uncover them.

She gasped in horror when he did.

Brandon identified the families. Scorched beyond recognition—the acrid stench of singed flesh made her stomach groan. She gagged and ran away—vomited uncontrollably.

She startled after Randvior's face appeared on the opposite side of the tree she held on to. "Don't sneak up on me like that!"

"Sick?"

"Yes," she snapped, "obviously."

She could tell he was trying to gauge her mood.

"And you should be ill, after seeing and smelling that … that hellish stench."

She retched again.

"You've thrown up quite a bit over the last few days," he observed. He felt her forehead and cheeks, checking for fever. "Are you dizzy?"

"No." She pushed past him.

He followed on her heels and offered a wineskin. "Rinse your mouth and take a deep swig. Liquid strength bolsters any man's spirit."

I'm not a man. She gargled and spat the mixture on the ground. As her husband suggested, she took a drink and handed the skin back.

"Is your heart made of stone?"

He looked at her levelly. "Stone, no." He snatched her close. "But hardened after years of war and death," he admitted. "These are my brethren—irreplaceable subjects who depend on me for protection. Thrall or freeman, if one is harmed, the cup of my wrath *shall* runneth over."

This was not the homecoming Randvior had envisioned.

Newly married, he wanted to celebrate, drink, and feast until his insides ached. He toured the grounds, stopped, and talked to the men on patrol. Brandon and Aud had wisely dispatched the remainder of the available soldiers to keep watch. Fifteen thousand acres was too large a swath for only a handful of men to protect. He returned to the hall and organized two more teams from amongst his tenants and slaves. Every available man was needed for defense. If he judged correctly, these bastards wouldn't dare attack the main house, only the outlying grounds.

The war council met in the great hall, and Randvior slammed his fists on the table. "Aud!" His temper had reached its limits. "Take two men and ride to my father's house. Bring my mother—either voluntarily or at the end of a rope. She will answer this night for her betrayal and high crimes."

Aud was especially adept at handling Lauga's manipulative mouth, almost handled it as well as Brandon. And unlike the men who lived within miles of his lands, Aud didn't fear her magic.

"I should have let them burn her at the stake years ago in Scotland, after the priests accused her of witchcraft," he fumed. "Should have let the winds carry her ashes to the four corners of the earth." He hated her now. Nothing could repair their relationship. No one would ever hurt Noelle again. Oh, he knew who sponsored Brian and brought him to Norway.

And no one challenged his decision. Lauga's dark magic … A mother should be the wellspring of her family, not cursed by her only son. He reminisced about his childhood—remembered a far off time when Lauga had been kind.

It shattered his heart.

He offered nothing further. Ordered most of his men to stand guard throughout the night and promised to rejoin them once he settled things with his wife. He went upstairs. Noelle was taking a bath in a large tub set in the middle of her room.

"Leave us." He shoved Katherine outside.

"Finish quickly and gather some belongings—enough to sustain you for a few days."

"Where are we going?"

"*We* aren't going anywhere," he snapped in a brooding rage. Noelle seemed unaffected by his sour mood, thankfully so. He softened his voice. "You are joining the women in the cellars and I'm staying aboveground to protect us and capture the bastards that murdered our tenants."

She nodded and made a last pass with a soapy sponge over her delicate skin. She braided her hair and dressed while he watched. He gave her a leather bag and she chose an extra gown and clean leggings, packed her jewel box, two books, and a dagger he pressed into her hands.

He discarded the pack on the bed and lifted his wife into his arms. "I'm sorry." He twirled her braid around his fingers. "Once this is finished, I expect you to return with me to our little cabin in the woods."

She smiled.

It would be a lot easier if he had been matched with a shrew. The kind of woman who once the marital vows were taken clamped her legs shut as tightly as a cell door. He had lost his strength to resist her and carried her to his room. She waited patiently while he put on his armor. Strapping his helmet on, he gave her a serious look. Together they went to the stairs and stopped. He saw the glow of what he thought was admiration on her cheeks and realized she'd never seen him dressed in full armor.

The welcoming heat inside her mouth as he kissed her made him reconsider his goals. A quick detour to the bathhouse wouldn't hurt a soul. He shrugged her bag off his shoulder, took off his helmet, and dropped it to the floor. God, what he could do with that little body in just ten minutes …

With some hesitation and more than a little regret, for not having the time to make love to her, he pushed the thought out of his mind, picked up the bag and helmet, and escorted her downstairs, straight to the cellar. Guards were already posted at the door. His men saluted and opened it. Randvior grabbed a torch from a sconce on the wall and went in. The passageway curved left and opened into a wide stairway. The main room had a high ceiling with plenty of light. A hundred women and children gathered around them.

Questions were hurled at him all at once. *Where had he been for so long? How long would they be locked in the cellar? Who burned the cabins?* He listened until the last woman had an opportunity to express her concern. He shushed them as gently as he could.

"There are no definitive answers, only strong suspicions. We know these families were targeted because of their relationship to me. Once the guilty are apprehended, I promise to mark days of mourning and all of my household will honor the dead. Odin hears their cries for justice and my sword is his answer."

Whispers among the women went on for a while. Some of the women and children were directly related to the victims and they wept for their loved ones. Randvior's words were accepted and eventually they quieted, but the sound of weeping ripped through him. This had always been the most difficult part of his duties and he hated it.

"I have brought my wife to join you." He pulled Noelle to the front. "We married four days ago in a secret ceremony at the standing stones. Who shall I entrust with the responsibility of looking after my bride?"

Unnr Raske raised her hand.

"Unnr," he acknowledged, reached out, and pulled her from the crowd. "I give her over to your capable hands." He joined his wife and Unnr's hands as if in formal pledge.

Before he departed, he walked with Noelle toward the back of the room. "Once I leave these rooms, I will lock the door from the outside. Only I have the key."

Her face flushed, and she spun slowly around as if memorizing the dimensions of her prison, or looking for an escape route.

Noelle did not like tight spaces or the idea of being locked underground. "There is a secret passageway meant for the women and children if an emergency arises. I know of no grown man who can fit through the door to get inside the tunnel. It stretches for over a mile westward—*only* to be used as a last resort. The older women know the signal to listen for to use it. These guards ..." He pointed at his men. "... will stay with you."

Her color improved.

"But this ..." He placed the bottle in her left hand and forced her fingers closed around it. "... is a means to a painless death if our enemies prevail. Don't be afraid, my love. I'm sure even your White Christ would forgive a woman for protecting her virtue." He felt a slight tremor in her hand as he let go.

"It's common practice—all the women own one." He attempted to convince her of its usefulness. "The threat of slavery or rape is beyond the comprehension of free Norse. Thralls face no such threats, would only be used in the same manner they are accustomed to in another man's household. *Promise me,*" he said with gruesome finality, "that if the situation arises, you won't hesitate to use it."

She stared past him, unblinking, searching the faces of the women and children, then looked back at him. "Only once I have seen to the needs of the others—I am their mistress now."

His mouth twitched. *Brave to a fault.* Randvior walked away, appreciating his bride even more than before.

CHAPTER TWENTY

Remember

BLOOD LUST GRIPPED Randvior's soul. Families were slaughtered for nothing more than a personal vendetta his mother held against his choice for a wife. Six children and four women, their homes burned to the ground. Even during his darkest days, pillaging in Western Europe, he'd never forgotten his morals or approved of unnecessary slaughter. Women and children were forbidden targets and if his men disobeyed, they'd suffer his wrath. Yet today he had failed to protect them.

The victims' bodies were relocated to Odin's altar. Funeral pyres were constructed in the clearing, one for each family, to be kept burning in memoriam. He didn't allow the bodies to be cremated yet. Not until the guilty were apprehended and forced to kneel before the pyres. Forestalling funeral rites was considered dangerous. It might delay the crossing-over of their souls, possibly imprisoning their spirits on earth forever. A chance he'd take for now.

In order to appease Odin, he brought a pregnant mare to the altar. His guards and slaves gathered around as he tethered the animal to a stake.

"Hear me great Odin. Grant me one gift—to see my enemies for what they truly are. Give me wisdom to judge fairly the men and women who seek to destroy these lands. Gift me the fortitude to see this through, even if I must sit in judgment of my own flesh and blood."

The horse reared and whinnied frantically as Randvior came near. Dark eyes grew wide in fear. He comforted her by running his hand over her broad chest, moved slowly downward until his fingers traced the outline of her belly, praising her spirit for being chosen for sacrifice.

"Run free in Asgard forever," he spoke quietly. "You are valiant, honored as any brave warrior in battle. An ordinary death is no end for a creature as beautiful as you."

Only a few of his men overheard these words as he unsheathed his sword. Slitting the throat of a pig or ram to entertain his patron was one thing; driving a broadsword to the hilt, through the muscled chest of a beast larger than a man to appease his god's wrath, was a rare demonstration of strength. Odin's stamina overtook his body and his blade cut through thick flesh and bone. The mare swayed and snorted. Randvior stood strong, looking her straight in the eyes.

Her sides heaved for air as she scraped the frozen earth with her front hooves.

"*La dette blodet gaven vise vårt engasjement og påskynde Odins hevn,*" Randvior said, and knelt before the beast. He reached blindly, grasped the handle of his weapon, and with all his might ripped the blade free. The mare teetered, then crashed to the ground.

He addressed his slaves first. "Guard these fires and the bodies of my kinsmen with your lives. There is no rest for their souls until we've destroyed our enemies."

He looked to his guards next. "If one of these bodies is moved, you will all be held responsible."

When Randvior returned to the great hall, his captains and men were waiting. He considered their grievances, mostly complaints about his delayed response to the attack. With his face and armor streaked with wet blood, he knew he resembled one of Odin's sons. A thrall brought a basin of water and towels to clean Randvior's face and hands *as he* counted his remaining fighters—

fifty. He assigned them positions.

"I believe this night will pass uneventful—our enemies are cowards and know I have returned." Randvior sat down on his throne and wiped his blade clean.

After guzzling his wine, he headed for the stables. His team followed. His first destination was the cabin where he honeymooned with his wife. They had left their belongings behind and he wanted to retrieve her gifts and his weapons. It would also give him an opportunity to inspect the bodies of the men who tried to kill him. He believed his mother's petty jealousies had finally caught up with her. *Soon, Lauga will stand before me and I will personally condemn her so all the Trondelag knows who she really is.*

Noelle paced the earthen floor. Even under Unnr's unwavering care, she still couldn't accept being sequestered underground while the men defended her home. Most of the women sat in groups. The younger girls knitted together in a corner, and the elders chattered amongst themselves, throwing looks her way occasionally. It made her uncomfortable.

Lauga's doing ... Even out of sight, the woman might as well have her hands wrapped tightly around her throat—slowly choking the life out of her. Noelle folded her hands. A pretty girl she'd never seen before was seated by the guards near the stairs, staring at her. The type of girl she feared her husband admired. But she couldn't be more than fifteen.

"Who is she?" she finally asked.

"Lauga's protégé. The girl she wanted her son to marry."

Some men preferred their girls young and compliant. Thank God, her father had never forced his daughters to marry at such a young age. She frowned at the thought, then she vomited on the floor at Unnr's feet. Noelle cradled her sour stomach with both hands.

Her friend ordered two thralls to clean up and draped an arm about her shoulders. "How long since you've bled?"

Her stomach groaned. "Over a month."

"Is the *jarl* aware of your condition?"

"Maybe." Noelle shrugged. "He thinks I'm sick."

"Aye, men overlook everything important unless it smacks them between the eyes." Unnr nodded sympathetically. "The dizziness comes and goes, eases with time."

Noelle gawked stupidly at her. "But you have no children."

"No living children," Unnr corrected. "I gave birth to five sons, but none lived beyond infancy."

Noelle wanted to slap herself in the face and deeply regretted saying a word. The strain in her friend's voice broke her heart. She grabbed Unnr's hand and squeezed. "Please forgive my insensitivity. I am terribly preoccupied with concerns about my husband's safety—and this." She hugged her stomach. "And now the discovery of my rival ..."

"Forget the girl," Unnr waved a hand dismissively. "She's bedded more men than I have in thirty-four years. I am sure you came to the jarl's bed unsullied."

Heat rose in Noelle's cheeks and she lowered her eyes. Unnr smiled and tugged Noelle's chin upward.

"You are a rare flower growing amongst the weeds and brambles. Never mind what these women think or say. The *jarl* chose well. Father Odin saw to that. And now, his heir grows inside you." She touched her stomach affectionately.

"You need sleep." Unnr took her to a small subchamber off the back of the main room. Clean hay covered the floor. "Time is of little concern underground. Rest and I'll go get blankets."

The night passed uneventfully, just as Randvior had predicted. Daylight was always a refuge. He dismounted and stomped into the hall. Thralls were setting out kettles of hot pork stew and bread. Randvior sat down at one of the lower tables and poured himself a glass of wine. He devoured a bowl of stew and signaled for a second serving.

He had reached the cabin quickly last night, and his men buried the bodies of his assailants. No prayers were offered over the unmarked graves. Let them burn.

Noelle's gifts were safely recovered. He rubbed his chin as pleasant memories of his short-lived honeymoon filled his mind. That tiny cabin had a long history. The former owner's family settled those lands centuries ago. Unfortunately, the last male heir died recently, and his childless widow sold Randvior the property on his promise that he would let the cabin remain.

He gulped down the last of his wine and stood. He stretched, twisting and groaning, and then eyed the cellar door.

Aud strutted through the back entrance of the hall like a rooster. "Come with me."

Randvior and a dozen soldiers followed him outside. A group of saddled horses waited near the stable. His mother sat rigidly atop one harnessed to a long sled.

He studied her face, hoping to see an ounce of compassion. But she returned his stare with icy-cold eyes. He turned away as his gut tightened. Randvior noticed a figure wrapped in layers of thick furs and blankets inside the sled. His face brightened when he realized it was his sire. Anundr Sirgurdson grinned ear to ear. By the gods, he hadn't seen his father in over a year. How he respected and idolized this man.

He walked to the side of the sled, fell to his knees, and bowed his head. No shame in demonstrating his obedience to the man he loved more than any other. Anundr was a living legend in these lands, a famous warrior who single-handedly slayed dozens of Varangians. Injuries left him crippled, but the man lived to tell his own story.

Strong hands rested on his head. Randvior looked up to see the rare glimmer of paternal pride in his father's stark blue eyes. He imagined there was a pair of lips buried somewhere underneath the thick curls of his beard. Randvior laughed at the golden beads decorating the braids on his face. After all this time, his father still chose to adorn himself like their ancient forefathers.

"You have prospered, my son," his father said, appraising the outbuildings. "While I squandered my wealth, you practiced frugality. If not for your mother's skills as a spaewife, we might have been begging at your door."

"What is mine is always yours." Randvior leaned over the sled and embraced his father in a bear hug. "Are you aware of why I summoned my mother?" He let go and sat back on his haunches.

"Aye," Anundr nodded. "Your ever-faithful captain explained everything to me. I demanded to come along as the legal representative of my household. Regardless of her deeds, Lauga is still my wife. If these charges are true, your mother has shamed me."

Randvior stood. With a stiff nod, he turned and unhitched the sled from the horse. Aud picked up one end and Randvior the other. They carried it inside to a thickly padded chaise lounge that one of the slaves placed on the dais. He lovingly lifted his father and settled him in the chair. Anundr arranged himself and sat back with a deep sigh. Furs from the sled were brought for him and spread over his legs. Randvior pushed an ale horn into his father's hands and excused himself.

Formal preparations must be made immediately. Although his father's visit was unexpected, he deserved every special consideration. "Announce my father's arrival, welcome all who wish to enter this hall and feast with him," he instructed his men.

When he unlocked the cellar door and started down the steep stairs, Randvior nearly fell, he was so distracted by the joyous occasion. He desperately wanted to share this moment with his wife. Women and children flocked around him when he appeared. He wheedled his way past them and searched for Noelle amongst the sleeping bodies that littered the floor. He finally found her curled up with Unnr.

He paused over her. *Odin, have mercy.* He knelt and brushed her cheek with the back of his hand. "Time to wake up."

Thick lashes fluttered open as delicately as butterfly wings. Once she realized who it was, Noelle shot up and flung her arms around his neck.

He smiled. "Important guests await your company upstairs,"

he informed cryptically. Anundr's presence made him feel like an awkward boy again. How he wanted his sire to fall in love with his wife.

Noelle and Unnr scrambled to their feet and smoothed their skirts.

"Who has come for a visit?" Noelle asked.

"My father."

"Your father?" she repeated.

"Aye," he confirmed. "I am freeing all the women and children. We are safe for now. Few people have had the opportunity to meet my father and will want time to prepare. Never fear, my love," he pinched her cheek. "My sire is composed of the same flesh and bone as me. His presence in my home is an honor we must celebrate. He is worthy of the highest esteem. I want him to meet you." He picked sprigs of hay from her hair and chuckled at her general state of disarray.

Noelle disappeared behind a far wall and changed into the clean dress she had packed. He nodded approval and reached inside his pocket when she emerged. Much to her delight, he had her morning gift. The stones reflected beautifully in the torchlight. He hooked the necklace around her neck.

"I feared it was lost forever." She fingered the stones lovingly.

He smiled. "Not a chance."

Both his wife and the necklace had cost him a small fortune and he'd be damned if he'd lose track of them again. His heart pounded furiously as he stepped back and admired her.

After a long moment, his smile faded. Unfortunately, there were more pressing things to discuss.

"After I left, I decided it was time for my mother to answer for her crimes. Many have gathered to hear her testimony. My father, who hasn't left the privacy of his home in many years, found it important enough to travel with her. Few nobles face a judge—especially in a kinsman's court."

This news should make her feel better. Instead, her eyes darkened and Noelle looked away.

Randvior took her hand. "I may ask you to testify."

She faced him again and visibly stiffened.

"No one will ever harm you again, I swear it."

His tiny Valkyrie had killed a man with no fear and stitched up his body without batting an eyelash. But she hated being the center of attention, especially in a public setting. Randvior moaned and pictured her tiny hand plunging that knife into the man's back. It sent shivers up his spine. He had no right to make more demands, especially where his mother was concerned. Noelle had been a victim of her viciousness for weeks. Yet, he believed his people would respect her more if she had the courage to speak up.

He placed her hand in the crook of his arm. "I will be your strength."

CHAPTER TWENTY-ONE
The Reaping

THIS WAS THE moment Noelle had waited for—assuming the role as mistress over her husband's household. It was an immense responsibility she had only considered in theory—until now. Familiar faces and strangers alike were gathered to witness this spectacle of a trial and to greet Randvior's father.

She cast a worried glance at her husband, who kept a firm grip around her waist as they walked. Women and children congregated along the back wall and slaves stood wherever they could find space. That diminutive chair next to Randvior's throne was adorned with flower wreaths and pine boughs. Decorated for her? A single strand of silver medallions, similar to the ones that adorned his chair, was draped across the back.

"Your seat is ready, my lady." Her husband made a sweeping bow.

She could scarcely take her eyes off him. After weeks of feeling the outcast, she was no longer considered the vile English harridan. Everything she wanted was looking her directly in the eyes. His love surpassed anything she'd ever known. And this house … She adored it, feeling a connection stronger than that of her birth home.

As often practiced in her homeland, her new steading deserved a name. *"Steingard. The Stone Farm,"* she whispered in Randvior's ear and he nodded approval.

"Which stones inspired you?" he asked wickedly while he helped her onto the dais.

Mortified by his question, she jabbed him in the ribs. Movement in her periphery grabbed her attention. The man she spotted needed no introduction. Their eyes met. His were as beautiful as Randvior's.

"Flesh and bone you say?" she teased looking between them. "You grossly under-described your sire—the resemblance is uncanny."

Anundr chuckled and offered his hand. She leaned over and affectionately cradled it in hers, feeling as if she'd known him all her life. If she couldn't gain a mother, please let this man be her second father.

"My son didn't exaggerate a bit." He eyed Randvior. "Your wife is as beautiful as the *alpenglow*."

Too embarrassed to admit she didn't understand the word he used to describe her, Noelle simply smiled.

"'Tis a great shame she cannot fully appreciate my compliment. *Alpenglow* is the golden-red light that illuminates the mountains at sunset," he explained. "It's nearly as radiant as Gabriel's golden mantle." He turned his face to Randvior. "Hire a tutor to teach her our language."

She appreciated the biblical reference. "You flatter me overmuch."

"No," he said most seriously. "Once, long ago, I too brought an English girl home." Anundr gazed at something far away. "She was nearly as breathtaking as you. But ..." He sniffed. "Lauga interfered, and I'm afraid I lost her."

Noelle nodded sympathetically. Never could she have imagined stomaching the idea of adultery. But for his sake, she did. An immediate kinship had been established between them. It baffled her how different Lauga and Anundr were. Randvior seemed disturbed by his father's confession. Perhaps he never realized how much his father loved the girl. Not that it mattered any more, the poor girl was dead. *Another victim of his mother's violence.*

While Randvior and his men discussed defense issues at the high table, Fald Ovesen entered the hall through the back doors. He was alone. What blood vengeance might his old ally harbor after learning his eldest son had died for kidnapping his wife? Although his son had committed a grievous crime, the *jarl* was prepared to pay a generous *weregild* to pacify his friend and foster peace.

Their eyes met as Randvior stood. He did not perceive him as a threat. In fact, the older *jarl* opened his arms. Confused by this, he asked Noelle to stay seated. He went to his friend with hope in his heart.

"My brother ..." Randvior greeted him. Fald gripped his shoulders. "What news has reached your ears?"

"Everything." Fald bowed his head, pain evident on his face. "I know my eldest son is dead."

Randvior felt his pain. If he could alter the past, he would.

"Much is changing in the Trondelag. Spies and backstabbers have infiltrated every court—traitorous fools who relinquish Thor's hammer for a cross."

Randvior nodded. "Are such men amongst us?"

"I cannot say. But two of my own fledglings are guilty," he admitted. "The gods blessed me with three sons, and two are traitors. And I swear my youngest will never see the light of day until I am convinced the old religion is deeply rooted in his heart. Sveinn deserved death."

Randvior couldn't believe what he was hearing. Never had he witnessed a father disinherit his own son. Aye, times were changing for the worst. Fald stared over Randvior's shoulder at his wife.

"Forgive me," Fald said, walking around Randvior, toward Noelle. "My family owes you a penance of great measure. I will do anything to set things right between our families. Sveinn's ambition drove him to madness."

Noelle accepted his apology.

It seemed many people were keeping secrets in the

Trondelag. Fald's pained expression confirmed his innocence. Randvior believed he didn't know what his sons were doing. Fald turned and addressed the crowd.

"My two eldest sons, Sveinn and Tyr, secretly converted to Christianity. They constructed altars dedicated to the White Christ and blackmailed my slaves. If any refused conversion, a painful death was promised as punishment. These tactics are openly taught by Olaf Haraldsson. He's polluted the hearts of our children and has the balls to proselytize in public."

Randvior's world was unraveling right before his eyes. He never thought he would live to see the day when a father must choose between his gods or his sons. Instead of feeling betrayed by Odin, Fald embraced the truth. Randvior felt nothing but deeper admiration for him. Lesser men would have found relief in the bottom of an ale horn. But one thing still deeply troubled him. "Where is your son, Tyr?" Randvior asked.

"Gone."

Not dead. He offered his friend a seat at the high table. Peace would remain between them. For now, a common enemy threatened them, the White Christ. Determined to flush out any remaining traitors, he looked to his own father for approval before he proceeded with his mother's trial. Anundr nodded.

"Lauga Sigurdsson."

Heads turned as Randvior's mother came closer, looking her part, half mother and half Jezebel. She wore what Randvior considered her finest apparel.

"I am here," she said.

"Aye," Randvior acknowledged her. He should be cruel, but wasn't. Instead, he mentally compared her to his beloved wife. Lauga paled in comparison. "Do you know why you're here?"

"Your captain, Aud Magnusson, has read me your charges."

Randvior suffered a moment of disappointment when he saw that his mother remained stoic. Even under the strain of being formally charged with high crimes she managed not to crack.

"You claim to be in possession of evidence to condemn me.

Don't waste my time with these unnecessary formalities. Speak your mind—there is no proof, I assure you."

For the first time, he saw her for the liar she was.

"No proof?" he scoffed. "Do you see the masses gathered in my hall today? Who amongst them is here to defend you? Let them come forward without fear of reprisal."

Much to his surprise, many hands went up.

No matter. There were fifty men to the one who would swear allegiance to her. And they wanted nothing more than to rip her heart out and feed it to the pack of wild dogs roaming the forest.

Randvior called the first witness. She came forward. The same woman who advised Noelle not to drink Lauga's wine in the weaving room. He watched Noelle's eyes blink nervously. Randvior patted the girl's hand reassuringly. She was a talented seamstress, well respected among her peers, and had no reason to perjure herself.

The spaewife who attended Noelle testified next, and by the time she had finished speaking, half the crowd clamored for Lauga's blood. More damaging testimony followed, although the finer details differed slightly from person to person, fifteen witnesses provided enough evidence to charge Lauga. The woman had a questionable history and a bad reputation for playing both sides of a coin, setting people against one another for her own amusement and benefit.

Before Randvior could leave to contemplate judgment, additional witnesses came forward and accused Lauga of consorting with Olaf Haraldsson. They swore on Odin's head that they had personally seen his mother accompanying Tyr and other notable men to political meetings.

"When did you last see her?" Randvior questioned.

"Only three nights ago, she passed me on the road. I recognized her horse and the silver saddle she uses when she rides to distinguish herself."

For once, her vanity would cost her dearly. A foolish act for sure. A plain saddle and dark clothing would have been wise if she wished to remain anonymous on the road. Perhaps she wanted to get caught, for his mother possessed the wisdom of a seasoned strategist. How long had she held his people in a death grip and divided his household? He dismissed the last witness and turned to his mother.

"Have you anything to say in your own defense concerning these new charges before I pass judgment?"

Lauga nodded slowly. "Only this. Your wife worships the White Christ." She pointed angrily at Noelle.

Randvior covered his face with both hands. *Yes, Noelle worshipped the Christian god, but no blood was ever shed over her faith.* "She is not a convert, nor is she guilty of treason," he retorted.

"Does this make her any less of a threat? Can you guarantee she will never lead these people astray or try to convert your men?"

It would be well if his mother shut her mouth. Hatred welled up inside him. "She is an innocent, completely blameless—born into her faith." He needed a drink to settle his nerves. "Bring me wine!" he commanded.

His ancestors would roll over in their graves if they heard their kinswoman speaking such falsehoods. *My mother is a heretic—a traitorous bitch. Who planted the seeds of deception and bitterness so deeply in her heart? An Englishwoman, you fool.* He stared heavenward. *I swear by my own life to never forsake the vows I spoke on my wedding day. Father Odin, destroy me if I fail to honor my wife.*

"Your father raised you as carelessly as a wild ass in the woods." Lauga scowled at Anundr. "See what comes from handling your child so liberally? A disloyal boy."

"Enough!" Anundr silenced her immediately. "How dare you stand before us and offer these lies up as truth? For years, you fed me draughts of sleeping potion to keep me from discovering your corruption. My legs are crippled, woman, not my wits. I know your heart better than you. Salvage what dignity you can by admitting your guilt. Offer your prayers to whatever damned god you choose, but leave these children in peace. I gave them my blessings. What father denies his only son's happiness? Look at them. What mother begrudges her child true love? You black-hearted wench."

Randvior stood, but held his tongue. His mother's eyes opened and closed, opened and closed. *How long had it been since his father spoke of any tenderness for his wife?* he wondered dismally.

"Plead guilty and I will consider leniency."

Lauga was slow to respond. "Would it matter if I did?"

Randvior rubbed his chin wearily.

"You condemned me long ago. After years of loyalty—after delivering countless tenants' children, healing the broken bodies of your soldiers with my own hands, this is the courtesy I'm shown? Do as you must, *blood of my blood*. Cut off my hands and feet and bury me alive as you have done countless times to your enemies. Whatever you choose, be quick about it."

Hopelessness and despair filled Noelle's heart. The memory of her own mother picked away at her thoughts and she tried to forget. It didn't work. *I never had the privilege of knowing my mother and I mourn her loss every day.* She wished with all her heart she was bold enough to speak out and encourage her spouse to make peace with his mother before he punished her. Forgiveness ... But the Norse rarely exercised mercy.

Good sense must prevail.

Randvior must have sensed her discomfort and leaned closer.

"Have you anything to add?" he asked.

Noelle wrung her hands and stared at Lauga. A shred of kindness from the woman would motivate her to intervene. Just as the Lord showed mercy in Nineveh, if Lauga repented, she would shield her from Randvior's wrath.

But a face as hard and bloodless as stone stared back at her. The scarlet shade of Lauga's gown accentuated the delicate color of her face. With her hair pulled high, she appeared years younger. *Any* man would be easily tempted.

Beauty lies in the eyes of the beholder, and even a deadly spider has her charms. Noelle's face hardened—she refused to be a victim any longer.

"Why?" she blurted out. Lauga did not answer, only stared back.

"Answer the lady of Steingard," he commanded.

Lauga laughed mockingly. "Steingard? How very charming. Only the filthy English give pet names to sticks and stones."

Lines marred Randvior's face. "I believe my wife asked you a question. But let me rephrase it since you seem so unwilling to answer. Why did you hire assassins to kill me, pay for Brian Sinclair to travel from England to murder my wife, and consort with Christians in a place where Odin's law is the heart of the people?"

The question upset the crowd.

"Kill *you?*" Lauga faltered. "I did no such thing—they were supposed to kill *her.*" The affirmation burst from her lips, seemingly involuntarily. She gasped and covered her mouth.

"Thrice you have attempted murder on my wife."

Sickened by her demeanor, Noelle shot up and interrupted her husband.

"I strove to win your respect from the moment I met you. In obedience to my husband, I made peace with these women and accepted what small role you were willing to assign me. If we had settled our differences, even agreed to exist side-by-side with mutual tolerance, I would have been satisfied. There is always hope where God reigns true."

Without warning, Lauga charged the dais with a knife.

Randvior blocked his mother's path; she screamed as his massive hand closed around her throat.

Men below pulled their swords and attempted to shove their way through the crowd. But Aud and his men stopped the attack. Three men collapsed on the floor after the brief conflict ended. Noelle rushed to Anundr's side; he quickly grabbed her by the wrist and pulled her behind his chair.

"Stay by me." He pulled a long knife from his belt.

She wanted to close her eyes and will this nightmare away. But Lauga had tried to kill her—again! Not even her Christian upbringing could overshadow the fury she felt in that moment. Herbs and powders, magic spells, and consorting with witches, all offenses punishable by death in Christian lands. Eighteen men were marched to the front of the room. Lauga was still caught in Randvior's unforgiving grasp. Her knife lay on the floor. Aud scooped it up and placed it on his weapon belt for safekeeping.

"Silence!" Randvior commanded.

All the excitement upset Noelle's stomach again and a burning pain spread across her chest.

Anundr narrowed his eyes. "What ails you?"

Not wishing to alert him to her delicate condition, she scooted away from him and found Unnr, who encouraged her to sit and recline on her chair while she gently blotted sweat from her forehead with a handkerchief.

"Violence can give anyone serious indigestion. And while you're pregnant, expect it even more. This too will pass."

Knowing what would happen next as her husband confronted the men who tried to attack him, Noelle could hardly keep her mind focused on one thing. She watched as Aud whispered something in her husband's ear.

Randvior exploded. "Insurrection is punishable by death, take them away."

The muscles on his face flexed as he stared at her, as if he were making sure she was listening. "Hang them until they're dead," he told Aud. "Leave their bodies in the forest so the beasts can pick their bones clean."

Enough violence and death. Enough pain and suffering. Enough misplaced allegiance. She had never seen so much brutality in one place. There was nothing for her husband to prove. She knew he loved her. He chose her over Lauga, killed Brian, and sought to avenge the deaths of his tenants. Randvior was no longer the soulless sinner in her eyes. His fierce loyalty astounded her. She had put all her faith in the right man. But now she wanted peace. Not for herself, but for the safety of her child.

Undeniably shaken, she knew unfinished business remained between her husband and his mother.

He spoke to the crowd again. "If there are others amongst us who wish to stand with my mother, do so now!" Randvior prowled. Searching and stopping—looking for signs of faithlessness on the faces of his tenants and guests. No one seemed safe at the moment.

Lauga stayed silent.

Aud and his men pushed the offenders toward the main doors. Women cried out and ran to Randvior. Four dropped to their knees in front of him, blocking his path.

"Favor us today kind master, spare our husbands. They were hypnotized by your mother's promises of wealth and prestige if they served her well."

"I am fresh out of mercy and tolerance. Let this serve as a severe warning." He flushed with obvious displeasure. "Aud, do as I commanded."

Guards removed the hysterical women from the room. Randvior headed for his seat, but checked on his father first. Anundr pointed at Noelle. *This is it… he'll find out I'm pregnant before I have a chance to tell him myself.* With all the misery, she didn't want to share this joyous news yet.

Raising his brows, Randvior asked, "Are you sick, Noelle?" He palmed her forehead. "You look thinner and pale."

"She's with child," Unnr revealed without hesitation.

Noelle straightened. Her friend had spoken without batting an eyelash. Everyone within earshot waited breathlessly for the jarl to react. A private matter had just been made public. Noelle fisted her hands in bitter disappointment. She had envisioned a quiet evening curled up on his lap, with her head resting over his heart so she could feel it skip a beat when she told him. She wanted to see *and* feel his joy.

He stood dumbly in front of her and thumbed perspiration from the tip of her nose.

"Thank you for providing me with clarity of purpose." Without another word or acknowledgement of her condition, he sat.

He raised his arms and the droning of voices subsided. "I am ready to rule on my mother's case."

Before he spoke again, Randvior stared at the ceiling. Her heart ached for him. No matter what he decided, Randvior knew, beyond the shadow of a doubt, that his mother was guilty. She couldn't begin to imagine what it felt like to face the woman who gave birth to you in such grim circumstances.

"Because the Thing does not convene until late spring, I am entitled to act as judge. By my mother's own pathetic admission, she plotted many times to kill my wife. And now she has deepened her culpability by striking out in front of everyone in this room. She has not denied the allegations linking her to the Christian rebel Olaf Haraldsson. Rarely have I seen a more corrupt person."

He acted more the avenging angel than judge. Sitting so close to him, Noelle could feel the heat radiating from his powerful body. Although her child was little more than a flutter inside her womb, she had held out hope that Lauga would be a part of their lives someday, if only for the child's sake.

However, it would never be …

Randvior pronounced her sentence in one word. "Banishment."

As tragic as a death sentence. She'd fare better facing the hangman. Aud braced Lauga's wilting frame against his body.

Randvior's voice blared as loudly as a war horn. "You will no longer call me son, and I shall never again refer to you as my mother. You are without family or friends, and no longer have roots in these lands—no kinsmen will ever shelter you. Odin will blot the sight of you from his eyes."

Noelle clutched her husband's hand. He spread his feet wide, dropped her hand, and folded his hands behind his back, looking as impenetrable as a fortress. His threatening stance elicited murmurs from the crowd.

"You will never see the next generation of Sigurdssons grow and prosper. Be gone from me before I change my mind and have you hung beside your fellow traitors."

Those were his final words. He turned his back on Lauga and so did every man, woman, and child in the room. Only Noelle faced her. *So this is what it feels like to have your life erased.* Despite Lauga's horrendous crimes, Noelle's heart ached for her.

"Why do you gawk at me girl?" Lauga hissed.

She sucked in a breath and held it before she could bring herself to answer.

"I pity you," she said at last. Lauga's eyes revealed the immeasurable depth of her hatred.

"I don't need your pity, nor want it. I am free now."

CHAPTER TWENTY-TWO

Tidings

T HE ATMOSPHERE INSIDE the great hall changed once Lauga Sigurdsson vacated the premises. For the first time since she had arrived in Norway, hope colored Noelle's world. Gratitude crept into her heart—Randvior had made the ultimate sacrifice.

Pleasurable aromas from the kitchen drifted into the room and made her mouth water. She didn't understand how everyone could return to their duties so easily. Thralls brought food and drink. Happiness surrounded her. A tragedy had occurred here today, not something to be taken lightly in her opinion.

Once again, Unnr tried to comfort her. The woman could read her almost as well as Randvior.

"Norsemen rarely show emotion. It took a great amount of courage for Jarl Randvior to punish his mother. He has gained immeasurable respect by rejecting his own kinswoman. Only a man guided by Odin's hand can find the courage to do such a thing. Wisdom is a divine attribute."

"So is mercy."

"Aye," Unnr agreed. "But did Lauga show any?"

"No."

"Odin has. See how loved and admired you are."

"Odin?" Noelle looked surprised. She was stunned an English woman felt anything for a pagan god. "Why would you attest to Odin's charitable character?"

"Because, I too, worship him."

As amusing as it had been watching Noelle struggle after Unnr made the unexpected announcement about her pregnancy, Randvior decided it was time to set things right between them. He took her to Odin's altar to pray for their unborn child's life. Promises had been made there weeks ago and he believed his patron would protect his family.

"Why did you wait to tell me?" he asked.

"I have hardly seen you over the last few days. And between the attack and Lauga's trial ... I didn't want to share such wonderful news at such an unfortunate moment in our lives."

A plausible excuse.

He stared at his wife. All this time he had carried doubt in his heart. Jealousy had eaten away at his flesh and darkened his soul. No longer, he would learn patience and dedicate his life to mercy.

"Mercy on your enemies, too?" a voice interrupted.

He drew his weapon and tucked Noelle behind him. "Who is speaking to me?"

His pulse accelerated. Hadn't there been enough surprises for one day? Noelle stared at him, then they both searched the clearing. He shifted his gaze toward Noelle again and she started to say something. He held a finger to his lips.

"A man without children has no purpose. Your sons and daughters are your future," the voice continued. *"Carve out a new existence for yourself. You are not meant to die. I have plans for you yet, Randvior Sigurdsson."*

Whose voice dared invade his head? His wife couldn't hear it; he pushed her protectively behind the altar stone. His eyes swept the area again. Not a blasted thing seemed out of place. And his slaves and guards remained where they belonged.

He sheathed his weapon, scratched his head.

"What troubles you?" Noelle asked.

He rubbed his chin and started to question his own sanity.

"Sometimes ..." he started. *It is impossible to put this delicately.* "It's rumored the gods may speak directly to you if you listen with your heart."

"Aye, the saints were blessed by intimate conversations with God."

She didn't need convincing, *he* did.

"*Why deny me?*" There it was again. "*Enjoy the pleasures I give you, Norseman. Hear me. Soon these lands will be obliterated by martyrs' blood. You aren't meant for this battle. Leave. Take your family and sail the North Sea to a new land. I will follow. Wherever you erect an altar in my name, I will come.*"

Randvior ran his fingers over the peak of the stone. He never doubted Odin's spirit resided in this place, but to hear his god's voice … to experience something so incredible had never been in the realm of possibility. Such a privilege should only be reserved for the greatest warriors. The warning—command ignited a spark in him. His steely faith and willingness to protect the religious rights of his brethren had always captured the respect of his peers. Apparently the gods had taken notice, too.

The only hitch: abandon the lands he had poured his life's blood into over the last eight years. Of course, Randvior admitted ruefully to himself, starting a new life in a new place appealed to him after everything he and his young wife had been through. If they could settle in a place closer to England, where Noelle might have an opportunity to visit Margaret and worship her god without fear of reprisal, he knew his family would flourish. Especially now that Brian was dead.

"I will heed your warning, Odin," he said aloud. He took Noelle's hand and kissed her fingers. It was time to make this dream a reality. They started for the house.

"*Where are you going, Viking?*"

Randvior swung around and flashed a smile. Staring at a hunk of rock didn't bring him any closer to Allfather.

"I've paid a great price, honored my departed friends, disenfranchised my family, executed a dozen of my men, and killed my wife's only brother. I need peace and maybe a bit of pleasure before I lay plans to leave this place."

Noelle was his greatest hope, and their unborn child his future. He would appease Odin … in time. Sometimes his patron played games. Allfather possessed many countenances, a god of war and poetry, and a skilled prankster.

Together, they entered the great hall. Women surrounded Anundr, and he drank from two ale horns. One gripped in each hand. Randvior laughed. His father was making up for lost time, happy to be free of a woman who had dominated and destroyed his spirit. Their eyes met, and Anundr's face lit up. Did Odin want him to take the old man along?

"I said your family."

Guiding his bride to their suite, they stopped at the top of the stairs and embraced. Too many diversions had kept him away from her. And all this death. He opened the door and went straight to the hearth. By the time he finished building the fire, she was stripped half-naked. Her lovely, full breasts rose and fell in a hypnotic rhythm. Her gown bunched around her knees. The soft thatch of hair between her thighs glistened and she touched the special spot in the middle.

"I love you," he choked. "Immeasurably."

Noelle stepped out of her dress. Her pulse skated as he kissed her neck, his fingers caressing her belly. The world was ripe with opportunity now, and Randvior Sigurdsson would never allow anyone to interfere with their lives again.

Publisher's Note

I hope you've enjoyed this story.

Violetta Rand was a very important member of Dragonblade Publishing. In fact, it was because of Violetta that I started the company—she hadn't had any luck at shopping a Viking series around and asked me if I'd publish it under my personal imprint at the time, Dragonblade. I agreed, the series launched successfully, and I realized that what I did for Violetta, I could do for other authors. This was around 2016 when visibility was becoming increasingly difficult for new authors and Dragonblade Publishing, Inc., was born with the goal of helping authors expand their readership.

Violetta was very passionate about her Vikings. I think that's evident in every Viking book she writes. She was equally passionate about Historical Romance as well as the publishing industry in general. She was extremely savvy about publishers and how it all worked, what was selling, what wasn't. One of her favorite things was to sign authors she'd long loved reading to Dragonblade and we have her to thank for many of our successful veteran authors.

Prior to being a published author, Violetta led a very interesting life. Her degree was in Environmental Science, so she was a scientist by trade. She and I would have a lot of conversations about things other than publishing. She was a friend to so many and when we lost her in July 2023, we lost a true friend and advocate for Historical Romance authors, everywhere. But she left a lasting mark on the industry by being an integral part of Dragonblade Publishing and also in the books she wrote for other publishers, and there were several. She lives on through her words.

Thank you for reading this book, one that Violetta felt was part of her favorite series, and thank you for helping us continue Violetta's legacy.

With warm regards,

Kathryn Le Veque
Founder and CEO, Dragonblade Publishing, Inc.

About the Author

Raised in Corpus Christi, Texas, Violetta Rand spent her childhood reading, writing, and playing soccer. After meeting her husband in New England, they moved to Alaska where she studied environmental science. Violetta spent a decade working as a scientist before quitting her day job to pursue her dream as a full time writer.

Violetta still lives in Anchorage, Alaska, and spends her days writing evocative contemporary and historical romance. When she's not reading, writing, or editing, she enjoys time with her husband, pets, and friends.

www.ingramcontent.com/pod-product-compliance
Lightning Source LLC
Chambersburg PA
CBHW051046050726
47592CB00002B/407